D0677898

The Guardian and the King

J. Carter Merwin

The Tales of Earden

The Swan and Arrow
The Fledgling
The Guardian and the King
The Seer

Copyright 2016 – MacGregor House Publishing, Castleton, Vermont, USA
ISBN – 13: 978-1534848 719
ISBN – 10: 1534848 711

No part of this book may be reproduced in any form without written permission of the publisher except by a reviewer who may quote brief passages.

The oil painting on the cover is 'Tristram's Death' by Marianne Stokes, 1855 – 1927. in the public domain.

Acknowledgements

Thank you to my friends and family for all their support and encouragement.
Thank you to these websites I used in my research and the people behind them:
www.localhistories.org/surgery.html
urmc.rochester.edu/neurosurgery
www.thearma.org.
And a special thank you to Henrik Granlid of the Modern Medievalist for his helpful advice on swords, armor and combat.

"Many prophets and kings have desired to see those things which ye see and have not seen them; and to hear those things which ye hear and have not heard them." Luke 10:24

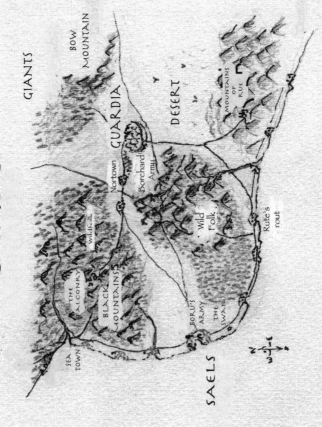

EARDEN

GIANTS

BOW MOUNTAIN

GUARDIA

Nortown

Borchard Army

DESERT

MOUNTAINS OF RUE

wildfolk

THE FALCONRY

BLACK MOUNTAINS

Wild Folk

Rute's rout

SEA TOWN

BORU'S ARMY

THE SWAN

SAELS

Table of Contents

"...Three leaders, two against one,
Four fathers and three bastard sons…
Five women bound to four men
Three warriors and three die for them..."

Rue the Seer

The Guardian and the King

1

"You must not despair..."

The cold sea air coursed between his primary feathers as Monk climbed above the long line of soldiers, wild men, falconers and their horses. In his excitement he flew higher than he'd ever flown before. The wind was strong and would have blown him far beyond the cliffs if the angry cries of the gulls hadn't warned him back. Taking a last look at Arius, Monk swooped on ahead. He was the first to see the city and the multitude stretching across the plain before its gates. He squawked greedily as the wind switched directions and he caught a whiff of the cooking fires. Scanning the thousands of soldiers and refugees going about their daily chores he hovered on an air current looking for his other human companion, the one with red hair.

"Coom down from there...you'll fall an' kill 'yerself!" Jors yelled above the wind. His little sister Brilliana stood on a block of the crenelated stone wall, her arms out-stretched as if embracing the palace, the city and the wide plain beyond. Her long black braid streamed out behind her as her new rose-colored gown whipped about her legs. "A fine picture you look!" he said reaching out to grab its hem and pull her down.

"Yes, don't I? I'm beautiful! Look at me! Leave me alone if you don't like it! Yer' not me Moother! I kin do what I please! He said so! That Boru lord. Ah'm 'is little princess 'E said! We 'ave the run of the place!" the little girl shouted looking down at her brother angrily. Tossing her head she clambered up onto a higher block and turning round, faced him with her hands on her hips. Pulling the wild hair out of her eyes that the wind had set free, she leaned over and stuck her tongue out at Jors. "We live in a palace now! An' Lord Boru's m' father!"

"Yer not! 'E's not! 'E's not yer father! Brillie! Damn you...you little shite!" the boy shouted slapping the top of the block hard with his hand coming down next to Brillie's little foot. "How dare you say that! Dah's yer father! Take it back! What you said! Our Dah's not dead!" Jors eyes filled with tears and he turned his face from the wind.

Every day he grew more and more afraid and angry. If his sister could so quickly forget their father as his mother seemed to have done, then might he not indeed be dead? Did that mean his brother was dead too? They were both still missing. If you forgot about a person, did they somehow disappear? Cease to exist? Brillie had warmed up so quickly to 'That Man', his mother's lover. When, because of the war, they had been persuaded to leave their home and come to the palace; he had watched as Brillie became more spoiled and more fearless, running loose every day. Her reckless bravado reminded him of Young Boru, and he missed his older half-brother terribly. Instead of following along behind him on missions of discovery and mischief he was saddled now with watching his trouble-making little sister. What bothered Jors even more was her growing fondness for Lord Boru. He seemed to be taking Young Boru's place in her heart. Brillie had followed her elder brothers everywhere but especially Boru. Now she stalked this man about the palace every chance she got. 'Fickle woman!' Jors thought. Like a kitten, she ambushed the man for kisses, following him from room to room in his private apartments. Once Jors had even caught her sitting on the Lord Protector's lap with her head lolling against his chest. 'A pretty picture that had been!' he thought to himself with Lord Boru's arm snuggling her in close and 'That Man' smiling across the room at his mother. That it was the image of his older brother's smile cut Jors to the quick. That was the worst of it. His older brother was Boru's bastard son. He could not wrap his mind around it. Yet it was true. Through his mother's love they were all tied to him, tied to this stranger and his own father lost, perhaps forever.

"Oh...do what you like!" he yelled in frustration. "Ahm' goin' in! Bloody wind! It's too damn cold out here!"

Suddenly all the bells on the city's northern towers began to ring with a clamorous noise.

"Wait! Look! I can see Arius!" Brillie pointed north, shuffling her feet on the gritty surface of the stones until she was standing right up against the edge.

"Get back!" Jors cried.

Brillie's braid whipped around her head and across her face as a gust of wind puffed up beneath her gown lifting the little girl sideways across the block. Brillie screamed. Jors gasped and reached out, but it was too late. The red fabric flashed against the sky and was gone in an instant. The sound of crashing rubble followed and then there was silence. All he could do was cry out for help in panic and despair. Guards came thundering up the stairs abandoning their posts and out onto the ramparts.

"She's gone!" Jors said feebly pulling a soldier over to the edge of the wall. The boy tried to climb up and look over the battlement but the man held him back. A horn sounded from somewhere below as soldiers began swarming along the banks beneath the wall.

Aolwynd ran out of the stairwell soon after and threw her arms about Jors. He collapsed in a flood of recriminations and apologies as his mother held him, until nothing but tears and incoherent gulps were left to give.

The Lord Protector heard the horn and came out of his tent on the plains below. He heard the cries of his soldiers and looked toward the northern horizon. There was Arius riding down the last slope toward camp with a great host behind him. His pet crow and companion, Monk flew above them. It was not long however, before Boru realized the cries of his men were not in celebration of these northern legions come to join their ranks but from some calamity closer at hand. Following the other men running to the base of the wall, Boru stood silently watching, as soldiers removed the broken covering from an old well. Falling stones had shattered its boards. Men were already retrieving rope to descend into its depths and search for the child.

Far removed and circling above the excitement something diving through the air had caught the crow's eye. It was not red like the hair of Arius' mate, Ruby, but almost that color and he flew toward it. Boru watched as Monk spiraled down and landed, inserting himself somewhere half-way up the palace wall, disappearing completely from sight. After a few moments he re-appeared, almost magically, flew off, came back, landed and disappeared again. The next time he came out of the crevice, he flew down, landed briefly on Lord Boru's shoulder, gave a sharp cry and flew immediately back and into the wall.

Boru called for his horse and in a few minutes he was through the city gates, up the stairs of the People's Palace in the great square and running out onto the wall walk. Aolwynd immediately clutched at him sobbing. Jors crawled away from the couple and put his back against the wall, hugged his legs and staring straight ahead. His grief and his guilt suddenly overwhelmed him. He prayed to the gods to let him sink into the stones and disappear altogether. "Please, don't let 'im see me..." he moaned.

"Get me ropes!" Boru shouted to the guards. "Jors! Come here!"

Jors shrank away from him. 'Will he hang me?' he thought.

"Come here!" Boru shouted. "I need your help." Still the boy did not come. "Be a soldier lad..." the man said casting a glance at Aolwynd and holding out his hand to Jors.

"For me..." his mother pleaded.

Slowly the boy got to his feet. Boru grabbed him and fashioned a harness out of the ropes, strapping them around the boy's waist and under his groin. Boru lifted the youth onto the battlement slowly pushing him backward toward the edge. The boy's eyes grew wide with fear. "Be strong now, I've got you." the man said as he forced the boy to lean out over the stones, use his legs as if walking and begin to rappel, coaching him in his descent of the outer face. Playing out the rope slowly, while soldiers on the other end wrapped it about their waists and anchored it fast, Boru called down to Jors. "Can you see anything?"

"Noothin'." Jors called as he inched his feet, shuffling slowly down the wall with his eyes shut tight. A dizzy sensation flipped his stomach as the wind whistled about him. After a moment Boru popped his head over the edge. "Open your eyes boy! Look about you!" Ashamed, Jors opened his eyes. All he could see at first was the wide blue sky. The wind buffeted his eardrums. A feeling of awe began to bolster his curiosity and he started to trust the rope that held him. He leaned back and began to relax.

Aolwynd stood against the inside of an archway, out of the wind, her face pale and her eyes closed.

"Anything yet?" Boru called over the edge.

"Lower!" Jors called back. "Wait! There's a hole, no there's a kind of a balcony must 'av bin, all walled up like, an' a bit of a ledge stickin' out here...if I can joost...let me down...a little more...Hold! There! Ah' kin see her dress! She's in here! An' so is tha' damn crow! Get out, yah' dirty bugger!"

Monk protested loudly and hopped up and down on the ledge flapping his wings with excitement.

"Can you get her out?"

"Aye. I'll get 'er. Oh Brillie!" The boy's voice suddenly cracked and became the cry of a child choking with emotion.

"Don't lad, be a soldier now." Boru warned him.

"Ahm' alreet." Jors said gulping and taking a deep breath. "Ahv' got 'er. Pull us oop."

It took many minutes for the soldiers to raise the two children. They did so slowly, trying not to yank too violently on the rope or cause it to swing. Jors face was white with exertion as his arms clung tightly to his little sister.

Lord Boru took Brillie off Jors' shoulder and laid her down on the pavement. Aolwynd knelt by her side as Jors was untied from his harness. "She's still alive." she said.

The boy lay flat on the stones looking up at the sky. His arms sang and pulsed with pain. Monk was swooping and diving above them jubilantly.

"Best apologize to that crow." Boru told him.

"Open those curtains!" Mother Brilla, Matron of the House of Good Women, said with authority, striding into the room and throwing her cape on a chair. "Let us have some light and see what can be done."

The little girl lay on Lord Boru's elaborately carved bed, motionless, barely breathing. Like some abused doll her pretty red dress had been cut away and lay in rags on the floor.

Aolwynd was kneeling there. She raised her head from the bed and blinked at the strong afternoon light. "What time is it?" she said. Her face was almost angry with sorrow. "Brilla! Save her! Save your name child!" she cried out upon seeing the matron of the great hospice of Saels.

"Has she made any movement? Said anything?" Brilla asked.

"Nothing."

"I will do what I can. Please..." She motioned to her bag. Aolwynd got up from the floor and retrieved it. "Now do me one more favor, bring me towels and a basin of hot water, then go to your room and refresh yourself. Leave me. I work better alone."

Aolwynd's mouth dropped open but she did as she was told. She was getting used to this new more abrupt voice of her friend but sometimes she still saw, with affection, the impetuous, young nurse who had befriended her years ago. The lilting speech of the common people came and went now, replaced by a much haughtier tone.

When she was alone with her patient Brilla lifted the girl's shift to examined her. One leg was broken near the hip. "Ugh. Nasty. We'll 'av ta straighten tha'...I fear she may hobble all her life..." Brilla mumbled, her true self and her old voice slipping out with concern. There were bruises and scrapes everywhere on the tiny body. "Eh...those will heal. Don't you think?" She said as if to someone. Turning her attention to the girl's head and neck, she moved her jaw carefully, looking in her mouth. Her fingers moved swiftly, feeling Brillie's skull, lifting her eyelids. One pupil was slightly bigger than the other. Brilla grunted. There was a large bump beginning to swell behind her left ear. "I doon't like the look o' that. Oh Rue...I wish you were here..." she whispered.

Boru, Aolwynd and Jors came back into the room as she opened the doors for them.

14

"She will have to be moved to the hospice, I need to watch her carefully and I need my Good Women and my books." The matron's clipped and precise voice was back again.

Late in the day a strange sight brought citizens to their doorways. A large wagon moved slowly through the streets of the great harbor city and up the steep streets toward the House of Good Women. A soldier stood on top of a load of hay forking it over the sides and down onto the cobblestones. a smaller cart, its wheels covered with skins stuffed with straw crept along behind. On a mattress in this cart, like a sleeping princess, the little girl lay surrounded and hemmed in by pillows lest she wake and try to move. Her brother sat beside her. Next rode the Lord Protector and beside him his lady, the one they called 'The Swan'. Aolwynd was too distracted to notice the gossiping and pointing amongst the crowd but Jors heard the words they whispered: 'Jem the Councilman's wife', 'Boru's mistress' and another word that he did not care to hear but understood. His face flushed and he turned away crouching down inside the cart. Some of the city folk began to follow them as news spread of the little girl's fall. The juicy story of the crow who had lead them to find her and her brother's rescue spread from tavern to tavern by nightfall garnering eager audiences.

Brilla stood on the steps of the hospital between the palm trees and watched the procession as it drew close, waiting and worrying.

That night, candlelight flickered about the walls of the Matron's study, casting a thin wedge of light into her sleeping chamber. On a cot next to her own bed, Brillie lay much as she had been when she was brought in that afternoon. Yet now she was feverish, her neck and skull slightly more swollen. Brilla sat at her desk surrounded by volumes of medicine written and collected by the previous head of her order, Lauro. The woman had been a formidable physician and an agile and gifted surgeon. Gifted in all the ways Brilla feared she was not. Over the years she had learned much, but the business of running a hospital had slowly turned her into a person of records and accounts. Diagnosis and treatment of patients was left to others. She missed Lauro and now missed Rue even more, for the anticipation of her help had been much on her mind. They had long prayed to the Great Mother for a proper doctor to replace Lauro. Finally one had been granted them and then swiftly taken away

15

again by death.

She pored over the pages pertaining to head injuries growing more and more unsure of herself. "Oh Rue! This would have been so simple for you!" she lamented.

She stood and gazed out a window at the darkness. Beyond the gardens she knew that the tiny cemetery was waiting to take her name-sake if she failed to save her.

"Mother Brilla...we have faith in you...you must not despair..." came a calm melodious voice, one she remembered but could not place.

"What?" Brilla turned and walked to her bed chamber door. A whisper dissipated into the dark corners of the room like a fog as she entered to check on the child. There was no one else there.

"Prepare...you know what must be done..." The lips of the sleeping girl moved yet it was not her voice. It was like a faint wind blowing across the fabric of Brilla's mind, or an echo from the distant past.

"...We will help you..."

Brilla's knuckles were as white as her apron. She hung onto the countertop in the surgery staring into a cabinet filled with tinctures, bandages and instruments. Her breathing was shallow and it was all she could do to stop her whole body from quaking. She tested her hands for steadiness by letting go but quickly grabbed the counter again. She was near crying with fear. 'How will I ever do this?' she thought. 'I'm no more than a clerk. Better to let the girl go in peace.'

The great copper barrel in the corner of the room hissed as a flame beneath it boiled water. Two women moved silently in and out bringing towels and setting up a tray with scalpels, tweezers, picks, a drill and a small hammer, putting them near the long operating table. A basket of bandages sat at the end.

Brilla took a jar of honey and a bowl of softened willow bark out of the cabinet and set it down on the counter with a clunk.

Her Good Women looked up at the noise and glanced at each other.

'At least I have Cere and Lyla...' Brilla thought, glancing back with a weak smile. Lauro's assistants had stayed on with her after Lauro's death. They, more than any of the others had taken on the

16

burdens of diagnosis and treatment. Their calm, efficient demeanor was a great boon over the years of Brilla's reign as matron. Yet they had gradually been relegated to the more menial tasks of bone setting and mid-wifery. Lauro's spacious surgery had been quiet for years. Difficult cases had gone elsewhere. This call to action had been a surprise. Their eyes watched Brilla's every move with suspicion. They had never gotten over Lauro's suicide. Besides being their friend, it had shaken the foundations of the entire order, the hospice and goddess temple. It was only Brilla's down-to-earth, some said "plodding" ways that had kept everything and everyone going. For that they were grateful, but a surgeon?

"We will get the girl…." Cere said quietly coming over to Brilla and putting her hand over hers. She felt it trembling. "You are sure about this?"

"Yes." Brilla said with a start, clearing her throat.

Cere and Lyla stepped out of the room.

"We cannot let her do this!" Cere said forcing Lyla to the wall. Lyla took her lover's face in her hands and kissed her softly on the mouth. Cere relaxed somewhat and leaned into her arms.

"Even Lauro hesitated before opening a skull..." she whispered.

"The girl will die anyway, my love, we may as well let her try."

"I miss her."

"I know, but it must be done...now. The pressure is increasing, have you checked that girl's eyes? Lauro is not here. This is the only way."

"Brilla is terrified. Just look at her." Lyla whispered. Brilla was in the same spot as when they had stepped out of the room. From the crack in the doors they could see her standing, head bowed, her hands gripping the counter top.

Cere jerked her head in Brilla's direction. "She has no choice. She must do something...Aolwynd is her friend…,this is her name child..."

"...and we must help her, my love." Lyla sighed.

They stood in the corner near the door for several moments, embracing, their foreheads touching, then walked down the hall together for a stretcher.

When they returned the doors had been propped open for them and Brilla stood at the table in the center of the room. They laid the girl out on the cold metal and Brilla immediately put her ear close

17

to the girl's lips.

The sun poured in from the tall windows and bathed the scene in light.

Brilla looked up and gave them clear and succinct orders. The startled women went about the business of washing the girl's swollen limb and strapping her down to the table. Brilla watched them, all attention, like a predatory bird.

"Cere, you are best at setting bones, I will let you direct us." Cere nodded, raising her eyebrows at Lyla who only smiled. She worked quickly, identifying the break, feeling its contours, then she ordered Brilla to hold the girl's head steady while Lyla assisted her in pulling the broken bone apart and manipulating it back into place as best they could. When this was done they set the splint.

"Good. Now please shave her head and call me when you are ready." Brilla spoke in a strong tone and walked over to the glass doors looking out on the sea. She stared at the empty cot on the balcony outside where Rue had died soon after her arrival in Saels.

When the women had made Brillie ready they turned and saw Brilla already walking toward them. She was speaking softly to herself staring at the girl on the table.

"Yes...yes...alright...and next?" She seemed to be taking instructions from someone.

"We are ready..." Cere said softly, staring at her.

Brilla raised her index finger in the air signaling them to be quiet. "Yes...alright...carefully. Yes, boring the hole...yes..." She turned and smiled. There was a calmness in her manner unlike the woman they knew. Her hands were steady and she moved with great assurance but seemed unaware of their presence. She merely pointed at the tools she needed or spoke their name and waited with an outstretched hand. Cere and Lyla marveled at her precision, it was as if Lauro were standing beside them again.

Quickly opening the skin over the little girl's skull she created two flaps with a scalpel and nodded as Cere secured them back with clips. Lyla daubed away the blood. Using a trephine Brilla carefully drilled a small disc near the swelling, stopping the rotation of the instrument just before she broke through the bone. Then with a careful tap from a very small hammer she opened the hole. Blood spurted up in a thin stream making her two assistants jump back. Brilla stood quietly as the stream pulsed to a trickle and

18

then slowed till it oozed.

"We are finished. Clean her up and bandage her, use the honey and willow strips to make a poultice over the wound then bind it with cloth. Quickly, I don't want her coming back to us on the table." Brilla spoke in a voice of authority familiar to them and yet refined, so like Lauro and yet different, but certainly not Brilla's. "Take her back and stay with her, I must go to the palace."

Lyla grabbed Cere's hand and squeezed it, her mouth and eyes wide open in gob-smacked astonishment. They both stared after Brilla as the matron stripped off the blood-soaked apron, threw it in a clot on the floor and walked sedately out of the surgery.

2

"My lady's son."

When Arius arrived at camp with the new recruits Ruby came running over to him. Raising her arms in greeting she stopped short in surprise as he grabbed the pommel and swung his leg over the saddle. He was balancing something carefully in the crook of his other arm. Moving the bundle to his shoulder he approached Ruby, a timid look on his face. The baby mewed and stuck one little arm out of its swaddling blanket.

"What th'...What d' ye' think yer doin' with that babby?" she cried taking it away from him in a rush. "Coo! It's terrible young, init?" she said hefting it in her arms.

"Ruby, I've got to tell you something..."

"'Ere!" she said, her eyes wide with suspicion. "This isn't yours, is it?"

"Ruby, wait!"

She loped off into the camp and sat down heavily on a log just outside their tent. Arius grabbed the pouch of meal and baby things and trotted over as Ruby undressed the baby. Finding it wet and dirty she proceeded to clean the child and paid no more attention to Arius till the task was finished, only holding out her waiting hand like a surgeon for a wet cloth.

The falconers sat on their horses and watched with interest as Arius dealt with his lady love. He had been all business and full of his new command on the way back from the Black Mountains, so unlike the cowering youth they had known that it gave them cause to laugh. They watched him struggle to gain her attention until he caught them sniggering.

Spurring their horses they cast about for a place in camp to call their own amongst so many soldiers and refugees. Feeling like strangers they aimlessly wandered the aisles till they found themselves across from Arius again and in front of The Lord Protector's great tent.

Arius and Ruby had their heads together so the men took it upon themselves, and as if it were their right and their duty, to surround the larger tent with their own smaller ones in a semi-circle. They spent the rest of the day setting up their birds, perches and cook fire. When they were done, Boru's tent took on a certain wild grandeur, guarded now as it was by fierce hunting birds and hoary mountain men. They sat by their fire watching Arius and Ruby across the aisle. Grumbling already, they wondered just what they were doing there so far from home and what this war had to do with them.

Boru's two camp guards looked on from their posts by the flap of his tent with chagrin and after a few minutes turned their backs to it all.

"So, who else have you had besides yer' sweet Rowan that Ah' doon't know nuthin' about?" Ruby asked when she was finished wiping the child's buttocks.

Arius stayed her hand with its dirty cloth. "Ruby..."

"I suppose yer' goin' to tell me it's not yours?"

"Ruby. It's not mine it's your father's."

"Blamin' my Dah, Mooncalf? Shame on you." She hissed at him, all the while cooing at the child.

"Ruby...it's your father's. This is your half-brother."

Ruby stopped and stared at him.

"What are you sayin'?"

"By the Gods, Ruby! How much clearer can I make it? If you don't believe me you can ask Boru. He saw them together! It's my sister Fern's child and your father's."

Ruby just stared at the small thing in her arms and said nothing.

"Listen to me." Arius said."I had to take him. He has no one. My sister died and he's not wanted. I told you how I was treated, how I grew up, it'd be the same for him. If you don't want the little bastard I'll take care of him." Arius spat out the last words. He was close to tears. All the years of loneliness at The Falconry came flooding back to him, the abuse, the names he was called. "He's part mine anyway, my nephew, I'm part of him. He's part of me." Arius said nothing about his mother, for him, the pain of her death as well as Fern's was still too fresh. He poured all his unhappiness into the child's fate. He imagined lying in Ruby's arms later that night and whispering of his sorrow to her then. But not now, not in the daylight, in front of his men or the soldiers.

Ruby sat quietly looking at the little boy. "Well, 'E's part mine too, then. I guess that makes 'im ours more than anybody else's. Lor! What a mess. Dah! Where are you, what have you done?"

Arius stared at her, his eyes sparkling.

"What?" she said trying to read his thoughts.

He stood and pulling her up from her seat left her standing as he ran across the aisle to the falconers. Leaning over them he said something in a low voice. A roar of laughter erupted as he was handed a ribbon of leather from the pocket of one of his men. They all rose and followed him back across the aisle to Ruby and stood behind him in a semi-circle like a delegation.

"Ruby..." Arius said, clearing his throat. "give me your hand..." Ruby held it out to him with an impatient look as she dandled the baby in the other arm. Arius took the thin leather strap, split one end with his dagger and poked a hole in the wider end. Then he wrapped it about her wrist, pushing one thin piece through the hole and tying both split ends together in a knot. The men whooped and threw their caps into the air, hit Arius on the back and called out for meat and drink.

Ruby looked around bewildered at the ruckus and celebration now spreading amongst the soldiers and their wives. "Arius...what just happened?"

"We're married...Black Mountain married...I've married you. That's alright isn't it, my love? To marry you?"

"Mooncalf." she said, her throat constricting and her heart beating fast. "What 'ave you gotten yerself into?"

***

"'Ere! This one can fight! Git out o' that cart you! Yeah, you!" Tanner was prodded by a guard then dragged out and made to stand in the front row of new recruits with two other prisoners. On the other side of the fractured land of Earden, Guardia's jail cart moved off slowly heading back toward the Western Gate having delivered its allotment of suitable men to the Supreme Guardian's army.

The expression on the face of the officer in charge of training was grim and un-impressed. As he limped along the line of men he cursed and scratched his greying beard. He had seen too many seasons in the Supreme Guardian's service, and his body showed it. Still he was a formidable hulk of a man and did his duty as he sized up the new recruits with a practiced eye.

The men slumped and coughed, stared at their feet and up at the walls of the city, any place but into the eyes of this man. Tanner tried to mimic their sloppy, shirking attitudes but years of soldiering had made his back straight, his face alert and expressionless. He stared straight ahead.

"So, yer' the fighters, eh? But what kind o' fightin', Ahm' wonderin'? Eh? Taverns? Street corners? We need soldiers fer this war, not no drunken brawlers! Argh, take 'em away an' git 'em settled." the Captain said to the guards as he spat on the ground. Two soldiers escorted the crowd to their campfires.

As he walked along between the aisles of tents, Tanner recognized several faces from past campaigns. His years as Boru's 'strong right arm' and second in command would make it hard to hide even amongst the thousands of new men gathered there. There were too many old friends amongst the companies. Too many memories. He hung his head and walked in the middle of the recruits. He bedded down that night as far away from the men as he could and kept to himself.

In the morning Tanner set aside his own name once again, left off shaving and in his place "Andrus Pitt" emerged from the tent and joined the others for breakfast. His disguise was further enhanced by a leather cap with long ear flaps he had 'borrowed' from someone's sack the night before.

After porridge, the men were called to train and those with some experience were paired off to spar with swords. The Captain watched them closely, walking up and down beside the partners. Those that knew nothing were soon told to keep out of the way and watch from the side lines.

It was too hard for Tanner, now Andrus, to hide his many years of skill. Wielding a sword came so naturally to him that he made the right move without even realizing he had done so. Instinctively he parried or thrust home and his enjoyment in his art was evident.

"What's yer name, soldier?" The Captain finally asked, stopping in front of him and shoving away his opponent.

"Andrus."

"Well, Andrus, what's tha' thing yer usin'? Go find a better, they're all inferior, but pick one." Tanner walked about the circle of men with a cocky smile on his face and his brows drawn together. The men held out their weapons for him to choose from. He pushed their arms away till he found a blade that suited him. It was light, with a needle point and gathered momentum as it swung.

"Whar'd yah git this, lad?"

"Mah grand dad."

"I'll give it back ye, then." Tanner whispered, walking away.

The Captain drew his own sword.

Tanner made a clumsy thrust.

"Don't you hold back, yah bastard! Ah' know better! Ah know what yer made of! That's as good as a lie ta' me an' I'll kill yah for it..."

The Captain was as good as his word. He came at Tanner in a fury with a grim smile on his face. For an old man he moved like a bull, powerful and surprisingly quick. The men stumbled and pulled back in a wider circle with astonished looks as the contest grew more and more fierce. The sound of strike and counter strike shifted the attention of more troops about the camp until there was a large crowd surrounding them. Tanner gave up any pretense and threw himself into the glory of single combat. All his "rustiness" fell away as his muscles warmed to the task. His hands had been itching to swing a blade for months and here was his chance to let fly. Tanner grinned back at the officer, breathing deeply and licking his lips. His hands clasped the grip, even though it was wrapped in leather, the hardness of the metal was unforgiving when it struck. The vibrations shot up his arms like a drug and he laughed out loud.

The Captain seemed to be putting him through some kind of demonstration of his prowess using all the basic stances and guards one after another for the benefit of the new men. Tanner fell in with him and easily anticipated his moves, warding off and side stepping with ease. He liked this new blade for its follow through, it seemed to have a will of its own, taking hold of the cut and not letting go until it was complete. From the crowd now filled with old professional soldiers came the names of the moves and guards loudly called out; "Look! 'The High Tower'", "High Horizontal!", "Low!" or "The Plow!", "Middle!" or "Chest!" and "Tail!". The men cheered and hooted each time swords clashed together. Finally Tanner stepped quickly aside holding his sword flat with the blade pointed toward the ground. Deflecting the other weapon it sent the Captain head-long into the crowd. When it was all over, Tanner stood leaning on his sword like it was a fence post in the middle of the men, breathing heavily from a smiling mouth, his eyes never leaving his opponent. The blood in his veins pulsing and his skills honed once more, his mind was sharp as it always was after a battle. His body coursed with energy, everything around him looked brighter, sharper. 'To hell with them!', he thought, not caring anymore if he was found out. Resolved to discovery or worse, 'I'll take him with me if 'E knows who I am!'

The Captain hobbled up to him, equally spent, threw his arm over Tanner's shoulder and announced boldly to the crowd; "Meet your new sword master, men!"

They all cheered.

As Tanner went up to return the sword, the boy raised his hand. "You keep it..." he said "it were too heavy fer me, you'll do it proud."

"Come with me, Andrus." the Captain said. "We have much to discuss." As they entered his tent he puffed "Whoo! Tha' took it out of me. Ahm' gettin' too old fer this. The name's Striker, Captain Striker. What's yer story, then? I've not seen an arm like that since...well, not in many a year. Ah' mostly teach now. Nobleman's sons. Never thought I'd be back gettin' ready fer battle, not at my age...but still...surely you were Guardian, were ye' not? Ah' seem ta remember tha' last stroke...where 'av I seen tha' before...?"

Tanner helped himself to a cup of ale, averting his face. He sized the man up and decided to stay as near the truth as he could. "Aye, Guardian...but I'm a wanted man now or was till I left the renegades headin' west...I've got no cause ta' turn traitor...no use followin' tha' fool's dream." he lied.

"Tha's right enough. Look here...we're marching on Saels come spring. I need men at arms, warriors with skills an' I've got precious little time an' no help! Ah've got ta' turn these clods inta soldiers before the frost breaks. 'Course ah doon't expect ya ta teach 'em everythin', no use burnin' candles to the 'Twins' for that lot, eh? We'll see how much they kin learn. But you help me ready this here army so's they doon't cut off their own toes an' I'll see yah doon't hang, who ever y'are...or were, what ever you've done...Andrus." Striker said squinting his eyes and scanning Tanner's face.

Tanner could see the man was trying hard to remember him. He raised his cup in salute, hid his face behind it and took a drink.

"Dah! You should have seen it! By the Twin Gods of War! It was brilliant!" Jemson chattered away in the cook tent about the contest he'd seen earlier while he peeled turnips into a pot.

"Ere! Watch where yer' puttin' tha' knife!"

In his excitement the youth had cut his finger. He stuck it in his mouth looking up at Jem guiltily. "But Dah! They were like two bulls going at each other! An' the men were calling out the names of the strikes and the moves as they fell to it! It was like...noothin'! It was like war!"

"Aye." Jem watched the boy and he saw the light in his eyes with trepidation. This temperament fueled by excitement, action, the lust for battle, this was Boru's son alright. Jem sighed. "Joost get them turnips peeled will yah, we've got men ta' feed."

"Dah."

'Here it comes...' Jem thought, lowering his head over his work, the question he'd been dreading was coming right at him. "Aye?"

"I want to be a squire."

"Uh huh."

"I'll never make a soldier peeling turnips! Please Dah! One of the other boys is already squired to an officer! Let me go Dah."

Jem came over to Jemson and sat down opposite him. "Ahm, tryin' ta' keep you hid, yah' know tha', right? An' anyways, I wouldn't see you no more. You'd go away from me. What about yer poor moother? I promised ta' find you and keep yah safe till ah could get ye' back to her. An' yer too young. An' ye' canna joost wander oop ta some gallant an' say 'I want ta' be your squire…' Yah may get more than ye' bargained for."

"Oh Dah, stop." Jemson squirmed with annoyance."Nobody knows me. Nobody cares. You can help. You must know someone. An' we'll see each other. We're in the same army after all…" Jemson said in a voice he thought sounded very grown-up. Staring at his hands and the bloody finger he said quietly "It's something I have to do…Dah…I can feel it…this is my place…I'm meant to be a soldier."

Jem gave a sigh as if all the breath in him eased out at once, like someone slowly letting go, dying. 'It's in yer blood alright, damn it.' he thought, then after a moment he said "Give me a little time to think about it. I may know someone."

Jemson let out a cheer and threw his peelings into the air. Jem stood up and turned to walk away. The boy ran up to him and held him about the waist. Turning around, Jem let the boy rest his head against his chest.

'When did he get so tall?' Jem wondered in amazement. It seemed only yesterday this child had plopped out of his mother's womb into Jem's waiting hands.

"Dah…are you crying?"

"Only the onions son, the onions."

***

The Lord Protector of Saels stood with his arms out to his side while two armorers took measurements. He was being fitted for a new haubrick, a shirt of ring maille. Jors watched the men from behind a palm tree in the safety of Boru's private courtyard. Ever since his sister's fall he had been watching this man, how he moved, his voice, the way he commanded attention when he walked into a room and especially how he treated his mother. There was a gentleness and an eagerness to be near her, to touch her, that he had not seen in his own father very often, not like this. And then there had been his trust in Jors, his resolve and quick thinking when he had sent the boy over the battlement to save

Brillie. No one had ever trusted him with anything that dangerous before, he'd been treated like a man.

"Bring me some wine, boy." Boru called out to him. Jors jumped. He hadn't realized Boru knew he was there.

Jors walked in slowly from the garden skirting the walls of the bath and bedchamber like a feral cat until he reached the table with the wine. Pouring a glass, he slowly brought it to Boru holding it out with both hands like an offering.

Boru smiled. "Have you fitted maille to Pirate yet?" he asked the men.

"Well, My Lord, we're taking his measurements now. We'll start on the horse when we're finished with you. Is this your son, My Lord?"

"My Lady's son."

"Come here boy and hold these tools." one of the armorer's asked.

Standing beside the men, Jors held their pincers, file and measuring cords.

The two men lifted the heavy shirt of metal rings over Boru's head and dropped it carefully onto his shoulders. It fell to just below his groin. One man set about removing rings on the open sides until the fit was neither too tight nor too loose. The other man slipped a long rectangular piece over Boru's arm, attaching it at the shoulder by leather straps and lacing it together to form a sleeve. Next they made note where extra rings needed to be placed beneath the arms and down the sides. Jors poked his finger through one of the rings and looked up. Boru was watching him.

Aolwynd entered the room taking off her gloves and cape.

"How is the child?" Boru asked.

"The same. She sleeps on."

Boru walked over to her leaving the armorers standing in the middle of the room. Aolwynd lowered her head and turning away leaned against a cabinet. Boru came up behind her and placed his hands over hers shielding her with his body from their eyes.

"Don't ever...don't turn away from me. Everything, we share everything together...do you hear?" Boru pushed his face into her neck and breathed the words.

"Yes...everything." she said.

The armorers looked away pretending to be busy while the two embraced.

Jors felt suddenly lost and alone. He ran over to his mother and put his arms about her waist burrowing between the amorous couple. Instead of being pushed aside, Boru made room for him. He felt the man's hand softly laid on his shoulder and instead of shirking it off in anger as he had done before, Jors let it stay. He didn't feel right about it but he let it stay.

"All will come round." Boru said softly."Today I hold my council, would you both like to come for a ride?"

Jors nodded shyly without smiling. Boru grasped his shoulder hard, pinching till Jors flinched and chuckled in spite of himself. Boru's strong hand spun him about on his heels and sent him out into the center of the room. Jors laughed, then looked back in surprise at his mother. All these years and their mother's favorite game had come from this man after all.

Aolwynd took Boru's hand across the space between their horses as they rode sedately out the Eastern Gate and onto the plain. Passersby gazed at the couple. Jors noticed some of them were not smiling. He stared angrily at those in the crowd who were watching, daring them with his eyes.

As they passed the little guard house Jors shouted from his pony.

"That's where you killed the pirates an' saved the city!"

Aolwynd shushed him.

"Yes, your mother was very brave...she took my breath away that night."

"My knees were knocking..." she whispered.

The three rode out of the gate and into a storm of humanity. Thousands of people milled about on the plain outside the city, across the sloping hillside and all the way to the forest a mile away. Children and dogs outside of tents, horses, carts filled with provisions, all manner of obstacles forced them to ride through the aisles of the camp carefully and slowly.

"I've been thinking about the last time..." Aolwynd said."the siege towers, will they come again?"

"No doubt."

"We must find a way to prevent them, and all these refugees... where can they go? They cannot stay here. This is a killing field."

"Can they all come within the city?" Boru asked.

"Well, they must go somewhere, I will ask Brilla."

"So many questions...I miss Tanner."

"Who is Tanner?" Jors looked over at the man.

"My strong right arm, my oldest friend, my lead man. Good council."

"We will help you...won't we Jors?" Aolwynd said.

"I miss my brother." the boy answered with a scowl, shifting his eyes away from her.

Dogs and children ran around them as they stopped in front of Boru's tent. The falconers were busy feeding their birds and shooing away this crowd of small annoying enthusiasts.

Boru's commanders were also waiting there for the council to begin and badgered him with questions before he even dismounted. Aolwynd and Jors were left to themselves as the leaders entered the tent. Monk flew down from a flag post and landed on Jors' shoulder, cawing cheekily.

"Go and find Arius." Aolwynd suggested. At the mention of the name Monk flew off and Jors went chasing after him.

Aolwynd opened the flap of the tent and went inside. The men stood up politely as she entered, waiting for their leader's mistress to ask her question and leave. Instead, she looked around, and pulling up a chair sat down next to Boru. Eyebrows were raised, a few frowns formed, but no one spoke. Boru cleared his throat. "Eight years ago this city was besieged by pirates..." All the men had heard of his first great victory and they nodded to each other. One man who had been there sucked in his cheeks. He knew what was coming. "...if it had not been for the Lady Aolwynd there would have been no swift victory. It was her daring plan to set fire to their ships and she who saved this city. There would have been a long siege otherwise, pestilence, many more deaths, including my own brother's. She stands...or sits beside me, and her counsel is welcome here." Boru kissed her hand.

After that surprising speech, the council began in earnest. Many things were discussed concerning the manner of provisioning, training and organizing the army. Time passed and Aolwynd sat quietly listening, observing each captain's remarks and demeanor. Only when they pulled out a map did she spark up, rising from her seat and studying it carefully.

When the meeting was finished, one officer asked courteously if she had anything to say.

"No..." Aolwynd smiled "but may I borrow that map?"

The captain rolled it up and handed it to her as he left the tent.

"You are mysterious this evening." Boru said pouring them both a cup of wine. "I think they expected you to ask a lot of foolish questions."

"Yes, I could see they were not pleased to sit with me."

"They will learn to respect my warrior. What will you do with the map?"

"I will check it against my father's collection first...before I tell you anything."

"First? You are mysterious..." Boru sat down on his cot and took off his jacket.

"I remember a simpler tent, when you were only a captain." she said looking about. "No embellishments. This one is far more spacious, finer...as befitting their Lord Protector."

"I remember it too. I would have that old tent and that night back again." He said draining his cup.

Coming over to him, she cocked her head and smiled. Unwinding a long green ribbon from her hair she shook the black curls free. Kneeling down next to the cot she quickly wound the ribbon about his wrists. "I also remember." she whispered.

Boru's eyes twinkled and he lay back on the pillow. "What? You would capture and ravish me? Here? Now? After a war counsel?"

"Ravish you? I only thought to tie you up..." she mocked. Smiling, she unlaced her outer dress and pulled the green silk over her head letting it drop to the ground.

"Should I be frightened of this warrior I am 'bound' to?"

"Perhaps..." she said laughing. She unbuckled his breeches and tugged at them. He stared into her eyes as he lifted his buttocks off the cot. Aolwynd pulled off his breeks and straddled his hips, pulling the circle of his arms over her head so that his hands fit the small of her back. She lowered herself onto him and took him in quickly with a gasp from her open mouth. Slowly, forcefully, she pressed upon him as she moved, keeping their bodies close so that every motion of their joined flesh gave her pleasure. Boru held her tightly helping her and she pressed her forehead against his. Swept away by their passion they did not notice the rocking of the cot. Her eyes were closed and her mind was far away. His eyes were on the ceiling of the tent as it wafted up and down, remembering another night long ago.

Suddenly the legs of the camp bed gave way. Aolwynd yelped and went rolling off taking Boru with her. Boru took his advantage with a laugh and kept her rolling till he was kneeling astride her. Kissing her mouth hard until she pleaded for breath he pulled his arms out from under her and held his hands in front for her to untie. Rubbing his wrists he said, "That is why...my love...I spread my cloak upon the ground that night. That cot has seen one too many campaigns." he smirked as Aolwynd pouted. "Battles, I mean. But I like your jealousy...now give me that ribbon, it is my turn and I will get our old friend the cloak..."

The next day Aolwynd went first to visit Mother Brilla and her sleeping daughter. Later, she took Jors and rode out to the inn for her father's manuscripts.

"Moother...I'm scared." Jors said looking up at the empty villa as they pulled the cart into the courtyard. Leaves swirled about the pavement stones and the dark windows stared back at them.

Aolwynd strode up the steps and unlocked the door. The inn's great hall smelled of must and damp. 'How quickly a house loses its warmth, its cooking smells, the sounds of its people. It has become some kind of brittle envelope without content.' she thought.

Almost in a kind of panic she mounted the stairs expecting to hear her husband's voice calling for a towel from his bath. Even Gerda's voice, her dear nurse, dead these nine years, haunted her from the hallway. Overcome with emotion, she took a deep breath and opened the bed chamber door to her father's old room that had become hers and Jem's after Folpas' death. They had spent their wedding night there. She remembered only a little of it. They had danced until dawn. Jorus the gardener had played his lute. Their guests had fallen asleep at their tables or crawled away home as the sun rose. What happiness there had been that day, like a final chapter in one of her father's manuscripts where all the threads of the story had come together in a knot of happy endings.

The newlyweds had fallen asleep in each other's arms after the house was empty and the courtyard silent. The neighbors had taken everyone away, her father, Mam, Jem's mother, even Aolwynd's baby. When the lovers awoke, they whispered in a silent house, made plans for the inn, and complained about their heads hurting from drink. Finally they drifted down to the kitchen and made an enormous breakfast. Full of bread, honey and berries, sausages and eggs they looked across at each other. With one sweep of his arm Jem cleared their feast and grinned at his wife.

In the afternoon, when the guests began to return to take up celebrating where they had left off the night before, they found Jem whistling to himself and making a bonfire with the remains of the broken kitchen table.

Aolwynd came back to the present with the sound of her son counting the flagstones and skipping in the courtyard. The high bed with its deep red curtains had become streaked with gray from the sun. After the children had left for the palace the servants 'must have run for their lives.' she thought. She closed the shutters and left the room.

"Come in here!" she called to Jors as she went back downstairs to her father's study.

"Nay. I'm not comin'...there's 'haunts' in there..." he said sullenly.

She looked at Folpas' daybed and the faded green silk that covered it. She had to agree. The room looked disheveled, her father would have despaired, he always kept his library so neat. It had been ransacked, she thought 'by the servants, neighbors...who knows. Of course. If anything of value were in the house it would be here for the taking. Good luck. There was nothing left of his gold and I had no jewels.' Yet someone had been through her father's scrolls, searching, and a few were missing. 'The servants...' she thought and she knew just which ones would have been taken...Folpas' collection of erotica, and anything with naked bodies, medical or historical. He had always let the servants borrow whatever they wanted, hoping to teach them their letters which brought him more joy than they. She could not help laughing to herself, for through the years the grubby and frayed ends of the erotic scrolls showed just which ones were in constant demand. She had hoped to save his vast library of other works, the histories, the poetry, for her children but the damp had damaged them all. Taking a basket from under the work table she began searching for the maps. There were none. 'Soldiers!' she hissed. Then her eyes sparkled with intent as she remembered where she

34

had hidden her favorite, a very special botanical and geographical work that she loved looking at as a child. Pulling out a heavy cabinet she reached behind it and found a large scroll in a leather case. She sighed happily. The man who drew it had taken years walking the landscape and countryside of Saels. There was nothing like it for detail anywhere in the city's library or in Boru's possession.

"Ah!" she said, touching its smooth vellum surface. "We shall see...yes, we shall see."

Coming out into the hallway with the case under her arm she passed the kitchen door. A shiver ran down her spine and she immediately began to whisper a prayer. "Mother goddess, keeper of the hearth, say 'good rest' to my father, 'good rest, Gerda my sweet', my brave, only mother of my childhood. Please, 'good rest to you, Mam', and if you must, blame only me and try to forgive me for all that has happened to your son. I thank you all, and may you serve the gods." She knew Gerda and her father would forgive her anything but she felt Mam's anger crash against her, real, alive and cold as a wave from the sea.

"I want to see my sister." Jors whispered to his mother that night before bed.

In the morning he sat quietly beside Brillie's cot playing with the fringe of her blanket. Monk flew in the window and hopped from his shoulder onto the foot of the little bed. He stalked along its top, pecking at the wood.

Mother Brilla and Aolwynd spoke in hushed voices, fussed about the room and finally disappeared into the study.

Jors pulled something small out of his pocket and carefully opened his sister's hand. Placing it in her palm he closed the delicate fingers over it.

It was a small ceramic figure of a horse and rider jumping. He had found it outside in the dirt of the courtyard where he had buried it. It was one of Brillie's favorite trinkets and he had stolen it one day in revenge. Its front legs had always been missing but the rider and horse reared none the less heroically for all that. She had prattled on about some fool thing Boru had done so much that Jors had been fed up to the teeth with her hero worship and had taken vengeance.

Monk jumped to the window sill and sat happily warming himself in the late autumn sunshine.

Jors listened to the drone of the women's voices and finally laid his head groggily on the coverlet and went to sleep. Coming back over to Jors' shoulder, Monk pecked at the boy's hair. Jors cried out in pain.

Suddenly Brillie sat up in bed staring with un-seeing eyes. All the terror of her fall came back to her with a gasp of her breath. Monk flew up into the air and the girl screamed in panic for her mother, waving her arms in front of her face as if to ward off the dark wings. Monk flew out the window with an insulted squawk.

Jors heard soft crying in the doorway and saw Mother Brilla holding Aolwynd in an embrace, they were both looking at the girl. Brilla was smiling.

Brillie had fallen back onto the bed, her eyes closed. Her face had life and color in it for the first time in many days and she seemed peaceful. Jors took her hand, which felt warm. It squeezed his gently. His chest swelled with joy.

"Dirty boys..." the little girl whispered, opening her eyes slowly and smiling at him, saying a phrase she used when she was angry at her brothers. Suddenly, without warning her eyes started open, she sat bolt upright and vomited across the blanket in a stream and all down the front of Jors' shirt.

"The gods! Brillie!" Jors said, pulling it away from his skin in disgust and making a face at the awful smell.

3

The Blue Goddess

By noon practice was almost over for the first group of green recruits in Borchard's army. Tanner laid down his shield and sword, waving the men away. Walking over to the water bucket he dunked his head and reached out for the towel which always hung on the fence post nearby. It was not there. Pushing the wet hair out of his eyes he saw a youth standing next to him holding out the cloth. The youth's eyes gleamed with admiration but it was something about his grin that made Tanner stand upright and stare.

"Who the hell are you?" he growled uncomfortably, grabbing the towel out of the boy's hand. "Don't ever sneak up on a man like tha', ahm tellin' yah."

The boy just stood quietly.

"'Ere what do yah want...an' wipe that garmy grin off yer face."

"You need a squire." Young Jemson said running to pick up the man's shield.

"Like I need an extra hole in my ass! 'Ere! Doon't...touch...mah... sword!" he shouted, poking in the air at the boy with the index finger of his big hand, emphasizing each word.

Jemson backed away obediently with his hands behind his back as if waiting to serve. Rooster, the army cook had finally taught him this after many curses and threats.

"Tha's sumthin' ye never do! Never! Did'nt nobody never tell you tha'? Tha's mah very soul, tha' is. Where'd you come from, boy? An' why doon't yah git on back there? I'm nobody's bleedin' nurse maid."

"My father works in the camp kitchen, peelin' fookin' turnips..." he said under his breath "but I want to be a soldier." thinking the harsh words would impress the man.

"Give over speakin' ill of yer Dah. He's doin' what 'E can. Coom back when yer tool rises an' yer old enoof ta' do the ladies some damage then I'll train yah. Git off now, ye skinny sprout, yer ony' in mah way."

Jemson refused to leave and watched as the next group of recruits slowly approached the training enclosure, dropping their shields and itching themselves under their new woolen shirts and leather armor. "I could fetch water! Carry things...anything, I'm strong. Please, let me stay." he pleaded.

Something tugged at Tanner, whether he was missing his own boys, or was it something about this boy standing before him...something he couldn't quite put his finger on?

"Oh hell. Git over there, out of oor' way an' doon't do noothin' to distract us, you hear?" he said pointing to the fence. Jemson ran to the side of the field and squatted down next to the water bucket jutting out his chin and smiling foolishly.

Practice was long and hard. Tanner drilled the men over and over till they began to strike and guard by instinct. He called out different combinations in a different order every time watching their reactions. He re-paired the fit and agile ones, moving them along faster and shifting them to the top of the field. Then he concentrated on the farm boys. "Clumsy moves'll git yah killed! Fluid! Smooth as silk from one strike to the next! Doon't you stop now you miserable chop an' chance its! Stand thar' like a stump 'an you're a dead man. Yer safer movin' than standin' still...remember tha'! Do sumthin'...anythin' till yah learn yer moves! Now, again!"

Tanner wiped his brow and nodded to Captain Striker as he rode by.

As soon as Tanner called a halt, Jemson immediately ran over carrying a smaller bucket, dodging like a puppy amongst the sparring men. Tanner grabbed him by the arm.

"Do you wanna git yersel' poked full 'o holes?"

Jemson stood stubbornly and offered the cup to Tanner.

"What's yer name, mooncalf?"

"Jemson."

Lord Faolan approached and walked through the middle of the combatants who gave way for the general to pass. "Let me see you for a moment, Andrus." he said gesturing to Tanner. He signaled the men to stand down and pointed at the water bucket. The men rushed over to drink and the boy jumped back out of their way.

"I heard there was a new instructor...I can't believe it's you! I thought you were in jail?" Faolan whispered drawing him aside.

"Ah was thrown in the army cart with the rest of the droonks an' pickpockets. But it's not safe fer me here." he said looking around. "I've too long a history, sooner or later somebody's bound ta' recognize me."

"Even with that beard?" Faolan laughed. "Lucky we have you for the moment teaching for our side, eh? So. What are your plans?"

"Biding my time. Must get away somehow. Must get Cherry out of that jail."

"Not by yourself you won't. But listen, it's about that that I wish to speak." They walked further afield, out of earshot. "The Jailor wants them moved out here to the camp. He can't feed all those families and he doesn't want the responsibility. And Rute, it serves his plans too. We'll guard them here in camp till spring, then they march with us...if they last the winter. Rute could care less."

"Cherry..." Tanner moaned.

"We must get them away."

"Aye. But how?" Tanner sighed and looked about him, thinking. "Do me a favor. Throw a torch off the north wall 'o the city tonight. I need to meet someone." The two men shook hands and looked up to see the boy creeping slowly along the fence toward them, drawn to Tanner like a worshipper.

"'E's like a leech that one. I can't get free of 'im. Go away with yah! Tell the men ta' head out fer supper...an you!" he pointed at the boy "Go on back whar ye' came from...the turnips are callin' yah. 'E wants ta' be a soldier." Tanner snorted nodding toward him. The boy ran off with a wave.

"Yes. Like his father."

"Nay, is' father's a cook."

"Tanner. Listen to me. Keep an eye on him. Don't let Rute get near him."

"Ahv' no intention of goin' anywhere near Rute meself. 'E know mah face too well."

"Keep the boy safe. I would take him into the palace but he would be too near his grandfather for safety. And there's no way to remove him without gossip amongst the men."

Tanner's eyes narrowed. "What are you sayin'...'E's yours?"

"I've never known you to be so dim before. Take a good look. What do you see?"

"But 'is father's a cook..."

"No Tanner, that's Jem...the boy's foster father...Aolwynd's husband."

Tanner's mouth dropped open and he stared after the boy. "Then that's...?" Tanner hit his forehead with the palm of his hand. "Of course he is...Ah couldn't see fer lookin' at 'im." He let out a deep breath. "Huh! Uncanny, even tha' devil of a grin." he finally said. "But how...?"

"Same as you, pressed for our glorious army." Faolan smiled. "Yes, there he goes, the image of my big brother, hero of my childhood back again. So...tell no one and keep him safe, I beg of you."

Captain Striker turned his horse away from the enclosure where he had been watching this intimate conversation between a mere soldier, one who'd recently been delivered from the jail and the son of the Supreme Guardian. He followed their eyes and focussed his gaze upon the boy disappearing between the long line of tents.

A flicker of light fell that night from the highest battlement on Guardia's north wall, but it was all that was needed.

Kora's men stood just inside the trees on an outcropping, watching and waiting at the appointed spot. Soon after midnight a man approached them on foot from the direction of the great army encampment. He skirted far to the west avoiding the sentries and took his time, using every bush and tree for cover as he moved.

"You look like my husband now." Kora said leaning against a

tree trunk as Tanner came up the hill toward her. Her face beamed and she grasped his beard on either side of his jaw. Tanner leaned in for a kiss but she only pressed her forehead against his and embraced him. "My brother...it is good to see you again." she said.

"My broother?"

"It is better that way. In front of the men." she said leading him to a fallen log. "Did you find your family?"

Tanner sat down beside her.

"Aye. Borchard had all the families of our troop jailed as traitors. He plans ta' use 'em as hostages come spring. March 'em right along w' the army to Saels an' turn Boru's own men against 'im. 'E thinks the soldiers of Saels will give oop, seein' their loved ones captive an' lay down their arms. Borchard thinks he can stop the war before it begins, at least that's what 'E told Faolan to get 'im to go along with it. It's a fair plan hatched by a foul mind and Rute had a hand in it fer 'is own purposes, I reckon."

"Rute again."

"Aye. Like as not he'll march them to their death before they even reach the battlefield. E' wants this war does Rute. He's a general now, y'know, him an Faolan."

"This Faolan, what is he like?"

"'E's a good man an 'E loves his broother. Trouble is 'E loves 'is father as well."

"Can we turn him?"

"Doon't need to. 'E's already against the war an' wants me ta' send you back with a message for Boru. But first we must think on the hostages. Faolan says their movin' 'em out here ta watch till the campaign starts in the spring. Very much to our advantage, tha'. If we plan."

"I would think they'd be safer in the jail. You'll start to lose them to the cold and pest out here before the march even begins."

"Aye, well, they're cold enoof now. An' the pest is no respecter of places, it'll coom to town or country. But it's just what Rute wants, I'm thinkin'. 'E wants 'is war, if they all die in camp or on the way, so much the better."

"We'll have to see that doesn't happen."

"Aye." Tanner said twining his fingers in hers.

"Tanner..." Kora said standing up and moving away.

"What is it luv? Not more of that 'dead man's wives' business

41

again?"

"No. Your wife. It's your wife I'm thinking of."

Tanner blew a cool note between his lips and stared out at the campfires below them.

"Tanner..."

"It's Andrus now, by the by..."

Kora sighed. "I cannot shift like you, my friend. And now a new name? I had a man, a family, they are all dead. It was the will of the Great Hunter. I had accepted all that. But then you came...and I never thought...never wished...such sweetness. She must be a queen among women that you love her so..."

"Kora..."

"No. We are not like you. We are like the trees in the forests of our home, cedars, strong and stubborn but depending on each other. Our ways are like that. Our roots are shallow but they spread across, twining together and we cling to the earth together to stay upright. So I must cling to my people and their customs. You will always be my friend and my brother, closer to me even than my husband was in many ways, but...I am wed to a dead man and always will be."

Tanner grasped her by the waist and pulled her behind a tree.

"That speech comes later..." he said pulling open her leather jacket to expose her neck. His lips felt like a brand from the fire in the cold night air. Kora's knees buckled as he curled his arms around her back and pressed her against the tall shaft of the pine. He kissed her lips and his hands pushed up the trunk of her body sliding against the leather of her jacket and squeezing her waist hard. Then, sinking his fingers into her dark hair he held her head in both hands. His thigh pushed between hers and pinned her till she arched her back, gasped and moved her body against it. Her eyes were closed, her lips open.

"Come with me now." he said taking her further into the dark woods until they found a clearing lit by a thin moon beam.

"Strip and let me see you naked once again." he said taking off his shirt and standing with it in his hand.

Her eyes scanned his muscled chest and finally her gaze left his body and focussed on his smile. The frozen breath escaped his lips as she let her jacket fall and unlaced her blouse. It slipped from her shoulders. Unconsciously she breathed in, raising her ribcage displaying her breasts for him.

He grinned with pleasure at seeing the deep blue tattoos that circled her midriff in a wide belt. The intricate geometric patterns rose in a point just between her breasts drawing attention to them but nothing marred their fullness or their beauty. Her skin appeared silver grey in the moonlight. Stepping out of her leather breeches she stood like a child holding them, only dropping them after many moments.

"Do yah have goddesses in yer people's religion?" he asked coming over to her.

She shook her head.

"Pity."

In the white light that fell between the pines they laid their coats down side by side and Kora kneeled down. "Tanner..." she whispered, helping him unbuckle his belt.

"Wait." he said, stepping out of his boots. He placed them fastidiously side by side.

"Soldier." Kora chuckled as she pulled down his breeches and he struggled to step out of them. Finally unable to wait any longer he fell on her, kissing her mouth to stop her from speaking.

The smell of pine and the crunch of the deep autumn leaves enveloped them as they came together again and again, violently seeking some position that could bring them closer than they'd ever been before, some union that would not fade away when it was all over. A pale fog rose and pulsed about them in the still night air from the warmth of their embraces. Finally, lying back against the earth, Kora snaked one leg inside his arm and rested her ankle against his neck, forcing him deeper inside her as she made ecstatic groans of pleasure. Tanner grabbed her leg and put it back down.

"Doon't." he said softly.

Shocked, she broke their union and rolled away from him. "Only with her?" she said. "Is that the reason you stopped? It reminded you of her?" Her eyes showed pain and disappointment. "She comes between us, you see..." Kora sighed with finality "as she should."

They dressed in a hurry, the sweat turning cold against their skin. Picking the leaves and bits of resin from each other's clothing they stood and held hands in the scant time left to them.

"That's that then." he said letting go of her and turning to leave.

43

"Tanner." Kora grasped him by both shoulders. He held his hands up in the air and let them fall again in a sign of surrender. He turned to face her.

"It's alreet. But it's hard on me manhood, y'understand? Yer the ony woman I've ever let get this close ta me, besides my Cherry...the rest meant noothin', just pleasure on the road...'an..." he paused "you're the ony woman who's ever said 'No' to me charms, ever." He turned and looked shyly into her eyes. "Ah' think it's the beard put you off."

Kora kissed him on the cheek. "I love you, my friend, but I'm neither a goddess nor your wife."

They walked in silence back through the woods and stood on the cliff looking out over the landscape below them.

"Look fer' anoother torch in a week's time. I'll speak with Faolan and then we'll send you back to Saels with a message and a plan." Tanner slipped down between the brush and the rocks like a fox and disappeared toward the camp.

Kora watched him, hugging her fur cloak against the wind.

"You are young and still have a soft heart, my son, perhaps I should not indulge you in this matter. There are lesser officers I could assign to this task." Borchard smiled, pacing about his private chamber in his nightshirt and robe.

"Let me have command of their safety and care, please, father. I would like to see them survive the winter and the journey to Saels. Otherwise, I do not see any sense in this scheme and little hope for the hostages. You should hear what the people on the streets are saying about your actions, father. They are not sympathetic to you. Better to let Boru's families stay at home in that stink hole of a jail then subject them to the outrages of hunger and un-protected cold. You yourself said that Rute would sooner see them dead."

"They have lost their claim to Guardia as their home! Boru's families? Boru's traitors, you mean! And they will be tented and fed! Our soldiers will spend the winter outside the city as well..." Borchard retorted.

"Different, and you know it."

"All right, all right, my monk! Truly you have missed your calling. If I had not trained you myself with the sword and know what you can do with it I would think you had rather wield a candle and a bell." Borchard sighed and turned to the open window. "Oh...speaking of sacred things...had you heard the witch is dead? Some kind of brain fever brought on by her father's potions. You were right after all. She was not long for this world. Pity, I hear she was a beauty."

Borchard turned to see his son standing as if dumb-struck, immobile, his face a blank.

"Well? Go about your new vocation, eh? My monk? Go shepherd all my little traitors to their new home out in the fields. Eh? That was good, Eh? Shepherd? Fields?" His jokes rattled around the empty room but Faolan had gone.

Faolan moved down the long hallways not acknowledging anyone, lord, lady or servant. He found himself climbing the stairway to the ramparts above his father's apartments. Walking in a daze he only stopped when he could go no further and his chest hit the stone of the wall. The wind seared his cheeks and a cold rain began to fall. Winter would soon cover the fields with snow. There he stood, frozen in mind and spirit looking west over the plain. The sun was low on the horizon when Rute found him.

"E's told yah then...about the Seer?" Rute said quietly, surveying his face. "Ahm sorry, truly. It's true then, what they've bin sayin', that yah loved 'er. Ah well, I know what it's like ta' lose the one yah love." Rute's face showed anger but his voice was resigned.

Faolan looked at him in surprise, listening.

"Aye, We'd been together many a year, Born an' I. Fought beside 'im and loved 'im. Almost ony friend I ever 'ad, and more then tha'. Yah doon't get over it, I hear. The pain. It fades, but it stays with yah. Fer you an' me it's all too fresh, eh? Like a wound, unhealed. An' I've got a score ta' settle. At least you don't have tha' on yer mind day and night. I'll get tha' little bastard. I hear the little bird 'as a troop of his own now. We'll see, we'll see. Then maybe I'll get me some peace."

"Rute..." Faolan started to speak but Rute just touched his shoulder as a friend might and walked back down the stairs.

When the watch took up their posts for the night, Faolan was still standing on the wall walk looking west.

4

War Council

Followed by her pack of Wild Men, Kora rode into Boru's camp as evening fell. She went immediately to his tent expecting to see him there. Instead she found her brother Bela outside it, talking proudly with the falconers, his bird on his arm. She swung her leg over the saddle and jumped down. The men turned and stared. Her brother watched the falconers' eyes drifting up and down her body, lingering on her breasts and hips. Their initial surprise turned into obvious enjoyment. This spectacle of a woman chieftain was new to them. They grinned and nudged each other as she stood and shook out her long hair making the little beaded braids dance and click.

Bela passed his falcon to one of the men and came over to her. He grabbed her arm and walked her away.

"Be careful, my dove. These men do not know you. You are no general to them."

Kora pulled her arm away. "Where is Boru? I must speak to him."

"He is in the palace with his mistress. You must go to their bed if you wish to find him, which I would not recommend, or you can wait until morning..."

Kora glowered at him. "I've just ridden hard for two days but I suppose it can wait till morning...what is all this?" she said, sweeping her arm about, taking in the hunting birds on their posts and the strange combination of guards and falconers.

"Arius' men...from the Black Mountains."

"Is that a baby I hear crying?"

Bela laughed. "Yes. One more thing Arius brought back from his visit home..." Bela watched his sister closely. "...Tanner's child, his bastard by Arius' sister." 'Was it just the night?' Bela thought sarcastically, or did Kora's eyes grow suddenly black as pitch?

The next morning Boru called a full council of his generals.

"It's no good." Aolwynd said to herself leaning over her map, waiting for them to arrive. After days of riding the hills east of the city, scrambling through the forest and scheming, she still had no plan. She arched her back and looked up as Boru's tent flap opened and his generals walked in followed by Boru, Arius and Bela.

Boru motioned for all to be seated then looked at Aowynd.

She cleared her throat nervously. "I have been comparing all the maps of Saels with my father's best. There were so many errors in yours, and so much had changed in his, that I finally made us a new one. I hope it will suit."

On the table Aolwynd rolled out a clean, brightly painted map on sail cloth. It showed the terrain reaching right round the coastline and extending to the eastern boundaries of their new country, elevations, buildings and roads were clearly marked.

"Thank you, this is indeed a wondrous gift. So this is what you have been working on so secretively as I slept." Boru whispered with a smile.

Aolwynd sighed. "But it is still no good. I wanted to find a way to defend the city somehow from the siege towers and other machines of war that will come...to change the landscape so that they could not descend onto the plain as they did last time. The best I can think of involves moving massive quantities of earth, following the forest ridge and extending it on both sides so that an artificial cliff surrounds the city. Yet this would create a kind of basin in which we would also have to fight, in short...a siege, or a trap, the very thing I wished to avoid."

"Aolwynd, my warrior. You do not carry this burden by yourself...and this plan is too complex, allow us to help." Boru said softly.

Kora stood in the doorway listening. She grinned her un-smiling grin, showing her canine teeth and taking a chair, tilted it back, rocking impudently.

Boru continued. "This is a war council and there will be more to come. It is not a place for answers yet, only voices, questions and possibilities. You have created a splendid map on which to plan our campaign when they come and it will help us answer our questions."

"Looking at this..." one general spoke "with its serene, pink-walled city...even the bell towers are depicted! Yet it brings to mind...I do not see...the thousands of soldiers, their tents, campfires, the families and dogs...the question of the refugees...Where are all these people to go?"

"The men are being gathered into our army, but the women and children must be removed..." another said.

"Mother Brilla and I have already spoken, they will be absorbed into the city somehow. She and Aolwynd will take charge of this." Boru said. "Let us set it aside for the moment and hear what Kora has to tell us, she has traveled far, seen the enemy and its numbers, let us hear of my father's army." Boru almost choked on the words.

Kora unfolded her arms from her chest and set her tilting chair back upon the ground. She looked about her with disdain. She had been waiting for a night and a morning to speak with Boru, now, when all his other generals were assembled as he had wished, she felt like a truculent child, unwilling to speak.

"I'll tell you one thing!" she said standing up and leaning her hands against the table. "You cannot wait for them to make their long march across the wilderness to Saels! You must reach out and strike them, and soon! This is no ordinary journey Rute has planned for your wives and children. Yes, he has rounded up all your families, cast them out of their homes and arrested them with Borchard's good wishes! All to punish you!" She glanced across the table at Boru who winced in pain. "This is a death march that suits his purposes very well! And all your soldier's families will be his victims." She strode a little away from the table then turned and said "Rescue them! Surprise raid on their camp, rescue and escape.

Take this weapon out of his hands. Borchard has promised Faolan that he will only display the hostages in front of your soldiers and they will lay down their arms, a bloodless victory for him. But this is not Rute's plan and I'm sorry, Boru, I do not think it is your father's plan either." Kora sat back down on her chair, recrossed her arms and leaned her chair against the tent post staring back at the shocked looks of the other generals.

Boru gazed at her intently, then smiled. "Thank you, General. I also do not want to fight our first battle on our own doorstep...tho' we may have to fight our last battle here. Yet I will not march against my father. I gave my word."

Kora jumped out of her chair. "Your 'word' as you say, was never delivered! Rute spoke for you, alright...on his return to Guardia he lied. You should have killed him. Your father never heard any of what you wished to say, maybe he did not care...maybe he leads Rute maybe Rute leads him...You owe him nothing. Your brother also sends this message: That he will help you in what ever way he can without openly betraying his position. It is important that he seem to be going along with their plans. He needs to keep Rute in check as long as possible, he has far too much influence over your father already."

"That my friend, is where Rute has made an error in judgement. My father is deeper than the mines of Magra." Boru said with pride.

"And Tanner will help us also."

"Tanner! You have news of him? Why did you not say so before? Where is he?"

Bela watched his sister sink back in her seat and pout. "Sister..." he said leaning into her ear. "if you wish to be treated like a man than act like one."

"Yes, my Lord..." she said rising to her feet one more time and giving her brother an evil look. "his quest to find his family took him round about the city and into Basin Town Jail..."

"Jail!"

"and from the jail to the army where he goes by the name of Andrus. By luck or the will of the Great Bear God he is sword master to the new recruits."

"He's training your father's army?" Arius said in amazement.

At this Boru looked stunned and the council was silent. Then he let out a belly laugh that shook the table. His joy and mirth ignited the generals with laughter.

"By his prowess I fear he will train them too well..." he said pouring himself a cup of wine. He raised his glass. "To my Prince of Schemers." he said looking at Arius.

The wine jug went round the table. "To Tanner!" they shouted.

Again Kora held up her hand.

"Whose running this council anyway?" Boru laughed, then raising his cup he pointed his index finger at her.

"My Lord, it is only a matter of time before he is recognized, he has seen many old faces, faces you and he remember from battles past, and though he wears a beard..."

"That I would like to see!"

"he fears he will soon be discovered. And there is another reason why we must strike soon. Your brother assured him that the hostages will be brought to camp and kept prisoner there. The jailor is anxious to remove them and Faolan knows Rute would like to see their numbers reduced by cold and pestilence over the winter."

"So..." Boru looked into the faces of his comrades and sighed "we have a choice to make, our first choice, and our greatest. Do we wait? Is this to be a siege against our city or do we ride out and meet my father on his own ground?" He had only to look at their expressions to find his answer.

"Right." he said with pain but resolve in his voice. "Next. Do we wait until spring, when they are on the move? It would be easier to separate a column of hostages from their hosts...what hostages are left for us to rescue. Either way the guardians will retaliate quickly. We will need our full force ready. It would likely turn into our first serious battle. Or...as Kora suggests, do we raid the camp before they march?"

"What! Slip hundreds of women, children and elders through the guards and out into the wilderness? In winter? And then what? Do they disappear? Do they fly away?" a general asked in disbelief.

"I do not need your help. These are my forests...My strike will be un-noticed until we are gone...we will send the enemy into chaos..." Kora said. "We will get them away somehow."

"So brave and so foolish..." Bela grumbled, then addressed the council. "No. That would only end in the death of the hostages."

Bela continued quietly and firmly. "You cannot attack an entire army by yourself, my Viper, though I know you would like to. If it is to work at all we must manage from the inside, then strike and disappear. We must rely on Faolan and Tanner to arrange things somehow. Then comes Lord Boru and our army. Already waiting. Your father will never expect you to come boldly knocking at his front door." he said looking at Boru. "He will expect you to shrink and hide with your mistress, waiting on him in your 'fish market of a city', as he calls it."

Kora jabbed her brother in the ribs with her elbow, a smirk on her face.

Boru's generals, glared uncomfortably at the siblings.

Boru laid his hand atop Aolwynd's and squeezed it to prevent her speaking.

Arius rose for the first time, his love and trust in Boru smarting at this insult. "Look outside if you think we will hide..."

Bela raised his hand. "Easy! Easy! I only repeat what I have heard out of Guardia, I am here, am I not?...To fight and die with you if I must."

Arius smiled sheepishly and coughed. "This is a raid on a sitting army...in its own territory, and close to the capitol but I will put my trust in Tanner, and you, my Lord Boru...father..." he said under his breath "and always will." Arius' eyes were glistening. "I say we go. But I have something more to add...if I may. My falconers. They grow impatient, they are not soldiers, I will give them a task if it please you." With that he sat down, having said what he thought was all that needed to be said.

Boru smiled at Arius and looked around the table. All met his eyes with a nod.

"It is settled then. Kora, how many men do you need?"

"Only my own."

"Don't be a fool." Bela whispered.

"If I must...fifty."

Boru raised his eyebrows and grumbling came from the other generals around the table.

"Any more and we will be seen from far off!" she said truculently.

"Fifty, plus your own men."

"Alright." Kora said hoisting herself out of her chair and

marching out of the tent.

Bela followed her outside. "I saw only the Mountain Road on her precious map as it crossed our lands. Where are all our trails and passages, are they not marked?"

"Secret, as they should be and will be kept that way, I'll not tell her anything. As you say, it is 'our country' whether she paints his name all over it or not. Ours. Not theirs." Kora said grimly. "Promise me something, little brother..." she placed her hands on his shoulders. "Lead our people and keep them safe if..." Bela nodded without comment.

The cool breezes of evening were a welcome relief from the day spent in a stuffy tent. The council members wiped their foreheads as they exited and paused to breath in the fresh air.

Ruby was pacing about with the baby in her arms.

"It's been hours! What on earth 'av ye been talkin' about?"

"War council things." Arius said importantly.

"You're goin' aren't yah? I'm goin' too, yah can't stop me! She's my moother held hostage! I want to help."

"Ruby, by the gods, were you listening?"

"Of course! An' we've never been apart, not since we met, well, almost, an' we're not goin' ta be..." her hot tears fell onto the baby's face making him blink and cry.

"It's not up to me..." Arius said.

Kora came over to them.

"Here, let me see him." She picked up the child and wiped its red cheeks. "He's teething." she laughed and stuck her finger into his mouth, massaging the gums. The boy grabbed onto her wrist with both hands greedily.

They sat down at the camp fire. "He has your father's proud forehead and his blue eyes." Kora said, handing the sleeping child back to Ruby. "Find someone to care for him, we may be able to use you."

Kora made her excuses and walked back to the tent.

"Ah like her. See? Yah can't get rid o' me..." Ruby said pulling seductively on Arius' belt and staring into his eyes.

"Aye. He warned me you'd stick." Arius leaned in and kissed her.

Boru came over to Aolwynd as she bent over her map.

"Proud of your handiwork?" He said tracing his fingers along her backbone and playing with the lacing of her woolen gown.

"I am." she said smiling. The brilliant green and gold border with its ships and sea serpents had taken her the most time, truth be told, but it had helped her to organize her thoughts.

"Where exactly do our borders lie?" he asked.

"That is for you to decide, my love."

Boru looked at her with a start. "No. I am no conqueror, do not look to me for more than a just ending to this war. I have your heart. If it were left to me we would be safe in some tower by the sea. No orders, no war and no other people."

"With only one entrance?"

"Yes. And a stout door that could be closed and locked from the inside."

"We must hold onto each other then and pretend the circle of our arms is your tower, for now."

"So." he sighed. "Where are my country's borders?"

Aolwynd put her finger on the map and traced it from the south coast to the north outlining a shape like a pregnant crescent moon with its back against the sea. Their narrow land bulged out in the middle reaching east to encompass Kora's Middle Mountains. Then she waved vaguely toward the northern wilderness.

"Not a very big country, is it?" he said, staring at the little painted city and harbor, flanked by fishing villages. Inland the pale green space of the empty plain was crested by the Northern Road. The south held only one passage along the coast, an insignificant little inn was drawn in loving detail beside it.

"Is it enough for you? This city state and the mountainous regions that surround it?"

"This is." he said taking her in his arms. His warmth intoxicated her, she dropped her hand from the map and laid her head on his shoulder. He rocked her gently back and forth as he might a baby.

A figure came out of the dark and approached Boru and Aolwynd as they were getting ready to ride back to the palace.

It was Kora. "I have something else to tell you."

"Yes?"

"It concerns your lady as well."

"What is it, my brave friend?"

"Your son..."

"Boru!" Aolwynd cried sliding off her horse and grabbing hold of Kora's shoulders.

"He is with the army, he is safe, Tanner is watching over him."

Aolwynd burst into tears and kissed Kora's cheeks. The General pulled away from her awkwardly. Her glance was cold.

"And my husband?" Aolwynd said, wiping her eyes and looking up guiltily at Boru.

"Yes. He is there too."

Aolwynd gasped.

"It is late." Boru said quietly helping Aolwynd back onto her horse. They rode off side by side in silence.

"No thanks for that bit o' good news, eh?" A voice from behind Kora sent the hairs on the back of her neck tingling.

"Stand back, who ever you are!" She said swinging around with her hand on the hilt of her knife.

"I meant no harm, your honor." The soldier said jumping back and taking up his post again by the side of the tent. He relaxed, leaning upon his lance. "Everybody knows their story, his an' the lady's, it's part of the city's history. Told to children, practically a bedtime story. Ah remember it. There's even songs about them. "The Captain and His Swan" an' "Jem the Pirate Slayer". Only now the bedtime tale is not something we'd tell to the children, eh? They're a bit different in the flesh, don't you think? Not so happy ta hear about the extra husband, I'll warrant..."

"You shouldn't talk about the Lord Protector that way."

"Why? I saw how you looked at her. I've said nothing that isn't true an isn't said by everyone else. She's not his wife...yet there she is, at the head of his war council, in his bed an' her husband still livin'."

Kora sighed and almost smiled. "She helped to make you free once, remember?"

"That were a long time ago. I were a child then. We don't forget, but no one muzzles us neither, not Guardian, nor king nor Lord Protector neither. It's why we're fightin', innit?"

"Perhaps." Kora said.

"An' he's a mystery yet to most folks here. He was holed up in his tent when he first got here, drinkin'. Ah saw him. An' some folk said he was shakin' when E' took the oath. Suppose he stays in his tent when we're doin' all the fightin'? What then, eh?"

"No worry there, soldier."

"Well, what makes you fight, my General?" he asked.

She could see the flash of his youthful smile in the light of the campfires, and just a flicker of mischief in his eyes.

"I fight...because it's all I know how to do, it's all I've done for years." This spontaneously honest thought was never meant to come out, yet she felt comfortable in the darkness talking to this young man, like an equal, just another soldier in the ranks standing night duty. A voice next to another voice, without his eyes upon her body like every other man she had encountered. She stared at the fires.

"That's a sad empty life for a woman, pardon my saying so. You should have a husband and a family, a beauty like you." The man in him said, coming up beside her so close she could feel his breath.

Kora snapped out of her fantasy. She'd heard those words before. He saw no 'general' standing next to him. He desired her. "Don't you worry about me, boy." She said bristling.

"Ahm' no boy. An' the name's Jak."

"Well, Jak. You're over-free with your tongue. Do your duty." With that she stalked away leaving him slack-jawed.

"If ever you need me, your honor...or me tongue, fer anything..." he called after her.

"I need no man." she growled at his invitation.

Arius' falconers sat around their campfire complaining about the food, the strange looks they got from soldier's wives and the fact they were treated little better than the Wild Men out of the forest.

"What are we doin' here? We're not soldiers."

"We follow Arius."

"Aye. The boy. Remind me again why?"

"Because we gave our oath ta' Anroth, tha's why."

"But what are we doin' 'ere, besides sittin' on our arses?"

"Let me worry about that..." Arius said sitting down on a log next to one of the men. "I've got an idea."

Two pairs of eyes watched Mother Brilla as she made her

morning rounds. Cere and Lyla carried the Matron's instruments and notebook just as they had done every morning for years. Yet now they scrutinized her every move, glancing back at each other to confirm or deny what they saw. She seemed to walk differently and held her head at a certain angle as she spoke with her patients. Every movement reminded them of Lauro's commanding manner. The two assistants spent their nights puzzling over this strange behavior, their foreheads together, sharing a pillow.

This mysterious change had been noticed by the other Good Women as well, for their Matron's instructions had become clearer, more precise. Most surprising of all, she had begun to prescribe with confidence, using combinations of drugs and herbs they had not seen used before. Brilla had always been over-cautious, almost timid about using the pharmacy and its myriad tinctures, poultices and droughts, relying upon the others for advice. She had never entered the room with its walls of shelves and cabinets if she did not have to.

One morning Cere found her amongst the bottles and flasks, not taking inventory but actually mixing a sleeping drought without the recipe book. The little girl's head could just be glimpsed above the counter and her squeaky voice was heard giving instructions. It surprised Cere so much that she dropped her basket of dried camomile flowers onto the floor. She spent the rest of the morning flicking tiny petal shards from her uniform.

Walking by the open doorway of the Matron's office the women often saw Brillie held on Brilla's lap whispering, going over the patient's charts together. Some nights when the hospital was quiet and all the wards were dark, these lessons would drone on and on until the little girl fell back, unable to teach any longer, her head drooping like a flower, exhausted.

Brillie suffered greatly from headaches the day after these all night sessions. She still slept on a cot in the inner room of the Matron's office. It had less light which was just as well. On these occasions the little girl screamed in pain whenever the curtains let in the sun. Only at twilight would the girl smile and ask to go outside. The women would find her lying comfortably stretched out on top of the Matron in her embrace. On the very couch where Rue had died, the two of them would gaze up at the stars. There they would rest, humming nursery songs, or stranger still, discussing patients until the girl's head stopped throbbing and they both fell asleep.

When Mother Brilla could not be found to sing to her, Brillie's screaming could be heard throughout the wards. She said later she dreamt of dark wings hovering over her or a poisonous throne that held her, its golden arms like human arms clutching her.

One morning, the Matron brought her a little silver box with a hinged lid. Inside on green velvet sat a pair of small brown glass disks framed and fastened together with silver so that they could be worn in front of her eyes.

"I had these made for you so that you may follow me on my rounds, and out into the sunshine, you are getting altogether too pale...and then there is this." Brilla handed her a necklace. A little disc of bone also encased in silver hung from it. "Some people wear them for luck." the Matron said with a smirk, fastening the tiny piece of skull around the girl's neck with a green ribbon.

As time went by the sight of the little shadow with a crutch and dark glasses limping along behind Mother Brilla became common place.

The pair were cause for much comment amongst the city folk, especially when it was known that they consulted in full view of the Good Women and their patients. The Matron spoke to Brillie as an equal, never as a child and found it necessary to reassure the women and their patients on occasion. This uncanny pair soon became the topic of a city council meeting but as no one had suffered from their care the matter was dropped. Besides, Brilla was in charge of the hospital and the girl was the daughter of the Lord Protector's mistress. No one wished to stir the waters.

Aolwynd and Jors came to visit and tried to persuade the girl to go back to the palace but she refused.

Instead of smiling and curling up in her mother's arms, Brillie walked to a window with arms folded and stared out at the sea, looking every bit like a grown-up. Finally she turned to her mother and said in a low voice, stern and commanding "Well my warrior...and how is your life going for you? Would it not have been better if you had joined us so long ago?"

Aolwynd stared at her daughter and backed out of the room. Taking the Matron aside, she whispered "What is the matter with her? Why does she speak to me so?"

"It may be too difficult for me to explain, I am afraid. I am not sure but it is not Brillie who speaks, not really. Something visits us, visits us both, and I hope means to help us. But I also hope it will soon go away...otherwise...it means...but do not worry yourself yet." Brilla spoke awkwardly, looking around as if she did not want to say too much or as if someone might hear that she did not wish to inform or offend.

"Perhaps she feels safer with you?" Aolwynd sighed, trying not to feel afraid or disappointed.

"Brilliana, would you not prefer to be with your family?" the Matron asked.

"No. I want to stay where I'm needed. I need time to do what I came here for. I want to help you, my friend." the girl said.

Aolwynd started at this and grasped Brilla's hand. This time a different voice had spoken, one she knew, younger, sweeter. The child's eyes were dark and luminous, all knowing, peaceful, yet her manner was so insistent that the Matron nodded automatically and turning to Aolwynd shrugged her shoulders.

"I am sure you are welcome here as long as you wish to stay." Aolwynd told the child glancing at Brilla. She fled the room, running down the corridor, hiding her tears.

Jors was not happy about his sister's decision the next time he visited and plied her with stories of a soldier's life. He told of the camp and Monk's tricks and the new baby that Arius had brought back with him from the Black Mountains.

"Is it a Wild Man's baby?" she asked.

"You might say that..." he lied, making sounds like a baby crying to make her laugh. "I'm going to squire for Lord Boru if you don' coom back an' I'll be a soldier then! You won't see me no more! Maybe I'll get kilt'!"

The girl just smiled at him. "No. I see something very different for you..."

Jors made a noise of disbelief.

"Well, you must do what you're meant to do, young man." Brillie said in a very grown up voice, soft but firm, taking his hand.

Jors steamed with anger and pulled it away. "Brillie! Tha's not what yer' meant ta' say! Yer meant ta' say 'Oh no Jors! Doon't go with that horrid man! I'll away home with yah right now an' we'll play our games again like we used to do!'"

His sister only laughed at him. "I can't my love...I've something else to do now. I must do something else, be someone else. My friend sent for me, she needs me still, and others may...be in danger." Brillie closed her eyes. Her voice was resonant and womanly and its strangeness frightened him.

"Yah' doon't sound right, Brillie, yer scarin' me, ye' sound like...I doon't know what. Ah' doon't like it. Give over talkin' lak tha'." He stood up and waved a timid goodbye.

"Don't be frightened...please don't be afraid of your little sister..." Jors heard the strange voice call after him as he ran down the hall.

"Feel that? The hair's all up on the back of my neck. Tell me I'm crazy. Tell me anything." Cere whispered, leaning into the pillow.

"Calm yourself, my love. There have been stranger things than this down these halls, remember? And what's the harm?"

"Years ago. Not for many years." Cere said.

"You're an old woman getting to be..." Lyla stroked her cheek.

"I tell you I listened and watched them tonight, sitting on the veranda."

"They do that every night now."

"But it was like the child is a 'Vessel', and not just one voice but two. That's the best way I can describe it. When was the last time that happened here? A Priestess Vessel...a true vessel, ages, long ages of men since we have had a gifted one...and two voices, like doctors. Using words and formulas I've never heard before! And the little girl, giving her instructions, surgical instructions! Casting her spirit into Brilla! I'm all over goose bumps!" Cere rubbed her arms beneath the covers.

"My dove, calm yourself." Lyla embraced her and kissed her neck.

"We must tell the priestess...what do you think? If the girl is...someone special...Watch with me, tomorrow night! See for yourself."

"I don't think I want to." Lyla turned over and punched the pillow.

"For me! Please!" Cere curled an arm around her lover's belly squeezing her tightly.

"Alright my love, only for you. But if she is..."

Boru called for men to join Kora's company and within hours all was ready. They left the plain of Saels as the first rains of winter fell. Bela and Kora lead thirty Wild Men and fifty soldiers through the main aisle of the camp.

Boru's own men remained with him to train the new recruits but would have had it otherwise. Their minds were focussed on their imprisoned families. They stood silently, hands raised in farewell and stared at the woman general on whose back the rescue mission depended.

Three wagons with provisions accompanied by twenty soldiers waited by Arius' tent. The falconer's loaded the last of their gear.

Arius had come up with a scheme of his own after the council and convinced Kora and Boru of its merit.

"Falconers and all those who raise and train hunting birds are under the protection of the nobility, they all, in a sense, belong to The Guardian and must have papers and be licensed vendors before they can sell. My falconers have those papers." he told them.

Boru nodded. It was one of the reasons he had gone after Arius' father in the Black Mountains although lapsed papers were minor in comparison with his banditry and complicity in murder. "Go on..." he said.

"So, I will take six of my falconers with us and we will look to be merely a caravan on our way through the market towns selling birds."

"What of the rest of your men? You do not plan to leave them here poking their fires, drinking and getting into trouble?"

"No. I have set the Eagle Masters a special test of their skill. They will start out with us, then go about their business. Give them some time and you will see the success of my plan."

"Time is one thing I have not a lot of. You make me curious. What do you think, Kora? Do you trust this youngster?"

"He seemed man enough to you when you sent him north."

"True. You've come a long way, my son. The grounds around my tent will be a sorry sight without the presence of your men; the birds on their posts, the noise and feathers flying..."

Arius beamed.

"Your guards will not be sorry to see them leave, however." Kora said. "They attract too many people, children and gawkers. Better to keep you safe. And by the way," she hesitated and then spoke without even acknowledging to herself why she said it "I'll take one of your guards with me."

"Take whom ever you want, you do not need to ask me."

"Good." she said and walked away.

Ruby placed the baby in the arms of a soldier's wife and climbed aboard the first wagon, taking the reins. Arius mounted his horse and rode ahead of her. Ruby snapped her whip and the oxen lurched, digging their hooves into the muddy track, beginning to pull. It was a sight to see the falconers join the column and the Eagle Masters lastly, riding out with their birds on their arms. Arius rode up and down the line, his chest out and his chin held high. When he rode past Boru and Aolwynd, Jors waved at him enthusiastically. Arius grinned and then assumed a more manly expression.

It was a cold wet march and the wagons only caught up with Kora's company by nightfall. They climbed ever higher out of the plain until the rain stopped and soft snow began to blanket the fields and hills.

On the third day out they came at last to the Great Crossroads high in the Middle Mountains. Two main roads bisected the realm and in good times travelers and merchants kept them clear. Both were now deserted in all directions and there were no fresh tracks. The snow covered the routes so that they could only be distinguished from the rest of the landscape by their relative depression. The coming of war and the "Great Separation" as it was now called had put a halt to commerce. Here the two companies parted. Kora, Bela and the raiding party took to the hidden mountain paths they knew so well. Their plan was to come down unseen into the heavily forested cliffs and hillsides just above the Guardian's city. The Eagle Masters followed Kora for a time on their own secret mission.

Arius lead his caravan to the Northern Road turning east on the route he had traveled when he first left home with Boru and his men. The small market towns and villages they encountered would protect their mission. The people were used to the sight of traveling peddlers. A caravan of falconers might be expected to journey in safety during winter festival to the capitol without interference or suspicion.

Ruby waved from her wagon as Kora cast a worried glance at them. The girl jerked her chin upward in an impudent salute and smiled. Kora smiled back.

"Who is that soldier riding so close behind her?" Ruby asked. "Almost like a bodyguard..."

"More like a puppy dog. See how he watches her. I don't remember seeing him before." Arius said.

Ruby stared at the young soldier with curiosity.

"He's young...Do you fancy him?"

"Idiot!" she said cracking her whip.

5

The Under-Hand Cut

Captain Striker interrupted practice one morning as the snow began to fall announcing a visit by General Rute. He would be surveying their efforts that afternoon. Tanner kept his eyes on the combatants and listened without expression. He called out the names of his best swordsmen and told them to give of their best when the time came or else. After choosing who would display their skills first and where they would stand he walked hurriedly to the Captain's tent. Striker was going over the practice records that Tanner had kept.

"Captain..." he began.

"What is it, Andy?" Striker looked up at him with surprise. "You've done a fine job. You're not worried about the men are you?"

Tanner shifted his feet uneasily and nervously grasped the pommel of his sword. "Nay, it's not tha'. But I moost get away, now. Make some excuse fer me."

"What? General Rute is expecting to meet you! He has heard of your efforts and wants to thank you on behalf of the Guardian."

"That's not all he'll do!" Tanner said under his breath. "Ah can't be here when he comes."

Striker raised his head from the log book with sudden enlightenment. "Ah...our little problem again, eh? Well, this is all very inconvenient for both of us and I wonder...yes, I have been wondering...just how close to the top are you? It comes to me mind now how friendly you were with my Lord Faolan...and I wonder if you've that same easy manner with his brother..."

Tanner leaned in over the desk inches from Striker's face and whispered with a grimace, his teeth flashing. "I'll kill you first an' bolt on outta here right now before I swing for a traitor..."

"Nay! Hold, my friend, I owe you something still. You've done fer me, I'll help you out. Yer worth more to me alive! I'll think of somethin'. Give me a minute. You know, ah like a good 'sit down', mah bones 'er too old fer this, ah should be home sittin' under me tree watchin' mah gran' babbies. I'd rather sit back and watch you turn those clods of dirt into soldiers than do it meself by a long road."

"You think of somethin' quick or I'm gone." Tanner walked out of the tent. Turning the corner he nearly fell over young Jemson. The boy's eyes were wide with fear. He'd heard every word. Tanner grabbed him by the collar and dragged him forcefully around the back of the tent. Jemson's toes trailed along the ground.

"What did you hear, son? Tell me!"

Jemson tripped and blustered trying to stand upright and think of something to say at the same time.

"Quick like! Or I'll drag yah' off and throttle yah in the bushes soon as look on yah...leave yah fer dead no matter who yer father was!"

Jemson's eyes went dark and he swung his fists at the man but Tanner held him just far enough out that he only spun around by the collar. Jemson stopped, puffing for breath and glared at Tanner suddenly realizing what the man had said. Looking about the camp with suspicion he whispered angrily "Whadayou know about my father? He's a traitor and so are you!"

"You shut yer mouth, you hear? You don't know nothin' about it." Tanner yanked the frightened boy further away. Jemson dug his heels in and slouched, making Tanner drag him across the snow. He threw the boy down on a clump of wet earth far enough away that his voice could not be heard.

"Sit doon there till I straighten you out! You got no idea what yer talkin' about." Tanner said leaning over the boy like an oak tree.

Jemson, still shaking, blinked at the man. Slowly a spark twinkled in his eyes. "Alright...I'll keep quiet. That's what you want, isn't it...on one condition."

Tanner made to grab the boy's collar again but Jemson flinched away.

"Teach me. Teach me to fight. Give me a sword and I'll keep quiet."

Tanner stood up and looked out across the plain toward the northern forest with his hands on his hips. Finally he took a deep breath. "Bloody fookin' hell...yah little bastard, ye' doon't give up do ye? Why should I do tha'? Besides, I've told yah, yer too young, yer bones are still sof', you'll tear yer muscles. Come ta me when yer shaft rises an' not before." Tanner couldn't help glaring at the boy but there was something in his eyes that made the boy smile.

"Then I'll tell everyone who you are...who are you anyway?" Jemson said, the threat gone in his voice and his curiosity taking over.

Tanner blew some air out between his lips and sat down on the wet earth next to the boy. "Ahm Lord Boru's second man that's who I am." he said with a sigh. "His right arm, second in command of the army of Saels, if you please, an 'is best friend in all this world. There's a prize for yah. Been beside him fer eight long year through every battle till 'E slunk all the way back to the woman he loves...yah, yer own moother, yah little shite."

Young Jemson's mouth dropped open and a slow wide grin swept across his face.

Tanner went on, "Wha's that'? Yer father's garmy grin? Give over! The gods! Yer 'is very livin' image fer fuck sake...spare it fer the girls, it'll no work on me." Tanner blew out his breath again and stared off toward the west. "'E never did want this war, it's Rute that's got this goin'...so you've nothin' ta' hate the man for, cept' his absence. An' I'll give yah one more nugget! You won't tell on me an I'll tell yah why. I'm a prize but your a bigger one! I'm Boru's Second but yer his son! If anybody finds me out I'll be in chains and then the rope but fer you...Rute'll parade you in front of yer own moother an' like as not slit yer throat in front of her! Pretty picture! But before that he'll squeeze every last concession out of yer precious city of Saels and 'E'll force yer father down on his knees to spare your life!" Tanner lowered his voice till it came out like a growl. "So you'll keep yer mouth shut young Boru...son of Boru, now Lord Protector and ruler of Saels, grandson of Borchard...Supreme Guardian an' ruler of Earden!"

Jemson sat shivering with shock and staring west beyond the white expanse of mountains. Somehow, running about the camp on errands for Rooster, doing chores with Dah, he'd never thought any of these strangers, Faolan, Tanner, Rute had anything to do with his life or himself. All he could think of now was to get up and run like a rabbit for home.

"Now, here's the bottom of it." Tanner said "I swore ta yer uncle Faolan I'd protect yah, not but what I'd kill anyone who tried ta hurt you fer yer father's sake alone...but ye've got ta' help me now. Be careful. Stick close to the cook tent or stick close ta me. An' stay clear of General Rute, you hear?"

Jemson nodded. "A sword. Give me a sword."

Tanner swiped the boy's head playfully with his hand. "Fookin' bloody hell. Hard as a nut! You don't give up, do yah?"

That afternoon a wagon left the encampment for the city and pulled into the gates of the great jail followed by twenty soldiers on horseback. A man and a boy jumped down and waited while the jailers assigned their guards and gathered the hostages together. The noise of crying children and the wailing of women rose up from within the walls of the stockade.

Tanner's heart cracked at the sound. He wondered how many of his children might have died within the walls of Basin Town already and whether he would be able to free what was left of them and protect them from re-capture once the raid was successful. If it was...

At last the heavy inner gates opened and a sorry multitude of gaunt figures emerged, moving with a shuffling gate and hanging onto each other for support. In their arms were babies as light as feathers and next to the women, the elderly stumbled, the old women fearful and confused, the old men defiant. Tanner searched the hollow faces of the crowd for Cherry. She passed in front of him before he even recognized her. She was staring straight ahead, the hand of her eldest son on her back and in her arms she carried the youngest girl. The other children stumbled along behind her. The baby was no where to be seen.

Tanner's throat constricted with anger and despair. He was relieved she did not see him and he turned away quickly to help the sick and feeble into the wagon.

"We'll take care of the corpses fer ye'." the head jailor said. He handed over an accounting of how many had already died and how many were left too weak to be moved. Tanner climbed back into the box and pulled the wagon out following the column through the streets of the city.

The sidewalks were lined with shocked citizens. No one spoke. He felt their anger and their hatred directed at the soldiers as they watched this ravaged legion of guardian's families shuffle past them. Suddenly every spectator was in motion. One person ran into his house and brought out blankets, then more and more brought food stuffs, candles, jackets for the children and thrust them into the arms of the victims.

"God bless Lord Boru!" a voice cried from deep within the crowd followed by curses and shouting as the soldiers tried to bring order. The prisoners passed beneath the city gates and out of sight to the sounds of anger and disbelief fading away behind them.

It was nightfall before they reached the outskirts of camp. A simple journey that had taken Tanner an hour had taken the weak legs and empty stomachs of his miserable flock all afternoon and beyond sunset.

"Striker, my old friend, you disappoint me." Rute entered the tent and sat down in the Captain's chair. "I told you I wanted ta meet this paragon of military skill oo's caused such a miracle amongst them lumps we started out with. Yet where is he?" Rute splashed wine into a goblet.

"Lord Faolan's order to retrieve the hostages took precedence, General, sorry. The order and your visit on the same day...bad timing."

"Or good timing...you're not hiding anything from me are you Striker?"

Striker turned his back and poured himself a drink.

"This is no ordinary soldier. Where did you say he was from? The jail? Drunken brawling, eh? Nay. I hear he keeps to himself and never drinks with anyone. Hardly likely fer a droonk, eh?"

"He's a loner, that's all. 'E don't like fuss."

"Commendable. However, those moves ah saw today, the way your men have learned to swing a sword. Ah've seen those moves 'afore. They're the tricks of a battle-hardened warrior. Those men 'av been taught things it takes years of fighting to learn...if y' survive to learn 'em that is. You know, Will, every man swings his sword his own way, unique, if you know what I mean. And I've seen that underhand cut to the side of the body...ony two times, used by the man that perfected it and used by the man 'E taught it to. Well, it's like a signature, innit?" Rute stood up and leaned over the desk with a snarl, "Tell me what you know..."

Dogs barked and ran along the length of the cold, bedraggled column as it moved out over the plain. The sky was leaden. Heavy snow would fall that night. The deep reds and greens of the pro-offered blankets contrasted sharply with the snow and the little grey figures that wore them.

They stopped outside the entrance to the prisoner's enclosure. It was set apart near the northern edge of camp and next to the training field. Faolan had seen to that. There was a wide swath of empty ground surrounding the area patrolled by guards. No one was allowed near the fence. Tents and campfires were already waiting. It appeared to be Faolan's over-protectiveness at work but it also created a clear run to the forest beyond.

Tanner slowed the oxen to a halt as each hostage was counted at the gate. Jemson was asleep, his head resting in Tanner's lap. Tanner peered into the gloom of dusk and the falling snow. A single mounted figure waited nearby watching the arrival. His arm rested on his knee and he leaned heavily on it. The hair rose on the back of Tanner's neck. It was Rute. He'd seen him sit in the cold like that a hundred times before. Then he noticed the soldiers standing behind him with their swords drawn.

"'Ere! Boy! Wake oop!" He shook Jemson till he rose groggily. "We're leavin'! You! Come up front!" he called to an old man sleeping in the back. "Can you drive this pair and wagon?"

The old man nodded.

"Come up here quiet like and take my place." Tanner grabbed the old man under the arms and pulled him forward onto the box.

"What's wrong?" Jemson asked rubbing his eyes.

"Ahm' savin' my neck and yer little pink ass. See tha'? There's Rute there a' waitin' on me. It ain't safe 'ere no more for neither of us. Coom with me now an' don't make no sound." Tanner pushed the boy into the back of the wagon. Clambering over the bodies of the sick and infirm they made their way to the drop gate. Tanner paused by a young woman who was big with child, came close to her face and took it in both his hands. The woman opened her eyes with a start and gazed up at him.

"Tell Cherry I'll be back." was all he said and with that he leapt out of the wagon and caught Jemson as he fell over the gate. They followed behind the wagon as it began to move again till they came to a hollow and some bushes, barely enough to shield them. One of the soldiers looked back scanning the column.

"Oy! Andy! What are you doin'?" the soldier yelled as he saw Tanner stand for a fraction of a second in the road looking at the boy. Jemson stared at Tanner, as if making up his mind, then shook his head slowly. The boy ran off toward the soldier, dashing around his horse and forcing him to turn round to look at him. The horse reared up and pranced to avoid stepping on the boy.

"Bad meat sir!" Jemson said, coming close and playing with the man's stirrup. "'E'll visit the bush and be right back."

"Oy! Sprog! Watch how you approach mah horse! Don't you konw no better than to walk behind? You'll get kicked!" the soldier said laughing.

"Yes sir."

Tanner slipped away into the darkness of a dry hollow heading north towards the woods.

Jemson walked along beside the soldier, jabbering about nothing, keeping him distracted. After fifty paces the man looked back and saw the old man still driving the oxen with no sign of Tanner. He looked down at his side to curse the boy, but he was gone.

"Find him!" Rute yelled to his men as the wagon pulled into the enclosure. The old man was yanked from the box and dragged in front of Rute.

"Where's the man who was driving this wagon?"

The old man shrugged and mumbled his answer.

"Get him out of here." Rute spat. The soldiers dragged him by the arms and threw him into the crowd beyond the gates.

"Take your horses and find him! He can't have gotten far! Even you lot can follow a track in the snow!" Rute turned his mount and rode slowly toward Striker's tent.

The Captain was sitting where Rute had left him. His face was bloody and bruised. Striker looked up defiantly. "'E got away did 'E? Good."

Rute fell on him cursing, knocking the Captain out of his chair. Striker drew a knife from his belt and pointed it at the General as he got to his feet.

Rute raised his hand and grinned at him while he placed his hand on the pommel of his sword. "Tell me, Will? How would you like to die? You can have it here, quiet-like or by the noose holdin' hands w' Tanner in front of yer own men. Which is it ta' be?"

Striker swung his blade across Rute's cheek and a ribbon of blood showed quickly. Rute drew his sword and hacked into the man's arm at the shoulder. Striker dropped his knife and held his arm, backing up against the wall of the tent and causing it to balloon out like a sail.

"Yer an' old man, Will. He was the best thing 'as ever happened to you...and my army, o'course. Thank you for takin' that chance, yah lazy bastard. 'E's trained 'em well, most of 'em. Even if he is a bloody traitor. But let me see, what do that make you? Oh. Right. I know, a traitor." Rute grinned at the man as he came forward with his sword to pin him through. Striker was pale from loss of blood, the wound and the bone showing through his torn jacket. He could hardly hear what Rute was saying, the effort to stay conscious was so great.

The General pushed his blade forward ready to pierce him.

"Rute! Hold!" Faolan's voice rang out as he ran into the tent. Crossing Rute's blade with his own he swung it forcefully toward the ground. "What goes on here?"

"None of yer' business..." Rute growled.

"Oh, I think it is." Faolan said.

"That's a traitor standin' there an' 'E deserves ta' die! He had Tanner here all these months an' said noothin' to nobody while he minced about trainin' our men right under our noses! Noothin'! We

72

coulda bin' murdered in our cots by turned men! A bloody mutiny on our hands! Treachery!"

"Don't act the fool man, panic doesn't suit you." Faolan said quietly taking hold of Striker and propping him up.

Rute realized he'd lost the upper hand. He'd used his skill to insinuate around Faolan but those steely-blue eyes had seen everything. No excuse could explain attacking a fellow officer. Not if you wanted to stay one yourself. Faolan stared at him and Rute backed away trying to hide his fury behind a weak smile. 'Same color as his bloody brother's'. Rute thought as they left the tent.

Stretcher bearers carried Striker away with Faolan loping along beside them. Rute cursed under his breath as he looked about for the training log. He left with it under his arm.

The next day all those who had been trained were shifted into the regular army and a new batch of recruits were moved in. A different trainer was assigned the men and the repetitive calls and the sound of sword and shield resumed without a break.

"You fool!" Borchard cried out as Rute made his report. The Guardian paced back and forth in his study. The pale winter light of morning made his face appear almost blue as he turned to glare at his General.

"Because he chose the best man to train my army you try to kill him?"

"'E's not dead yet, yer honor, I only taught 'im a lesson." Rute lied. "An' Tanner? What about 'im? Our enemy...or so I thought." Rute stared at Borchard incredulously. "Striker knew it, yer honor. More than takin' an awful chance, tha's treason, that is." Rute's voice grew soft and conciliatory.

"A matter of differing opinion...my son says..."

"Phaw!" Rute made to spit but looked around at the carpeted floors and thought better of it.

"Tanner, my Lord, Boru's man!"

"And once my friend as well as my son's. Could he not have been turned?"

Rute stared at the old man in confusion.

"Nay! Never! Loyal to the death 'E is..."

"Would that I had more like him..." Borchard sighed.

Rute grimaced. "'E's turned traitor like yer son...' Rute stopped in mid-sentence as Borchard's pale eyes sparked and turned on him. Rute finished his sentence."...an' 'E escaped twice."

"Yes, sloppy work, wouldn't you say?" Borchard cleared his throat. "Just how long was he training our troops, eating our meat and learning our numbers?" the Guardian said sardonically.

Rute fumed but said nothing.

"I'm sorry my friend, you seem to see things only in terms of black and white. Striker has more subtlety, a quality I much admire. But then, you are a peasant and must be expected to think like one." Borchard sighed. "Try, if you can...to think like a general in future. Always use what you have first, remember that. Get what you can out of a man or a situation, as long as you maintain control, and then deal with it. 'Suck the marrow out of the bone before you throw it to the dogs'. "

"You are fond of peasant expressions, my Lord." Rute grumbled.

"Yes, well, I am a man of my people."

Rute smirked.

Borchard looked at him with an expression of surprise and concern as if he were seeing Rute in a new light. "Now, see that you cripple no more of my captains. How are the hostages?"

"Who? Oh, settled."

"No doubt Faolan has seen to their needs."

"No doubt." Rute grunted. "One oother thing...Ah'v heard there were a lot of very angry folk in the crowds tha' lined the streets, yer honor...they weren't happy ta' see so many of their soldier's families treated like criminals."

"Not their soldiers any more...traitors."

"Aye...but they doon't see it tha' way."

"Perhaps I should send more troops into the streets to keep them quiet?"

"Ahm' not sure tha' would be taken the right way, my Lord, speakin' of actin' more subtle-like."

"Do I look like I care?"

Rute stared and shook his head. He found it difficult to navigate around the corners of Borchard's noble manner and mercurial nature.

"Rute! Find out who is openly talking against me and deal with them. That is a task more suited to your bold talents."

The man put his hand over his heart and bowed low so that

Borchard could not see his face.

The next day fear and rumor began to spread within the walls of Guardia. Soldiers patrolled the streets on horseback, lingering near taverns and market places. Warnings were few, the rebellious were swiftly dealt with and the bodies of five citizens who had spoken openly against Borchard swung by sundown from the Western Gate.

The Guardian paid a visit to Striker in The Mother House of Good Women the next day. It was the oldest hospital in the realm, only the former school of doctors in the Mountains of Rue had been older. "Heal quickly my friend, I have need of you." he said standing over the man's cot.

"Ah'm no use ta anyone anymore." A twinge in the wounded man's shoulder made Striker breath in sharply.

"Don't speak like that. General's do not have to swing a sword themselves, they need to think and lead others. Heal quickly, General Striker..." Borchard called over his shoulder as he left the ward.

Striker lay with an incredulous look on his face and smiled in spite of the pain.

Faolan stood on the battlements of the city's north wall that night staring out into the darkness. "If you can see this, my friend...." he said dropping a torch from the wall.

6

The Cooking Pot

"Dah!" Jemson whispered from inside the cook tent.

Jem and Rooster were busy serving meals outside as two lines of men passed by on either side of an enormous three-legged cauldron. The cook's foreheads were beaded with sweat from the fire and in their effort to get so many men fed quickly. Every night their ladles scooped 'Luck of the pot' stew as fast as they were able. Men shuffled past with a chunk of bread in the bottom of their bowls and held them out hungrily. Those that could hunt augmented their rations with rabbit or game birds and cooked their own meat over their fires but there was always porridge in the morning and something hearty at night courtesy of the army. 'Keep 'em fed an' you'll keep 'em near' Rooster was fond of boasting. It was better than coming right out and saying they were kept from deserting only by his food, but he held that high opinion of himself. Jem had to agree with him. Some of the men looked like this was the first time they'd "eaten regular" in their entire lives.

"Dah!" Jemson called a little louder. Jem raised his head from his task but only for a moment.

When the lines of men converged into one and some were

coming back for 'seconds' the boy raised his voice. "Dah!" he called.

"Ere! Jemson! Where've you been to?" Rooster demanded. "I coulda used you today!"

The boy squinted his eyes and with a serious look on his face jerked his head at Jem to join him in the tent.

"Oh go on...I'll take over from here...'E's in soom kind o' trouble, you can tell tha' from the look of 'im."

"Aye." was all Jem would say. He'd seen that look before on his son's face and it meant he was in over his head about something.

"Dah."

"What's the matter?" Jem said as the boy pulled him through the cook tent and out the other flap at the back.

"We went to the city today and brought back the hostages."

"Oh, aye?"

"An' when we got back close to camp Andy jumped out the wagon and ran off!"

"Wha'?"

"'E's in trouble w' General Rute..."

Jem just listened, bending over his son and walking him further away. He knew better than to confuse him by asking a lot of questions. Better to keep him calm and just let it spill out little by little.

"'Ow can that be? Isn't he doin' a fine job o' trainin' the men?"

"Yes. He was supposed ta' be thanked by both generals today but...an I knew I wasn't s'posed to but...I listened at the tent an' heard him talkin' to Captain Striker tha' he didn't want to meet Rute an' to send 'im away like, an Dah..."

"Aye?"

"He called 'imself a traitor an yah know what else?"

"What?"

"He's not "Andy" at all! He's the enemy!"

"'Ow do yah know all this?"

Jemson looked at the ground. "Oh, he caught me listenin'. An Dah...he's Lord Boru's right-hand man, his second in command."

"He told you that?"

"Yes. He made me promise not to tell. 'E trusted me, Dah. An' he knows who I am. He said I was joost as big a prize as him and that I wouldn't tell 'cuz I might end up dead an' fer me to stay clear of

General Rute. Then we went to the jail ta' bring back the hostages."

"So after you came back..."

"He saw the general awaitin' for him by the gate an' he up an' jumped out the back of the wagon an' I jumped out too. An Dah...he wanted me to go with him! But then a soldier spotted us and I decided to help Andy escape. I had to Dah, he's my friend, an I don't know...I just don't think he's bad. Am I in trouble Dah?"

"Might be. Coom on." Jem grabbed the boy by the arm and walked him forcefully behind the row of tents heading for Faolan's own and hoping he was there.

A few dogs barked as they passed a line of latrines and the open ditch that was the garbage tip. This section of camp was always active day and night with folk on solitary business of their own, soldiers walking back and forth, squires with piss pots and dogs scavenging for food. Two figures walking along in the shadows caused no comment.

There was no guard on duty around General Faolan's tent when they found it and all was dark inside. He was not there. His shield was not hanging on its post outside. This usually meant he was spending the night at the palace.

Jem walked swiftly up to the entrance and pushed his son inside.

"Doon't coom out, don't say nothin' ta nobody nor call fer nuthin'. Go into 'is sleepin' chamber at the back and cover yerself up with a blanket. Try 'in get some rest. I'll come fer yah in the morning when I've figured soomthin' out."

Jemson slipped beneath the flap and scrambled through the darkness to the interior wall that separated the outer chamber from Faolan's private space.

What little light there was came from an open flap at the top of the tent. The boy could see the moon pausing in its course to look at him through the hole. A camp bed stood against one wall and a low brass table engraved with hunting scenes stood next to it. On this stood a flask of wine, a cup and a matching brass box. Jemson looked inside. It contained honeyed fruits and nuts. The boy helped himself, sitting down on the camp bed covered with a blanket of skins. As his eyes adjusted to the light he saw a large satchel filled with scrolls, a chest in one corner for clothes and a stand. Jemson sucked in his breath and a shiver went down his spine. Faolan's helmet, his swords, vambraces and gauntlets hung from this wooden frame along with a coat of maille. It could almost have been the man himself standing there. The boy tittered nervously then cursed himself for being afraid.

Jemson poured a cup of wine and choked at the strength of it. He had never had wine as it truly was before, always his mother had watered it down. He grinned. This was heady stuff indeed. Warmth radiated through him in no time at all and he looked about him with an overwhelming feeling of manly happiness. He giggled and stood up, a little unsteady on his feet. He went over to the 'tree' and tried on the gauntlets. 'What joy!' he thought. 'This is what it's like to be a real soldier! This is all I want in all the world! A soldier's life!' Forgetting that this was the tent of a ruler of his country, not an ordinary soldier. The gauntlets chaffed his hands and fell off till he held them upright and marched about the room importantly. Finally he began to feel dizzy and had to sit down. He took the gauntlets off and pouring more wine, picked up his cup again. He swallowed it down in one long gulp as he had seen Jem do many times. Then he lay out on his belly with his head hanging over the edge of the cot. It was there he noticed two scrolls laying side by side beneath it. He reached for the first one.

It was a history of the great School of Healing in the south. The one that had been destroyed and its master physician killed just that past year. Many rumors of murder and kidnapping flew about its destruction blaming Lord Boru. It was one of the many reasons he had heard to validate the coming of war. 'Did this mean Andy was involved?' young Jemson thought, his head beginning to feel a little fuzzy. He concentrated on the illustrations of flowers and plants. At the end of the scroll were two portraits. One was of Master Doctor Cornelius Severus and at the very end of the vellum, its edges worn and ragged, as if viewed most frequently, there was another portrait. Staring back at him was a beautiful woman dressed in a dark blue gown seated on a small golden throne. Her hair fell in long ringlets and on her forehead was a diadem. Beneath her picture were the words "The Queen".

Jemson rolled the scroll up and put it under the bed. The other scroll he found much more enlightening and entertaining although some of it confused him and much of it made him feel uncomfortable in his loins. It showed illustrations of naked people, in every possible combination, involved in elaborate contortions,

80

some of them, he couldn't help thinking were very funny. They cavorted in gardens, on top of beds, in baths and waterfalls. Their faces expressed pleasure, but also surprise and sometimes, he thought, a kind of agony. Jemson was unsure and he puzzled over them for some time. He knew they were meant to be 'acts of love' for he and his brother had figured things like that out quite some time ago. He and Jors were 'men after all'.

He lay back on the cot missing his brother and his little sister. He choked back the sadness that suddenly overwhelmed him. He remembered his brother's dirty jokes and the way he willingly followed his every command. He thought of the pleasure young Boru got from teasing Brillie and her screams of delight when he crushed her in his arms. Then an image of their mother floated in front of his bleary eyes. Tears rolled down the boy's red cheeks and he sobbed quietly until sleep took him and his hand let the scroll drop to the ground.

Jem walked back to the cook tent but stopped when he saw soldiers near the entrance. Slipping around the back he crept in the tent and hid behind a pile of barley sacks and supplies. The soldiers were questioning Rooster.

"Ye doon't say? All this time? Trainin' our men?" Rooster let out a bark of incredulous glee. "It's enoof' ta' make a cat laugh, that is. An' the boy helped him escape? Huh. What do it mean? What are ye askin' me for? I don't know whar 'E is!" Rooster moved about the kitchen elbowing the men aside. "Ah tell ye I don't know nothin' more an' yer in my way!" He kept working all the while he spoke, chopping meat with an enormous cleaver. The sound of cracking bone and the heavy thud of the knife on the chopping block made the men jump.

"Stop tha' a moment if you please..." the lead soldier said angrily.

"What?" Rooster yelled laying his cleaver down and leaning with both hands over the bloody block. "Ah'm working on tomorrow's dinner fer you lot, there ain't noothin' more important ta me than tha'."

"Where's yer oother man, yer cook? 'E's the boy's father init?"

"Tha' might be. 'E was out back last I saw him."

They made to run out the exit.

"'E's not there now...yew great pillocks." he shouted.

"What else do you know about them?" the officer asked, coming back.

"'Ere! Ahm busy. Tell that general Rute I'll come by later, maybe I kin tell 'im soomthin' about tha' boy if I've 'alf a moment ta think...an' if 'E makes it worth my while..."

They nodded reluctantly and left the tent.

Jem waited till he heard nothing but the sound of chopping then he came out from behind the mountain of supplies as if he had just walked in. Rooster jumped when he saw him but quickly smiled.

"Whar've you been? Soldiers been lookin' fer your boy. What's 'E been up to?"

"Ah don't know." Jem said quietly walking up beside Rooster. Picking up a slab of meat he threw it on the man's block.

Rooster stood back eyeing him with his cleaver in his hand. "Thanks." he said.

Jem avoided his eyes. Walking to the other block he picked up his knife. Rooster backed away from his task knocking over a bag of beans. Jem put the pot of stewing chunks on the ground between them. Picking up the chunks he began carving the bones away, throwing them in a separate pot for broth. His eyes were black and he focussed on his work.

"Jem? We're friends, reet?"

"Aye."

"No harm, eh?" Rooster said, his face red and sweaty, his eyes darting about.

Jem kept working.

"Ah wouldn't say nothin' Jem. Joost tryin' ta' get them out of my kitchen. What do I know anyway?" the man babbled wiping his forehead with his arm. "So 'E's not yer son, eh? Plenty I know 'av an extra boy...I might 'av a babby or two meself I don't know about. What of it?" Rooster tried to laugh.

"Aye. Tha's right enoof."

"So yer friendly with Lord Faolan...the boy is his, Eh?"

Jem looked up at him without expression then down again at his work.

Rooster slipped on the spilled beans and steadied himself on the block.

"What I mean is...Jem...apart from sayin' I saw you out back with the boy, I've got nothin'. Ah'm just warnin' yah it might come back at you."

"Thanks, but I don't know nothin'. 'E came back and ran off again."

"Well...that's alright then!" Rooster relaxed, throwing his pile of meat chunks onto Jem's block and taking up another slab.

"Aye."

"So...tell me, who is 'E, that boy, anyway? Maybe I can help 'im get away. Why'd 'E help that man? If 'E's not Faolan's, is 'E Tanner's boy then?"

Jem looked at the man but kept his thoughts to himself. "'E's mine, 'E's roon off, I don't know where 'E is." he said quietly.

"Faolan's...?"

Jem stared at him for a long moment as if making up his mind. "Nay. Stop pesterin' me, yer like an ol' woman!" Casting him a nervous smile he beckoned with his knife. "Coom help me move somethin'."

"Sure, Jem, sure." Rooster laughed following him to the back of the tent. "But if 'E ain't yours an 'E ain't Faolan's nor Tanner's neither then..."

Jem was waiting for the cook as he came around the sacks. He quickly wrapped his arm around the man's neck and pulled his head back. Rooster's hands flew up into the air and he lost his balance falling backward. Jem braced the great bulk of the man on his hip as he toppled over. With a swift cut of his knife he sliced his throat. Rooster collapsed in a mound of flesh upon the ground. Jem dragged the heavy body into the shadows out of sight and covered it with a tarp. The only noises were the soft sounds of air leaving the man's lungs, liquid gurglings and gasses escaping his flaccid remains.

Strolling outside the tent he added logs to the dying embers of the cook fire, set the largest of their cooking pots over it and poured water from a bucket into the bottom. Then he went back into the tent.

7

Masters Bell and Devers

Faolan walked into the camp early the next morning, tired and dirty. His cloak was covered in burrs from the hedgerows and his boots caked with mud. The story he told was that he had gone riding, it was a new mount and he'd been thrown. Rute waved him over as soon as he saw him.

"The men saw you walking in from the hills this morning."

"Yes. Any luck finding my horse?" he said with a disarming smile. "What about the trainer?"

"Nay." Rute looked at him with suspicion. "And you? Ah thought you bein' a friend, 'E might a' met up with you someplace."

"What do you mean by that?" Faolan bristled.

"Yer not goin' ta' deny you've been friends this long many years? We all rode together from the mountains only a year ago!"

"Who? Andy?"

"Aye! But tha's no Andrus we're talkin' about, that's Tanner!"

"No!" Faolan said feigning innocence.

Rute stared at him with his mouth open, then a slow crooked smile lit up his face. "Alright." he said raising his hands and stepping away like a man who's just missed stepping on a snake. The wheels began to turn behind his bright eyes. "I almost forgot,

85

you're the man in the middle, aren't yah? Which way are ye' going ta jump? Make oop yer mind before spring comes..." he said with a friendly gesture, touching Faolan's shoulder. "Well...we've got more mysteries ta' solve than joost him at the moment."

Faolan looked askance, tapping his boot but did not pull his shoulder away. "Are you finished with your questions, my friend?" he said, and though his mouth was smiling his eyes were not. "As you can see I've spent the night in these wet clothes, I'd like to get to my tent."

"Tanner is still gone whether you're dry or not, that boy helped him escape an' now 'E's missin' too..." Rute sighed "...and we've lost a cook."

"Found a better position did he?"

"No."

"The new one or the old one?"

"Rooster."

"That fool? He must be sleeping one off."

"Nay. 'E had somethin' to tell me about the boy last night but 'E never showed up. Ah'v taken the oother cook into custody. 'E knows somethin' I'll be bound. 'E's the boy's father, after all. This is all mixed in together like a stew, I know it. Tanner, the boy, the cook, I'll beat it out of 'im."

Laying his hand on Rute's shoulder now, Faolan said in a voice meant to charm but with steel behind it. "Why don't you leave Jem to me. Maybe I can get more out of him than you. We've known each other a long time. You concentrate on finding Tanner. The boy will turn up when he's hungry."

"Aye. I was forgetting just how close you all are." Rute let a sly smile quickly pass over his face. Becoming bold he added "You need to decide, my lord, whether you're fish or foul, friend or foe..."

"Just what do you mean by that?" Faolan grabbed Rute by the collar and showed his teeth. "You keep your opinions to yourself. It's you that started this war, General Rute..." Faolan spat the words "for your own reasons! Don't forget I have influence yet with my father...What if I tell him about your 'translation' of my brother's message? Oh yes, I know about that...I'd say it was delivered differently than intended, wouldn't you?"

Rute stared at him.

"Yes. I'm not such a boy as you imagine. I have my agents too, and my own men. I can assure you there is nothing that my father hears that I do not also know, and many things you have yet to find out." Faolan let Rute go.

The man looked about him in embarrassment but they were alone. His mouth curled down in a sneer. Measuring Faolan's words, he nodded. "Alreet. I'll let you talk with him, but I'm not through with this yet, m'Lord." Rute bowed mockingly with a flourish of his hand. Walking away, he said under his breath "It stinks an' I'll find out why."

Faolan walked to his tent, worrying that he'd let Rute see too much of his mind. The man was getting under his skin. He was smart and far too devious. 'What did he want?' he mused.

As he entered his tent he knew someone was there. An overpowering smell of sick came from his sleeping chamber. There lying on the cot was Jemson holding his forehead and groaning softly, a dab of vomit sticking to his lower lip.

"Well, Good Moro." Faolan said surprised, relieved and amused all at the same time. 'How like my brother.' he thought.

Jemson winced at the light and sound as the man moved about his tent.

Faolan turned the empty wine flask upside down, shook out the last drop and lifted the cover of the brass box. "All my sweetmeats gone too?"

"Ohhwwww!" Jemson groaned, rolling over. He coughed and wretched pitifully on the ground but nothing was left in his stomach. "Ahm sorry." he said collapsing back on the cot.

"Clever boy to come here. No one would dare enter without my permission."

"No. Dah brought me. Where is he? He said to wait here till he thought of something. He was supposed to come get me..."

"Yes, we must figure out what to do with you both. You must get away from here, you and Jem."

"Where is Dah? What's happened?" Jemson sat up too fast and grabbed hold of the cot.

"Here drink this." Faolan handed him a cup of water. "Stay in the tent till I get back and don't move. Stay...don't move, don't say anything...bloody hell!" Faolan jumped back.

87

Ohhhwwwwwooof!" Jemson cried, sitting up and projecting the contents of his stomach across the room in a stream.

Lord Faolan ordered a guard to unlock the cell. Jem's hands were tied behind his back and he lay in a corner of the stock house. His damp shirt clung to his back. The only wooden building in the camp was set apart from the community of tents and surrounded by guards. Two other men lay on cots in his cell, still groggy with drink. The heat of the men's bodies during the night had made the air thick and smelling of sweat. Faolan walked over and pulled Jem to his feet marching him out the door before the astonished faces of the guards.

"This man is in my custody now." He said simply. Leading Jem away he immediately cut his bonds. "Come with me." was all he said. The guards did not dare to question his orders but stood silently watching the pair walk away.

Jem spoke first. "Ye' must get my boy away from here. It's ony' a matter of time 'afore he's found out. If I'd known it was Tanner trainin' him I'd 'ave kept 'im away. Ah' don't know what Rute would do if 'E knew who the boy was."

"Keep walking."

"Don't look ta' find Rooster...'E's dead."

"I thought as much. Where did you hide the body?"

Jem shook his head as they made their way toward the cook tent. Soldiers were helping themselves to something in the cauldron, laughing and holding out their bowls for seconds. Their morning barley porridge had been replaced by a hearty hunter's stew in the massive iron pot.

Jem jerked his head in its direction as they passed.

Faolan looked confused for a moment then he swallowed hard and setting his jaw, stared straight ahead. They walked on in awkward silence until they reached his tent.

Jemson recognized his father's footsteps and came running out of the sleeping chamber as they entered. He threw his arms about the man. Jem just stood there, one hand on the boy's head and the other arm draped over his small shoulder. He stared at Faolan without smiling. His eyes said everything.

Faolan nodded. "I understand."

That afternoon a covered supply wagon left the camp for the city with two passengers hidden amongst the empty barrels.

"He knew nothing about it." Faolan replied to Rute's angry outburst upon finding out Jem had been let go.

"Ahm' not through with him yet!" he shouted, pointing a finger at Faolan.

Borchard stood up from his desk and leaning over it he shouted back. "What do I care about the loss of a cook? Or two for that matter! Bring me Tanner! Train the rest of those men! Be ready to march when spring arrives! It's near time for Mid-Winter Festival. Rute! I'm depending on you. I know I can depend on my son." He waved his hand at Faolan. "And oh yes, come spring there'll be three of you. I've made Striker a general. We'll need his cool head as well as your heavy hand!"

Rute cringed but recovered quickly. "What about the boy?"

"Forget about the boy! Did you hear me? Tend to your army."

Faolan leaned against a wall with his arms crossed trying not to smile. His father had regained his old spark and vigor, a light shone in his eyes that had not been there for some time. His lengthy, vitriolic feud with Boru had sapped his strength, turning him peevish, even vindictive. This was not the 'old man' pining for grandchildren that the courtiers spoke of, full of remorse and resentment. This was Borchard the Great, Supreme Guardian of Earden, as Faolan remembered him. This war, unjust as it might be, had brought him back to life. 'Things are never black and white...I love them both. The gods help me.' Faolan prayed in a soft voice.

After the meeting Faolan descended the wide stairs of the great hall where preparations for feasting were already underway. Evergreen boughs festooned the balustrades, the hangings had been cleaned and strung with ivy and mistletoe. An enormous log was being dragged toward the fireplace while dogs nipped at the heels of the servants. Sugared fruits decorated evergreen garlands that ran the length of the tables. Candles were everywhere. Musicians were practicing traditional tunes in their balcony overhead. He whistled 'The Hound and Hare', his favorite.

As he strolled further through a maze of hallways, he came to a great staircase like a waterfall that descended to a series of enormous vaulted kitchens just below the ground. Opening off, one after the other, each was dedicated to a single purpose. All the cooks and apprentices bustled with activity within the confines of their particular sphere.

Oblivious to the serving girls who giggled and tripped over their feet every time they saw him, Faolan strode past the bakers and pastry makers to a connecting doorway. 'If it weren't for the delicious smells, the heat and shouting, the clashing of pans and voices raised in trivial argument I might be on a battlefield' he mused. He passed amongst the tables laden with platters of food in the 'Serving kitchen'.

These had always been his favorite places. He had been coddled and spoiled there by cook and baker alike. The interest he took as a child in all their recipes and preparations had endeared him to all. Just as Boru had gravitated to the armory and the soldier's quarters, so Faolan had found his solace here.

He searched the myriad of sweating faces until he saw a man and a boy tucked in a corner by the warming ovens. Jemson's head swiveled every which way. He was fascinated by the apprentices carrying platters of cakes and breads, the men with roasts of meat and the girls in their crisp white aprons waiting to carry.

Jem was watching his son with amusement. He stood up as Faolan approached and he pulled the boy to his feet also.

"Thank you, fer what you're doin' fer us." Jem said quietly.

"No. I thank you." Faolan said looking at Jemson. "Now let me introduce you to Master Bell, he's head of the kitchens and then Jemson, you come with me."

"Am I not to work with Dah?" the boy asked, his eyes tearing up immediately.

'No, I must bury you a little deeper.' Faolan thought to himself. To the boy he said "No, I have something else in mind for you."

Jemson tagged along behind the men passing through another doorway to a small open office in the 'Bloody Kitchen' where the meat was prepared. He noticed the staff glancing at them and also that no one from either kitchen passed through to the other sections. Each kitchen had separate entrances to the palace and separate sculleries. Only servers passed between. All seemed very well organized and clean.

In the Bloody Kitchen men were chopping meat on long blocks

and a stout man stood hovering over them barking orders. A fireplace that took up one end of the room was filled with game of every description roasting on spits. Apprentices, like small aproned devils stood with forks and basting tools watching and turning the meat.

Master Bell wiped his hands on his immaculately clean apron, doffed his small white cap to Faolan and bowed daintily.

"Young master! Good to see you again. How tall you've grown. Come into my office."

Faolan laughed. This was Bell's greeting every time they met.

Bell shooed a muscular orange cat out of his chair and sat down. "Git to work, Chores! Find me a nice big rat! Who's this then? This boy you've brought needs fattening up! I could use another runner. Midwinter Festival is nearly on us an' I'm desperate for help."

"No. He's not for you. I've brought you a fisherman and a cook."

"The Gods! But that's a miracle! If he can tell a good fish from a bad one we'll be ahead of the game!"

Jem snorted a little under his breath. "Ah should hope so." he scoffed.

"Master Fructus Bell, this is Jem and Jemson." The boy backed away.

Jem smiled and put his hand on the boy's shoulder.

"Well met, young man. Well met. So...Jem. Lord Borchard loves the fruits of the sea, but being far from it we haven't had a good fish cook here, oh, not fer a very long piece...not someone who can go to market and deal with them fishmongers...not get cheated, that is. Why last week we had ta throw out a whole barrel 'a smoked eels. Not worth the salt they came in."

Jem shook his head in sympathy and winked at the boy. Jemson was not impressed and stood in the doorway sniveling. Then Jem fell into intimate conversation with Bell about the calendar year of a fisherman, what was in season, what was running, what was not and what they might expect to serve. The two men walked away into a further room whose tiles were decorated with creatures of the sea. It was empty of activity apart from two boys shucking clams into a bowl. A long metal table with a lipped edge and an indented drain stood in the center surrounded by stools. Empty barrels were stacked in a corner.

The boy stood until Jem was finished talking then he ran to him.

As the two embraced Faolan gently pulled Jemson away and guided him back through the mob and out onto the stairs. Jem stood still and silent in the busy kitchen watching the boy leave as cooks and servants swirled about him. His look was solemn.

Faolan and the boy traveled through corridors decorated with tapestries, followed by the orange cat. Up two flights of stairs they went and around a columned balcony to Faolan's own apartments. The cat marched past them and dived in the door.

"Come, look out this window with me for a moment." Faolan said. "This is your city. Did you know that? And I am your uncle." Jemson stared at the cat as it made its way along the walls of the room and jumped up onto the balustrade. As it did so Faolan's words settled into his brain for the very first time. The boy stared back at him. "Trust me to do what is best for you. I will keep you safe at the cost of my honor and for the sake of your mother's friendship. Did you know she saved my life? But most of all for the love I bear my brother, because you bear his name and you are his son."

"I doon't know him. My father 's doonstairs in tha' kitchen." The boy wiped his running nose on his wrist.

"I'm sorry. I know how much you love Jem and all he has done for you." Faolan remembered just how much with a shudder. "More than you will ever know, I hope. But we must look to the future. That is why I have brought you here. But enough of that for now. You must obey me, do you understand?" Jemson nodded. "For the present you are still in danger, Jemson. Do not call me uncle, nor mention your real name or connection to anyone in my family, and stay away from Rute or his soldiers. It is not often that he comes to the palace which is why I have brought you here, but he has spies everywhere."

Jemson looked about the room wide-eyed.

"As do I." Faolan laughed. "Ah! Here he is!" Faolan turned to greet a tall thin man dressed in a floor length green tunic. His hair was cut to his shoulders like a page.

"Devers! Here is a new recruit for you. His name is Jemson. See that you train him well in the manners of the court and the niceties of dining, serving and dress. Do your best with him. He will wait on me exclusively during the Midwinter Festival."

Devers eyes flickered with interest as he bowed low.

Jemson stood with his jaw hanging open. Wiping his eyes, he gulped.

"Well boy! Don't just stand there like a carp with your mouth open! God's teeth! Bow to my Lord Faolan! See what he's done for you! You! The son of a fisherman! Ah yes, there's not much I don't know about in my little world. No! Not like that! Like this! With your hand over your heart, bend from the waist with a straight back, as if you meant it! Good the Gods! Alright! Let's go!" With that Devers, Master of the Household Pages rolled his eyes in frustration at Faolan and ushered an astonished boy out of the room.

Faolan turned back to the window, his smile fading and looked out to the east. The orange cat cleaned himself, balancing on the balustrade with one leg high in the air. Faolan could just see the fallow fields of Earden, shorn of their crops, his father's realm, his own he hoped and some day, Boru's as well. 'But how to make that happen, my friend?' he wondered, scratching the cat behind the ears. Chores allowed this show of affection, but only briefly, then jumped down and minced away.

All was white, quiet and peaceful. Then a howling wind drove Faolan back into the warmth of the room. Snow swept across the fields and into the city over the rooftops.

8

A Game of 'Catch the Prince'

Riding Faolan's horse Tanner made good progress even through the thick pine forests north of the city. The Three Traveling Gods were with him, he thought. A sharp wind blew dry flakes of snow covering over his tracks. At one point he could even hear soldiers out looking for him but their voices died off or were carried freakishly away upon the wind. He rode all night, not daring to stop. By dawn he came upon a trapper's road that lead out of the forest to the northern-most highway of the realm. This was the same road to the Guardian's city that he and Boru had taken Arius on when they left the Black Mountains only a year or so before. To the west it crossed the whole of Earden. To the east it dissolved into the wilderness of the Bow Mountains after first piercing the heart of the capitol.

Turning westward, away from the enemy he traveled until nightfall. His horse exhausted, he begged leave to care for it at a farm house and slept safe and warm beside it in their barn. In the morning he hitched Faolan's horse to the back of the farmer's cart and rode with him into market at Nortown. With a straw sticking out of his mouth, he smiled at the women and blended in so well with the crowd that Ruby did not even recognize her own father as her wagon slowly moved east along the main street. As the column of soldiers rode past him Tanner fell in.

"'Ere! You! What are you about? By the War God's ears and balls! Is that you Tanner?" a soldier shouted suddenly recognizing him.

"Aye. Keep yer voices down. How goes it? I see me daughter's drivin' a cart. What's she doin' here? Whar's Arius? No babbies yet?"

The men just looked at each other. Several of the falconer's turned their heads back, stared and laughed.

"What? Am I a grandfather or what?"

"Ask Arius." Came a voice from the falconers.

Tanner looked with concern. "What's he bin doin'? I'll murder 'im. Has he bin neglectin' my girl? Gone off with some wench? What?"

Arius rode up beside the men who had slowed the column with their talk. "What's going on?" he said in a stern voice. "Who's this? Tanner! By all the Gods!" His joy bubbled up for his old friend making him look and act like a boy.

Arius often felt like he was 'playing the part' of a man. He still jumped inside when ever they called him 'Captain'. Giving orders to gruff soldiers twice his age and his father's own men made him sweat more than he liked to admit. Even Ruby intimidated him although she reminded him so much of Tanner in her ways that she gave him strength as well. Arius loved the man and turned toward Tanner and his family like a plant facing the sun. "What timing!" he said. "What a man you are for showing up just when you're needed! Come! We'll rest, plan and have a feast! What do you say?" Arius turned round to his men. They laughed at his changeable soul, half captain, half youngster and heartily assented. The men nudged each other and pointed to a tavern sign as they passed through the market place.

Rather than arguing over a likely campsite, as usual at the end of a long day's ride, the soldiers stopped at noon and quickly agreed on a spot close to the outskirts of town. The oxen and horses were unharnessed and set to graze and a fire speedily built.

Ruby took up her basket with only a glance at her father and marched into town. Tanner watched the girl, then sat down in front of the fire. Arius joined him, poking the embers with a stick.

"Tha' was less than a lukewarm welcome I got from m' daughter. What's happened. Av' you changed towards her?"

"No..." Arius protested, then said softly "...it's not that..."

"Ah' see she's lordin' over you...what's she doin' here?"

"Kora thought she might have her uses and I couldn't stop her if I tried."

"Aye. Kora." Tanner sighed and looked off toward the forest.

"Tanner, I've got something to tell you and just as well we're alone."

"The babby?"

"You know?"

"Aye. The men told me. Did she miscarry? Don't worry son, it often happens."

"No." Arius said looking puzzled. "She's dead."

Tanner looked up at him. "What do you mean she's dead? I've just seen her!"

"No! Fern. My sister. She's dead."

Tanner continued to stare at him without enlightenment. "What do yah' mean, son?"

"The baby's your's, your's an' my sister's..."

When Ruby returned she seethed but showed nothing. She set about peeling vegetables into a pot, adding sausages and dried beans, then she filled it with water and set it on its tripod over the fire. When the men had finished talking she sat down on the other side of the circle of stones and watched her father out of half-closed eyes like a cat watches a mouse. Tanner sat stunned for some time, resting his arms on his knees and staring out into the fields. Arius unconsciously mimicked him in male communion. Seeing this, Ruby sucked her teeth and sighed. She pretended to ignore them, stirring the bottom of the pot or adding water from time to time.

"Come here, you." Tanner said grabbing his daughter and pulling her down next to him. He kissed her neck roughly. "So you've been lookin' after the wee might for me? You're a good girl."

"Someone had to." she grumbled.

"Aye."

"Dah...how could you?" she said softly.

"Doon't, doon't even ask tha', you doon't know me, lass, my life away from you, not really. Yer' moother...she...You've yer lad there, cleave to him, think on him an' leave me be." Ruby got up slowly and walked away.

"It's alright." Arius said. "She's good with the baby. She likes him. And he's my family too."

"A boy, then?" Tanner smiled and lowered his head on his arm for a moment. Raising it again he looked at the soldiers. "So, how far away is Kora and her men do you think and how many with her?"

"She should be coming down out of the mountains by now with eighty men."

"Where did you plan to meet?"

"Above the encampment. There's a ridge the Wild Men use on the edge of the forest."

"Aye, I know it. Too close. Too many. Let me think."

Ruby came back with bowls and spoons.

"Ah saw yer moother, once at the jail and then again when I lead them ta' camp. She didn't see me then, I didn't dare let 'er. She looks...well, she was alive when I left, an yer brothers and sisters too." He didn't tell her about the baby.

Ruby's eyes were full of tears.

"Ah'll get 'er, ah'll save 'er if it's the last thing I do. Doon't you worry."

"Oh Dah!" Ruby said throwing her arms about his neck.

"Arius! Captain!" a voice hissed over the drop gate into the depths of the wagon around midnight. Ruby grumbled in her sleep from somewhere inside.

"What is it?"

"You've got to come quick-like! There's been an argument about the price of birds." said a falconer slapping his sides in the cold and making a cloud with his breath.

Arius threw a leg over the gate and looked down at the man. "What kind of argument?"

"The men are still at that tavern, an' one of them townies started complainin' Burr wouldn't sell 'im a bird, 'an Burr said 'E couldn't, not wouldn't, then words were spilled an' now they're fightin'."

Tanner, Arius and the falconer ran back toward the town.

They heard chairs scraping, voices cursing and the thud of bodies hitting the walls even before they reached the house. Arius ran in first. The smell of spilled ale, sweat and sawdust hit him, then the accumulated body heat made him stop in his tracks. It was hard to tell at first whether there was any fighting going on at all, the room was so packed with farmers and journeymen all laughing and drinking. Somewhere safe in a corner, a musician tried hard to be heard, blowing into his flute till his cheeks were round as apples. At the far end, near the fireplace Arius could see the innkeeper in his white apron standing on a bench. He waved a bar cloth frantically at Arius.

"Cheery place..." Tanner said elbowing through the mob towards the back like a man pushing through a corn field. As they plowed through the crowd Arius saw three of his falconers and two soldiers fighting with the locals.

"They're all droonk, Ahm' not worried about the talk, joost let's get 'em out in one piece, eh?" Tanner cried above the noise.

Two men were rolling about beneath the tables throwing cack-handed blows at each other and men were egging them on and making bets. Another pair were up against the brick wall. Tanner pointed to them. A falconer was getting the worst of it as a burly farmer pounded on his already bloody face. His punches were taking their toll. Tanner jerked his head toward the falconer and Arius nodded. Tanner watched for the farmer to drop his arms then he pinned them against his sides solidly in a bear hug from behind. He locked his own hands in front of the man like a vise. Tanner lifted the man off his feet and sent him spinning across the boards. The innkeeper was only too glad to keep the man moving toward the door. With Tanner's help they held the farmer's head underwater in the horse trough till he came up spluttering and coughing. At the same time Arius pulled the falconer away and threw him at his companions. Everyone had stopped fighting to watch the spectacle except the two under the tables.

Arius went over to the men and kicked the falconer in the ass.

"Burr! Get up! And you! Get your sorry bones back to your wife!"

Tanner grinned from the doorway as Arius pulled the men apart and helped the farmer to his feet. He brushed off his jacket and picked up the man's hat. This combination of authority and

99

courtesy confounded the man and he stood there blinking. Finally making a small bow, he took the proffered hat and shuffled off.

The next day a pale sun like a thin lemon slice filtered through the fog of early morning. Tanner stood by his horse. Ruby hugged herself and stamped her feet.

"You'd best wait for me here. This market gives you good cover for now. Any closer and troops may get word of you. Tell the town you're waiting for a spot in the Mid-Winter Market at Guardia, an' what birds are left are all spoken for. Tell the men to keep their mouths shut and their hands off the women or they'll have me to deal with."

"That's rare comin' from you..." Ruby said under her breath.

"Doon't..." he said smiling and pointing a finger at her.

"You sound like your leaving." Arius said walking up to them and yawning.

"I am. I've got to talk with Faolan. Then I've got to find Kora and her men before they get too close to the city. I'll bring them all back here, in secret, I hope. There are still guardians out there searching for me. I've nearly spoiled our surprise. We'll have to wait till they give up looking before we can rescue..."

"Moother."

"Yes, your moother, an everyone else."

"Be careful." Ruby said.

"It won't do to stir the hornet's nest just yet. And you must be ready to move them as quickly as possible through the woods to the wagons. Is there anyone in the village you can trust? If they chase us, and they will give chase, we must find a way for everyone to disappear. Find out how the townsfolk feel about Borchard, if we can count on their help. This is a fool scheme, we need to plan and time is growing short. That's why I must need's see Faolan. He's the only one on the inside now unless I go back."

"Don't be daft! What are you going to do? Just walk back in and say you forgot your hat?" Ruby said.

"Summit like tha'." Tanner said smiling.

"They'll kill you."

"They've not got me yet." Tanner held out his arms to Ruby and they embraced. "Thank you." he said into her ear. Slapping Arius on the back he whispered to him "Go on back ta' bed, it's early yet, go make 'er one of 'er own ta' nurse. Then maybe she'll give yah some peace." With that he mounted his horse and disappeared into the fog.

Master Devers kept up a steady torrent of abuse as the pages practiced their duties for the night's banquet."No! No! No! Always stand on the lady's right, take her hand, smile...remember to smile...then guide her along to her seat. You are her protector! Her knight! See that she doesn't bump into anything as you navigate the hall. She must sail to her harbor like a queen...ship...well, you know what I mean! Lean over her and ask if she's comfortable...if she needs anything before you leave her, then come immediately back to this spot for the next guest! With the men...walk proudly...friendly...but not too friendly and to the point, no small talk, then get out of their way. You've been eating onions! Fix your tunic! Did you brush your hair this morn? It looks like a cock's comb!"

Jemson found it hard to keep a straight face and his mind was swirling with rules, taboos and duties totally foreign to him. He thought of his mother, of how she kept the inn running smoothly and all the guests happy without nearly this amount of fuss. This was like a great battle in comparison and Devers was surely the most nervous general he had ever seen.

"Wipe it off young sir! Wipe it off!" Devers pointed a bony finger at him. "Take that smirk off your face or I'll have you shucking clams in the kitchen with your father!"

Haughty laughter surrounded him. Jemson glanced angrily at his fellow pages. Their condescension was evident. Noble parentage prevented them from seeing him as any kind of equal and they stood apart from him at every opportunity. Jemson found it difficult to keep up from the very beginning and they made sure to make it so. At night they grabbed the first trays of food and the most prestigious guests to escort. He was left to carry the heaviest objects and walk beside the fattest crone or the most cantankerous old baron. When the guests had finished their meal and were nibbling on dainties or getting ready to dance, Jemson always seemed to be guiding bilious men to the privies or cleaning up after one of the hounds.

The only time he was free of rebukes and mischief was when he waited on Lord Faolan. Then he was left alone to do his duties, to stand and pour his wine or to fetch and carry to and from his chambers some article the lord had forgotten or object of beauty he wished to share with his guests. This special connection kept him from the usual fate of commoners lucky enough to join the household. These poor souls were regularly beaten by boys of higher birth and no one thought it strange. Only this mysterious tie to Lord Faolan and the fact that his fists were at the ready kept him safe from their abuse.

The days and nights of Midwinter Festival rolled on. Feasts and entertainments came and went. Jemson gained knowledge of things he had no desire to learn but his uncle seemed to think were very important. He learned how to cut up a roasted chicken and eat it delicately with his hands, he learned to dance, how to play a decent game of Kings Men and how to let your opponent (or your lady) win without letting them know. All the niceties of court etiquette pounded in his brain at night in Dever's reedy voice. As he lay on his cot in the page's quarters he often thought of home, of standing on the hill above the city with his brother and sister.

Yet good food, education (of a kind) and a warm bed soon gave him a healthy appearance which he further enhanced by better grooming and attendance to his costume. One had to admit Devers was a magician, for within a very short time he had made Jemson into someone who turned the serving girls' heads. Even though he did not know why they looked at him more often than the high-born boys, Jemson found it pleasing. He straightened his shoulders whenever they passed and met the girl's eyes with a grin.

Whenever he was free he could be found near the steps leading down to the kitchens. At first he hung about, hoping to see Jem but after the celebrations had started he seldom caught sight of him. The kitchens were far too busy. But there were other distractions. Chores the cat often sat beside him, flicking his tail, watching the comings and goings and then there was an ever-changing flock of serving wenches taking their meals on the steps. They preferred their own company to that of the big table at the back of the Serving Room full of 'old people'. Jemson was much favored by these good-looking girls and the giggling started as soon as they heard his footsteps running down the corridor. They offered him bites of their meat pies and dumplings if he would sit with them. What boy could resist? He grew brazen and snuggled next to whoever would let him. This he knew was "not manly" as the other boys shunned women's company like a plague. Jemson didn't care.

His loneliness was like a deep well that could not be filled. Jem was there, at the bottom of the stairs, he knew, far too busy to talk, yet Jemson was drawn there just the same. Also it seemed, when he did find him, his reactions were cool, not like the father he had known, almost like a friendly stranger. When he left, there was sadness and resignation in Jem's eyes. The boy could not understand it.

One night during an entertainer's long and tedious recitation of an epic poem he crept away from the main hall and the festival. The droning of the ballad singer grew fainter as he walked the corridors. He had listened to the first part about the founding of the city on the back of a dragon. After that it had seemed dry stuff full of ancient and forgotten names.

He came upon the knot of girls sharing a bowl of leftover honeyed fruits. Jemson was soon sitting in the middle of them being fed from their sweet fingers. He lay his head back on a lap and the girls exploded with laughter. Tempted by their giddy merriment he leaned around and squeezed the girl about her waist as hard as he could. His sister's squeals resounded in his ears and he was suddenly home with his family. Screams of delight came from the girl and were taken up by the others. Like a bevy of birds they jumped up, their skirts whirling about them. They ran up the stairs and through the long hallway with Jemson like a hound in pursuit. Calling it 'Catch the Prince' two girls linked their arms and captured him attempting to hold him back but he quickly ducked out of their embrace and chased one girl after another until he had squeezed them all. He had a funny feeling as he ran that they could all have evaded him if they really wanted to but the game was so much fun that he let it slip from his mind. With his arms about an older girl and his face buried in her bosom he did not hear the footsteps coming down the corridor nor did he recognize the voice until it was too late.

"How now, my young huntsman! What is this racket and who is making bold with my serving wenches!"

The girls bowed and scraped and within an instant Jemson was alone with Lord Borchard, Supreme Guardian and Protector of all Earden. The man stood with his arms folded over his voluminous robes. The gold seal hung about his neck.

"So, young page, the ballad was not to your liking? Is that why you decided to abandon your post and give chase?"

"If you please, my Lord..." Jemson remembered just in time to bow and place his hand over his heart "...I liked the part about the dragon."

"But the rest?" Borchard asked.

Boru shrugged his shoulders.

The Guardian looked at him for a moment then let out a belly laugh.

"I can't say as I blame you! Better a pretty face and a warm breast, eh? When I was just a little older than you I hunted the same hallways, but with better success I might add. You are too young yet, my huntsman. Where are your game birds now?"

Boru smiled shyly. "All flown. They're afraid of you."

Borchard arched his eyebrows and laughed again. "You're not, though, are you?"

"I guess not."

"Ha! A careful answer. You're a man to be reckoned with. Tell me, why are you not with the other pages? There's always a game of Kings Men on the board."

"They don't like me."

"Ah. And the girls do?"

"Aye."

"And you like them."

"They remind me of my mother and sister."

"Are you not of this city?"

"No my Lord, far away."

"Ah! You are Lord Faolan's new page then, are you not?"

The boy shuffled his feet nervously. "Yes, my Lord."

Borchard studied his face, lifting the boy's chin with one finger and turning Jemson's face to see his profile. "Tell me about your home..."

Jemson cringed a little with suspicion, remembering Dah's warnings and those of Faolan's. He sized up the Guardian, wondering whether it was safe to tell him anything.

"Come, come now...I am your ruler...you serve my son...you are protected by him, in fact...for I am no fool, young man...you have my blood. Tell me."

Flattered by the old man's attention, Jemson's lower lip suddenly trembled and his eyes welled with tears. "I, I miss them, my brother and sister, my mother, we had an inn...by the sea."

"Ah! That's why your...'father'...knows his way around my Sea Kitchen..." Borchard's eyes riveted on the boy's face.

Jemson shifted his gaze away and gulped, wiping away the tears. "Um, yes."

Clearly the old man was hinting at something. "Well," he said with a canny look "See that you serve my son...well, make your 'father'...proud." Borchard put special emphasis on his words.

The boy shot him a glance and bowed again. "My Lord?" he blurted out as the man walked away.

"Yes?"

"Is there really a dragon?"

Borchard smiled and coming back, leaned down to the boy's ear. "Yes. He protects the realm (and my family) from all foes."

Jemson's eyes grew as big as duck eggs.

"I must go back to my guests." Borchard said with a chuckle. "Do you suppose that man has finished his whining?"

"P...probably not, sire...um my Lord."

Jemson heard the Guardian's laughter echoing down the hall.

Like a flock of sparrows after the jay has gone the girls came running back. The eldest girl, Jenna, kissed him on the cheek. "That's for bein' our hero, yah little bastard." she said. The others laughed and ran back toward the kitchens. Jemson grabbed Jenna's hand before she could turn away and pulling her near, kissed her red mouth. It was sweet as honey.

"Hero? Is that what you think you are? To the serving maids…" Dane, the tallest and most senior of the pages came up to him as he returned to the banquet hall. They were waiting outside the doors for the close of the evening when guests might need to be walked or carried to their carriages.

"To a bunch of dirty common little bitches more like." said another.

"Tell me something..." Jemson began as the tall page leered at him contemptuously.

"What do you want?"

"Is there really a dragon?"

Dane put on a serious expression and looked around at his companions. He draped his arm over Jemson's shoulder and said in a low voice. "If you go to the guardian's archway, by the stables early in the morning, when everyone's asleep, stand near the palace wall, you can hear him breathing." Dane's companions chuckled softly behind their hands.

"Come away, Dane...leave this sprat, Devers is calling."

"Yes, you're just an ordinary sprat from the fishing villages and the smell of fish is still on you!" The boys waved their hands in front of their faces.

"Yes! Sprat! Phew! That's what we'll call him! Sprat!"

"Come here fisherman! Come here Sprat!" The pages pushed him one after another in a circle. Jemson tried to smile good-naturedly as guests were turning their heads but the pushing soon grew more vicious and he found himself on the floor.

"Owww! We've spilled a basket of sprats! Phew! The stink!" The tall page said laughing.

Devers sent them about their duties but not until several oaths were cursed, voices were lowered and barbed threats exchanged. Jemson answered them all back with every foul word he could think of.

"Remember, tomorrow, near dawn..." The tall page whispered to Jemson as they guided the drunken guests down the palace steps.

Early the next morning before the breakfast bell was rung for servants, Jemson stood breathing on his hands near the palace wall. He looked about at the archway where the palace guards came and went.

All was quiet in the city, it was that time, just before daybreak when not a sound could be heard, the streets were holding their breath, waiting. Soon the milk wagons and peddlers, soldiers changing their guard, servants and merchants hurrying to their shops would appear, all would be bustle and noise. But there, by the cold stone wall Jemson stood listening in silence.

'Wait! What was that sound? Yes.' Jemson thought, it was like breathing, though breathing deeper and louder that any animal he had ever heard. Jemson followed the noise around the curved wall of the palace until he came to a window covered by an iron grate. It was just above his height and he jumped up and hung onto the bars peering into the darkness. It was a shaft that lead steeply downward into the depths of the palace. Jemson shuddered. Warm, foul air hit him in the face and pulsed out at intervals. "The dragon..." he said to himself.

Course laughter came from behind him and a hand pulled him off the grate.

Dane stood laughing with his fellows. "What a little fool you are, Sprat! You still believe in dragons?" Dane wrenched Jemson by the arm and walked him away, through the guardian's archway and into the stable yard. With a push, he sent him spinning. The horses fidgeted on their heavy hooves in their stalls and snorted foggy breaths in the cool damp of dawn. Sparrows sat in a line on the ridge top as if waiting for the entertainment to begin. The orange cat sat in a patch of pale sunlight.

"Don't be afraid...It's only the bellows harvesting air for the prison down below...don't you know anything, Sprat? What, are you disappointed? Are you cold? Here, I'll warm your hands for you! Unless you'd rather I warmed you another way?" Dane made a gesture as if he were holding his own erect penis. Jemson scowled at him and backed away. The tall page took off his expensive tabard and handed it to another boy.

Jemson looked at his own, shabbier uniform and made to unbuckle it but before he could, the boy struck him full in the face, more of a slap than a punch. It was clearly meant to remind him of his lowly status. The cluster of boys laughed contemptuously. Then he was punched in the stomach before the shock of the slap wore off. Jemson took a deep breath, held his temper and jumped at the bigger boy sending him backward and nearly knocking him over. The sparrows popped up into the air and flew off noisily, away from the roof. Jemson grabbed the boy's shirt collar and holding on with both hands, head-butted him. He'd only done that once before to his brother Jors and it had been more of an accidental discovery but he knew it hurt and caused the tiny stars to swim about the head. Being shorter yet sturdier, he hit Dane squarely in the middle of his face. The boy bled most prodigiously from his nose and let out a wail of pain. Turning away, he signaled to the other boys.

Two of them jumped on Jemson and held him while the tall page wiped his nose with his sleeve and grinned. After they had beaten him as much as was to their liking they left him slumped on the stones.

Jenna came running out from behind a pillar as soon as they were gone.

"I hate them! The spoiled little terds!" She cried as she flew to him and kneeling down touched his already swelling cheek. "Can you walk?"

"I...I think so." he said with a grunt. She pulled him up to his feet and together they walked slowly up the steps and along the dark and sleeping corridors of the palace. Chores followed behind them. It took many minutes to descend the staircase that lead to the kitchens for Jemson took each step one at a time. Instead of going to Jem's room off the Fish Kitchen, Jenna stopped at a recessed doorway the boy had not noticed before.

Jenna knocked furiously upon it. A reedy voice called from within."Give us a moment! Goddess of Mercy! Give two old men a minute to pull themselves together!"

Devers opened the heavy latch and peered out in his nightshirt and cap. The cat slipped inside around his legs. "What is it Jenna?"

"Who is it my heart?" Master Bell's voice came from behind him. "Who disturbs us?"

"Please...masters...I'm sorry, it's me, Jenna. I've brought Jemson, I didn't know what else to do. He's hurt...I didn't want him seen..."

"Stop blustering girl! What's the matter? Bring him in." Devers took the boy's other arm as soon as he saw the drooping figure and guided the boy to a lounge chair by the fire. "Can you sit?"

Jemson nodded. He looked about at the well-appointed chambers and focussed on Master Bell standing with his arms akimbo, his nightshirt stretched across his prodigious stomach.

"What have we here?" the master chef spouted, more out of sympathy than humor. "A bloody mutton chop? A pile of sausage meat? Look at that face! What happened?"

Jenna explained in a dither as Devers brought out a wet cloth and wiped the blood from the boy's face. He poked and prodded him and worked his fingers one by one and then his wrists, arms and legs until he was sure nothing was broken.

"How's your stomach?"

"It's hard to breath."

Devers delicately lifted his shirt. A great red bruise was already forming on the boy's ribs. Jemson closed his eyes in embarrassment and winced.

"Hummph." Devers said. "A poultice I think, my love, if you wouldn't mind."

"Right you are." Master Bell said sharply and marched off to the kitchens swinging his arms like a soldier. "On parade! Willow bark, honey, what else?...I'll get your father, shall I?" he called back, popping his head around the door.

"No...please, don't tell him." Jemson said in a frightened voice.

"Here, drink this." Devers held a cup of brandy to his lips while the boy tried to sit up. Then the Page Master whispered something to Jenna and the girl disappeared.

9

The Memory of Rue

When Jemson awoke he found himself in his own cot in the page's dormitory. Chores was sleeping curled up in a ball at his feet. It was quiet and empty in the room save for one tall figure standing near a window.

"Well, huntsman, and how are you feeling this morning?" Lord Borchard said turning and walking over to the bed.

Jemson tried to rise but quickly fell back on his pillow.

"Stay! Stay! You've slain your first dragon! Rest, soldier." The old man chuckled. "How you remind me...So, that Bowmountain boy, Dane and his troop did this to you? Huh. Never mind. They are all from the same family, every generation and always the same attitude; stupid and self-important, heavy-handed clods the lot of them. They have only one solution for everything. They are noble only because their ancestors killed or married into all the other families on their gods forsaken rock. Ancient house my ass! It's not for nothing that their crest is emblazoned with a stone for that is what's between their ears!" Borchard watched the boy laugh then wince in his pain. "Now, you did not hear that from me, eh? Only between us diplomats." He said holding a finger to his lips.

"But isn't that the way you rule, my lord, war and marriages? Pardon...I only meant..."

Borchard sat at the end of the cot and pushed the cat aside. He looked at the boy for a moment and Jemson thought perhaps he had said something wrong. Borchard's brow furrowed and the corners of his lips turned down but then he smiled. "So this interests you? I suppose it may seem that way, war and marriages. That is one way to rule, when one has to. But there are times of peace as well, and then you must find common ground to share, contracts between peoples, handshakes, a constant exchange of ideas where all feel they have had their fair say, councils, plans, projects. I am the Guardian of their peace and the prosperity that comes with it. At least that was my goal, before...." Borchard watched the boy who seemed to hang on every word. Smiling he placed his hands on his knees and rose with difficulty. "But you are tired. Yes. War and marriages would be easier, tf that were all...wouldn't it?" he laughed. "We will talk again. When you are better. And here comes your warden with some soup!"

Jenna entered carrying a tray.

"Be good to my councillor." He said patting Jenna's rump as he passed. With that the old man left. Jemson could hear him whistling down the corridor.

Jenna rolled her eyes. "If 'E can still find my ass I guess he's not dead yet!" she whispered.

The boy tried to laugh but his ribs hurt too much.

"Here, sit up." Jenna placed another pillow behind his head and leaned over him, her breasts touching his cheek. She smelled of lavender and roses. The boy reached out and embraced her choking back a sob.

"Now then my hero, who am I, your girl or your mother?"

Jemson pulled his hands back quickly staring up at her.

"Yes, I thought so." she said smiling. "No more of that till you can tell the difference an' do summit about it. Now, eat your soup."

Lord Faolan strode down the hallway toward his apartments, his boots spraying bits of dried mud across the stone floor.

"My Lord..." a voice called from behind a pillar.

Faolan stopped, found the hilt of his dagger and looked about him searching the shadows cast by the early morning sun. Seeing the small figure his caution turned to curiosity. Jenna curtseyed and waited for him to come nearer. Faolan smiled and stepped behind the stone column.

"What would you, lass?"

"Your son, my Lord, has been beaten."

Faolan looked at her hard. "My son? I have no son. Who are you talking about?"

"The new page. The one you put forward. Jemson. He was beaten this morning in the horse yard. But he's alright, he's resting. Devers sent me to find you."

Faolan took a deep breath, his eyes narrowed. "Who did it? That Bowmountain boy I expect. Any worse than the others he's bloodied?"

"Oh much worse, my Lord, because he's yours. You should have guessed that would happen."

Jenna gave a sly smile and watched his face for a reaction.

"Jenna, I asked you to watch and report to me anything of interest that goes on here but you must not try to guess my motives or the reasons why I might assign a task to you. You are my little agent, are you not?"

"Yes, my Lord Faolan." Jenna smiled shyly now. He thought he could almost hear her purring as she spoke his name.

"And you would like to continue serving me?"

Jenna sighed. 'What I would not do for you...' she thought. "Yes." she said softly.

"Then be my spy and keep my secrets, but don't question me, Kitten."

"I thought so...he's yours...there's been a lot of talk you know. Why would you raise a fisherman's boy to a position only nobleman's sons hope to attain, unless?" Jenna played with the strap of her apron and tilting her head looked up into his eyes.

Just then a guard walked past them. Faolan pushed her further into the shadows and sheltered her with his arm. The warmth of his body, the smell of leather, horses and pine sap tantalized her. She made bold to grasp the pocket of his jacket and pull him in close just a second longer than was necessary as the guard continued down the hall.

"Jenna…" Faolan whispered "What are you about, my flower?"

Jenna swallowed hard and tried to regain her composure. "It's

113

just tha', he's a good boy. I don't want him hurt. Tha's why I followed them. I knew it was comin'. Sure enoof, the dirty little bastards came at 'im...I'll look after him, don't you worry...but 'E's not just a fisherman's sprat is he? Tell me. You owe me tha' mooch."

"Owe you? I don't owe you a thing, Kitten. You're too smart by half." 'And you don't know when I'm trying to keep you safe. Too much knowledge is just as dangerous as too little.' Faolan thought to himself but looking at her pouting face, he sighed. "Alright. If you must know, he's the son of a woman who saved my life a long time ago. I owe him a good start, as good as I can give him, and that's all. Will that satisfy my kitten's curiosity?" Faolan bent down and took her dimpled chin in his hand. Jenna swayed slightly, her head drifting back at his touch and her eyes fluttered shut for an instant.

"Jenna..." Faolan whispered letting his thumb play across her full lips, first the top and then the bottom until they were moist and parted. Unable to resist, he leaned in on impulse and kissed her mouth softly. Then as if he had returned from the depths of loneliness and had found his love waiting for him he kissed her harder still. With a release of emotion he had tried to put aside and feelings held in check for too long he took her in his arms. Lifting her slightly off the floor he held her against the wall, propping her up with his thigh forced between her legs. His mouth caressed her cheek and trailed down till he buried his face in her neck. Jenna gasped for breath, lost in love and swept away. She flung her arms about him as a child might do. Faolan tried to stop the memory of Rue from rising in his mind but her voice was in his ear whispering of her love for him. They held each other and Jenna counted the seconds, hoping it would never end.

"Jenna..." he said after a time, pulling her legs away where they had entwined about his back. He let her slide gently down till her feet again rested on the floor. "Forgive me. I should not have done that."

Faolan turned and immediately walked away from her, his hand to his forehead and a frown of confusion on his face.

Jenna stood by the pillar, staring after him, her heart beating fast and the blood pounding and coursing through her veins.

Jemson drifted in and out of sleep the whole day and it took the distant sounds of revelry and feasting from the hall to wake him with a start. The cat was gone.

Jem was sitting at the bottom of the bed. His head was bowed and he was staring at his hands that were draped between his knees, side by side. He looked tired.

"Where are all the others?" the boy asked, sitting up.

"Oh, they bin sent to the dungeon." Jem said looking round at him.

"What?"

"Oh. Lay down, Ahm' only jokin'. They're servin' I expect. You sure know how ta' make friends in a hurry...What was this scrape all about then, eh?"

"Dah, stop..." the boy moaned. "You're worse than..." he almost said 'Mother' but instead said "Dah, I've missed you."

Jem lowered his head again, looking at his hands, and a sound came from deep in his chest more like a groan than a sigh. Jemson had seen that furrowed brow before and knew better than to disturb his thoughts. He closed his eyes and reached out for the hand of the only man he knew as his father. Jem took in an expansive breath. Jemson opened his eyes, he knew something was coming.

"Ah well." Jem said as if his mind was made up and there was nothing more to be said. "Now listen, I've summit to tell ye'. Yah may not see me for a while, ah'm goin' away. There's business I need ta' finish, see thee, but I'll be back for you." The boy's eyes widened and he started up.

"Don't say anything about noothin' as 'appened so far. An' remember, if anybody asks you, you're Jemson is all, mine, y' hear, my son."

The boy threw his arms about Jem. "Dah! No! Don't leave me!" Jem patted his back. "Faolan'll look after yah, he's a good man and true." Jem's dark eyes glistened as he held his son back and looked at him. "I remember sittin' next to another rare fighter an' holdin' her hand after a battle."

"Moother?"

"Aye. She was fearsome brave. Gods keep thee." he said as if he could say no more. Standing up, he straightened his back with a groan and walked away without looking back at the shaken boy.

Faolan stood watching from the archway. Jem's face was grim

as he came up to him.

"Will you not stay?"

"Nay. I've got somethin' must be done."

"Jem. It's for the best, you understand that, don't you? Why I've taken over his care…why you must pull away from him."

"Aye. I understand alright, Yer' lordship. Yer precious heritage! Yer precious Guardian's seat! That's what it is, isn't it! Yer future. But 'E's a bastard, remember? 'E'll never reign after you! What do ye need 'im for? An' what's stoppin' you from marriage? Children. Then E'll be further down the line than a donkey's fart! Less than noothin' ta' anybody! Let me 'ave my son an' we'll make our way back out of here!"

"I can't do that, Jem. You're welcome to stay, but he doesn't belong to you anymore. He never really did."

"That's all you know! Nay! You can't keep me from my son!" Jem growled as Faolan pulled him back into the recesses of the hallway out of the boy's hearing. Guards came running and took hold of Jem's arms as he struggled to get free.

"Jem! Listen to me!"

"Nay! Give 'em back! He'll never be any use to you as long as I'm alive!"

Faolan stood quietly looking at Jem through narrowed eyes. His hand strayed to the pommel of his dagger for a moment, then he sighed. "Take him away. Take him to the South Gate, give him a horse, this letter of passage in my name and also this." He threw a purse full of coins to one of the men. "See that he does not enter the city again."

The soldiers dragged Jem off down the hall, put him on a horse and escorted him to the city gate where they handed him over. Jem heard their laughter as they rode away. He was asked politely, too politely he thought, to step down for a moment while the sentries examined his papers. They moved away and he listened to them argue back and forth amongst themselves.

"We 'ave orders to send every able-bodied man to the army, General Rute's orders."

"But this is from…"

"'Ah don't care. 'Oo would yah rather cross, Rute or The Monk, eh?"

There was some grumbling but before Jem could protest he was

116

hustled outside the gate to a waiting cart filled with men. Jem climbed in next to an old peddler and a youth who's downy upper lip proved he was new to manhood. Their satchels and aprons showed they'd been snatched straight from their shops and occupations without warning.

The cart pulled off toward the encampment. Jem looked back and watched as the soldiers stripped his horse and lead it away. They stood counting out coins to each other from the pouch Faolan had given him.

***

"Ow! Ow!" Brillie cried, dropping her crutch, grasping her cheek and falling forward onto the bed of a pregnant woman. The ward full of women began to wail and call out for the matron. Brilla came running from another room and picking the girl up laid her on an empty bed. "What is it my sweeting? What hurts you?"

The girl thrashed about on the bed as if she were being struck. "Stop it! Stop!" she cried out with each invisible blow.

"What is happening? Brilliana? Who must stop?"

The matron looked about her and quickly picking up the girl carried her out of the ward and down the hall to her study.

"They're hurting me!" was all Brillie could say as she curled up in pain on her own little cot.

Cere and Lyla ran into the room.

"Let her be...she sees something, I thought her injuries had returned but it is something else. Go back to our patients." The matron held Brillie's hand until her body uncurled and relaxed like a tiny fern. After a time her breathing slowed.

"Brilliana, what did you see?"

The girl opened her eyes and stared at the pattern of sunlight on the ceiling. Her chest rose and fell and she spoke softly with each out going breath. "My brother...I miss him...someone has hurt him...and someone misses me...I feel his heart against mine. Don't you feel it too?"

Brilla sucked in her breath, for holding the girl's hand, she had shared this vision, but for her it was as if she were in Rue's body and a man had held her close. Brilla shuddered. "Rest now, my love. Close your eyes." she said and covered the girl with a

117

blanket.

"No. No rest for us...we are all together in this..." Brillie mumbled, reaching out and grasping the strap of The Matron's apron.

***

On the last night of revelry Jemson limped into the great dining hall on Jenna's arm. She made him sit in a corner and then left. He did not wish to go but she seemed to think it was important for him to be there.

The musicians were playing a lively tune and two men were dressed in costumes as hare and hound. They danced between the tables as the guests clapped in time to the music. The youngest pages were passing amongst the crowd handing out little presents wrapped in red paper.

At the end of the room Lord Borchard stood wearing a long robe of red velvet trimmed with fur and drinking from a goblet. His chain of office sparkled on his chest.

"Tonight my friends..." The Guardian called out. At this the man dressed as a hare dived under a table full of guests bringing the dance to an end with much laughter and cheering from the crowd. "tonight we end the Mid-winter Festival and move onto a time of waiting. Waiting and preparing for spring."

"And for war!" someone called out.

Borchard raised his hand. "I thank you all for being my guests and also my family at this happy time of year." His face turned solemn. "I have finally gotten the approval of the Supreme Council." There were groans of sympathy and cheers of approval from the crowd. "Soon we will march on this rabbit warren, this "Saels" as it is called, unhappy may their outcome be." More cheering. "But we would welcome them back into our embrace once more, would we not?"

"Yes! And we are the hounds! We will 'embrace them' alright!" came a voice with much applause and pounding on the tables.

"Well, you know I am a man of peace...but I will keep the peace, and I would have our nation whole again, what ever the cost."

The drunken cheering and pounding continued until he raised his arms.

118

"So, even as our army sharpens its swords and prepares for war, we celebrate one more tradition as we have always done at the close of the festival. We perform the Ceremony of Induction. Will those pages who have been chosen to be trained in our School of Arms come forward when their names are called?"

A tall soldier dressed in full armor covered by the green tabard of Earden walked up and stood next to Borchard. Devers, also wearing a robe of green, crossed the hall and stood in front of the dais with a scroll in his hands. He began reading off the names of all the eldest pages.

Jemson watched the boys approach the dais, be greeted by the Master of Arms, kneel before him and be lead off by their noble sponsors.

Devers rolled up his scroll and looked at Borchard. The Guardian nodded.

"Dane of Bowmountain, come forward."

The tall page, resplendent in a new tunic of gold marched up the aisle between the tables of cheering guests, his chest puffed out and a grin on his face for his relatives.

"Kneel, and pledge fealty to your uncle the Lord of Bowmoutain, return home and train there. On your return may you serve us well." Dane knelt before his uncle with a surprised look on his face. His uncle scowled at Borchard, laid a gauntleted hand on his nephew's shoulder and made him stand. They both bowed and walked backward to their seats. His uncle's face was a mask of stone. Disappointment and anger boiled just beneath the surface of the boy. It was clear he was insulted and ready to shout or bolt. He did not expect to be sent home to train.

Borchard signaled again to Devers and he walked back down the room. Coming up to Jemson, the Master of Pages laid a hand on his shoulder.

"Jemson, son of Jem the fisherman, come forward." Borchard's own voice rang out across the hall.

The guests spilled their wine and set down their cups. All tongues went silent. The pages watched in amazement as a stunned boy in a hand-me-down tunic walked unsteadily with Dever's help up the center aisle.

"Kneel and pledge fealty and sworn service to Lord Faolan, Guardian and Protector of the realm of Earden, to be trained by his

119

own hand into the duties of a soldier of our nation. May you serve us well."

A gasp came from the guests and the boy heard The Guardian chuckle under his breath. Borchard raised the boy to his feet with his own hands.

The Bowmountain clan, enraged, could take no more but rose as one from their tables and left the feast in a fury, plowing through the other guests and servants to the doorway.

Dane and his Uncle stood like statues glaring at The Guardian. Lord Bowmountain opened his mouth to speak but Borchard turned away and left the hall without giving him a chance. Devers quickly guided Jemson out behind Borchard, down the long hallways and back to his cot. The boy walked all the way in a kind of dream. The pain in his ribs and his limp had miraculously disappeared.

In the morning he looked across the room at the pages waking from sleep. The three beds of the Bowmountain cousins had not been slept in and all their things were gone. Laid out at the bottom of his own cot was a squire's uniform of green, a leather jacket with a belt and attached to it, the sheath for a short sword.

Faolan walked into his father's bedroom. Borchard stood naked in a large shallow basin surrounded by servants and dressers holding towels and clothes. In his bed, one of the serving maids lay, asleep, curled up beneath the covers.

"Good moro, my son!"

Faolan had to smile. His father's body was still firm, perhaps less well-muscled than he remembered of old but for a man of seventy some years...Faolan nodded to himself with pride.

"What do you think, eh? Still able to wield my sword?" Borchard took his penis in his hand, waggled it and laughed. "How's that little wench of yours? Still following you around?"

Faolan raised his eyebrows but said nothing.

"It's time you married, you know, one bastard boy does not a family make."

Faolan smiled. So the rumor had caught and traveled like a burr on a dog's back. 'So much the better' he thought.

"She's a child, Father."

"Hmmm. My eyes see more than yours then. I did not think you

120

had it in you to father a bastard, my quiet monk! At least I know it can be done and you have the stomach for it! You make me proud! So, tell me, what did you want to speak to me about?" Borchard's eyes wrinkled at the corners. He stepped out of the bath and raised his arms. Immediately a linen shirt was put over his head and he was swathed in a rich winter robe.

"You've made enemies."

"Ah. The Bowmountains...the look on their faces, though...it was worth it. They were ever so, and they needed a lesson this time. Sitting up there on their mountain, trading with the Giant Men, robbing and stealing cattle from our folk whenever they feel like it. Sending their nob-headed sons here to be trained for nothing! Noblemen. Hah!" Borchard reached out his hand and a goblet of wine was placed in it. "And I like your boy...Jemson. He has courage and brains. Like all our seed."

"Yes, he reminds me of Boru."

Borchard cursed under his breath. "Do not use that name in my presence! Never mention his name again!"

"Father...even now...has he sent you any message? Let me send for him. We can end this before it has cost us many lives."

"I will bring them back into the realm by their ears, we will bring them back, the whole lot of them and we will grind them under our boots before it is finished." Borchard shot him a glance that brooked no argument.

Faolan sighed. "About the Bowmountains, then."

"Yes?"

"You have insulted them for the last time. They are like a boil, I fear, coming to a head."

"Then we will lance it!"

"I mean they will rise up against us."

"I know what you meant. Come! Come! You worry too much! I've already sent a few men to watch their cursed rock for comings and goings and report back to me. We will know if they do anything foolish."

"You are ahead of things as usual."

"Of course."

"Tell me Father," a hint of a smile returning to Faolan's face "what is the difference between you and a king?"

Borchard chuckled. "Aside from that cursed council of old

fools? Nothing, my son, nothing but the crown."

The wagon rolled on and the landscape about the camp beneath Guardia's stone walls became familiar. Jem's mind wandered into dark places and one thought overtook all others, to finish the job he had tried to do so long ago...to kill Boru. It had been all his fault, he reasoned, had started and ended with that man and started all over again, his separation from his wife, the war, his capture, and his son's. As if no one had control over their life but this spoiled nobleman.

Jem's mind ran over and over these sorrows like an oxen harnessed to a grain wheel. His will crushed it finer and finer into a single obsession. Aolwynd and her love for Boru never crossed his mind except as that single image of her standing alone on their hillside, year after year, waiting, always waiting. Nothing mattered now except to find Boru on the battlefield and kill him. ' So...' he thought 'back in the army. P'raps that's where I were meant ta' be all along. No more cookin'. I'll learn a few things an' maybe get my chance.' He gripped the rail and a grim smile appeared on his face as the cart rolled into camp.

10

Someone Without a Face

Jors walked along the sand at the bottom of the cliff beneath the House of Good Women picking up bits of shell and bone; presents from the sea to his curious nature. Brillie squealed in mock disgust and teetered on the rock she sat upon. Her crutch lay next to her and she lifted her face to the morning sun. Creeping up onto the rock, Jors menaced her with a leg joint from a crab's shell, waggling it comically. They dissolved into laughter.

"Aren't you meant to be in bed?" He scoffed at her cowardice while sliding back down and crouching to observe a sand dollar as it made its slow journey across the wet surface of the strand.

"What are you lookin' at?" she said in her little girl's voice and then in a loftier tone "...Everything interests me about this world. As it does you, my dear...like an unopened book, I can't wait to explore its pages, discover...and heal."

Jors stood up and peered at her with narrowed eyes. "Doon't talk like tha' around me Brillie, I've asked and asked. It ain't natural an' it gives me the 'haunts'. I doon't like it."

The girl only smiled.

"An' doon't give me tha' look like an ol' Good Woman neither! Ah doon't know who you are sometimes Brillie."

"Who does?" the girl sighed in a world weary way and looked out over the waves. Gulls cried and swooped. Brillie hugged her shawl about her thin shoulders and shivered as visions of black wings crossed her mind. "Jors..." she said struggling to her feet "...help me walk without that thing."

"Aye. Tha's why we're out here every damn morning, init?" Jors pulled his sister to her feet. He held her hands gently but firmly walking backward as she took her steps. She dismissed his gruff-mannered talk, for it meant nothing, his careful actions and affection for her meant everything. She lifted her bad leg and dragged it ever so slightly trying not to wince for his sake as she set it down.

"'Ere! You're stronger than yesterday."

"Am I?"

"Joost a little further, past that rock. Tha's right. Now this is farther than ye've done a' week!" he said proudly. "Now we'll go back."

"You're a good brother, Jors."

"Bulls bollocks. Ahm' yer ony brother, ony one you've got now. Make the moost of me."

"No, he's alive..." she said fiercely. "I know it. I feel his heart beating, his and another's." She placed her hand on her chest, closing her eyes and turning her back on the sea.

"Alright young man, hold your sword and swing across, keep it level, keep your elbows close together, you'll have more power that way." Jors hit the wooden pole with the flat of his blade and it bounced off.

Boru laughed. "Heavy isn't it? I know, you're arms will be on fire tonight. Let's see if you can treat your friend with a little more respect. He's not a paddle. Try again."

Frost shook off the pole as Jors struck it again and again. First he made a cut from the air, then swinging from either side, then

124

spinning completely about he spun and missed the pole completely. He watched the men from his spot at the back of the training field perform the same set of movements with far greater power and effect. Their blows resounded throughout the camp.

"I...I can't do it, ahm dizzy." Jors said laying his sword down and sitting next to it on the ground. "They're men."

"And so shall you be, someday. Sooner than you think. Rest yourself. You've done well."

Jors' gaze focussed on a beetle, struggling to bury itself beneath the cold ground near the post.

"Boru,,,My Lord."

"Yes?"

"When will you marry my mother?"

Boru looked out across the field and cursed under his breath. "I would tie that ribbon to her wrist in an instant but I cannot for now, you know that."

"Don't you love her?"

"More than my life...and all my life."

"But I hear people call her names...I'd like to cut them all down with my sword." Jors jumped up and hacked at the pole.

"Here! Stop that! That's no soldier! Save that sword!!" Boru wrested the sword from the boy's hands. "Here's your first lesson, one I taught your mother years ago. Keep cool, never let fear or anger guide your blade and by that I mean your head, or some one will chop it off for you."

At sunset, Brillie watched her brother parry and thrust with a stick along the beach as she hobbled toward him.

"I remember another brother doing that. An' I saw somthin', just then, anoother vision."

"Argh. Spare me." Jors moaned, rolling his eyes. "Oh, alreet..." he sighed "what is it this time?"

"He's got one."

"Wha?"

"A sword, his father's sword."

"Drink this." The Matron said helping a soldier in the men's ward to sit up in bed. His arms circled her waist in his delirium, crying out his sweetheart's name. Brilla placed her hands on the man's chest and held them there. His heart beat beneath her palms, warm and strong. 'How long?' she thought, had it been since a man last held her? Gradually his arms lost their strength and his pulse slowed. Something about the laying on of her hands made him sigh as he passed into sleep. She picked up her things and stood in the doorway watching him. This small act of comfort had disturbed her.

That night, as she lay in bed she caressed her own breasts and thought of Jem, guiltily and yet with pleasure, wondering what it would have been like to be loved by him. What if Aolwynd had gone with Boru instead of staying with Jem? How would he have touched her? Brilla sighed sadly and rolled over. Love, a house and a family around her at last. She laid her arm across her belly, holding it tight as if a man's arms embraced her from behind. She longed for someone to kiss, to curl up with at night, whisper the events of the day to and decide about tomorrow. Why had it ceased bothering her when she had been so lustful as a girl? She could still hear the voices of the older women laughing and chastening her those first few years. She had had men, and men had desired her. What had stopped it all from happening?

Simple. Lauro had died and the business of running the hospice gradually consumed all her time. As the years went by, what had happened to dull her passions? Other women had husbands or lovers that they went home to. And women like Cere and Lyla had found each other...why had she forgotten how to find love?

Her body was calling to her now, aching again, her pulse racing and throbbing again, ready to prove she was alive. 'That's just my luck!' she thought as Brillie's vision tormented her. 'Some ghost an' anoother woman's husband. Tha's all I've got to think on, Jem, even tho' she don't want him no more! An 'E's dead too, more like. Great Mother! What a mess.' Brilla tossed on her mattress, aroused and confused. She could not stop thinking of him. Raising her nightgown, her own touch finally gave her some relief, but strangely, by dawn she fell into a restless sleep in which someone without a face, someone she knew before, years ago, visited her and took her.

"There you are!" Cere said coming around the corner of the gardener's cottage. "We've been looking all over for you!"

126

Brilla lay on a lounge chair looking up at the sky admiring the clouds and the remoteness of their little home. Lauro had made a gift of this little house to the couple years before. It was just far enough away from the hospice community to provide the respect and privacy they deserved.

Lyla joined them, her notebooks and satchel of instruments already over her shoulder. "It's time to do the rounds." she said.

Brilla continued to stare and waved them away with a pathetic hand.

"Have you been crying?" Lyla dropped her heavy satchel and sat down on the end of the lounge. "What is it, sweeting? What's the matter?"

Brilla took hold of Cere's hand, pinching it. "You must take over for me, I will not be seeing to the men's ward for now."

"Why ever not?" Lyla looked at her. "Did someone accost you?"

"No!" Brilla puffed bitterly.

"Then what?" Detecting her mood and suddenly sighing Lyla knew. "Oh you poor soul."

"What?" Cere asked.

Lyla smiled and looked up into Cere's eyes.

"No."

"Stop!" Brilla said angrily, wiping her tears and turning away from them. "It's not that."

"Oh, it's very much that. She's found someone. And why shouldn't she?" Lyla crossed her legs and held them at the knees with her hands, bobbing the free leg up and down furiously.

Cere recognized it as a sign that Lyla had got hold of a notion. It was best to let her have her say or she would worry them until it was said.

"We are not made of stone..." she continued. "I remember a girl so lusty she flew at everything in a pair of troos, even your precious Aolwynd! Remember? The look on your face! You've buried yourself in nothing but papers and books for years. I don't wonder you're sick of it. There is someone...tell!"

"Who has brought you back to life?" Cere asked.

Brilla smiled, sat up and tucked her knees under her chin. "There is no one. It's no use, I'm hopeless. My looks are fading away. No man will want me now. I wish I had what you have found. How much simpler to find love here. So well matched, so good to each other."

"Humph." Cere said smiling and jerking her chin at Lyla. "That's all you know about it." she joked. "And anyway, this woman I love is no substitute for a man. I want no other. She is my great passion, and my dearest friend." The couple gazed at each other, connecting on so many intimate levels in only the briefest moment of time.

Brilla watched them. "I'm sorry, my friends, I didn't mean it that way. You have been so kind to me. Why suddenly I feel so hollow inside, I don't know. I won't deny I have been lonely. I watch the other women going home at night to their husbands...families. And I see you...what you have together...I would kill for! I think, why should I be alone? Is this what drove Lauro to her death? She did love once, I know, even if it left her empty inside. But I go no where, meet no one. Once a month I go to those boring city council meetings, give my report in a room full of fat old men. Jem was the only exception. My friend, a smiling face there, always glad to see me. And now he is gone. Dead. I do not even have that smallest of pleasures, seeing his face. Of course I am alone."

"So...what are we to do?" Cere asked.

"Just as I've told you. Take over for me, until I am strong enough to gaze at a pair of troos again." she smiled wearily.

"I see our Matron is back...do you think now we can get on with this morning's rounds?" Cere grabbed Brilla's hand and yanked her up playfully from the couch.

The women walked back through the herb gardens admiring the silver leaves of the sage and remarking upon its smell. They failed to notice the little girl following behind them, her crutch tracing a pattern of scallops in the dew-soaked lawn.

128

11

The Kitten and The Monk

Tanner jumped into the back of a covered wagon as it drew close to the northern gates of the capitol. Hiding amongst the turnip sacks he waited until he heard the sounds of the marketplace then he jumped out again and walked along the back streets till he reached his old neighborhood. Slipping in the broken pantry window of his abandoned house he was shocked to find that others had done so as well. Somehow he had pictured everything being left the way it was, not counting on the hunger and greed of others. Cherry's precious dishes were stolen or in shards upon the tile floor. Not a pot or a ladle was left and the food was all gone, of course. Mice skittered out of his way. He traced the dust with his fingers along the counter top he had made for her. He remembered watching her clean and polish its wooden surface with oil and the song she sang as she worked.

The great room was empty of furnishings. He imagined his children playing amongst their toys and pillows and walked quickly out of there. He stood at the stairs but did not dare to climb them, afraid of seeing the bed he and Cherry had slept in destroyed, or worse yet, not seeing it at all; the bed they had made all their children in with so much passion and delight.

He walked out the kitchen door and saw that the iron gates of his courtyard had been broken again and re-hung rather poorly. A new chain and lock held them in place. He walked along the garden wall and knocked at the door that he shared with his neighbor.

A feeble voice answered from the other side.

"Andy, it's Tanner."

"By the Gods, boy! Just a moment! Just a moment!" The door opened with the sound of several locks and bolts. Andrus stood, bent with exertion from working in his garden. Leaning against his hoe for support he reached out with one arm to embrace Tanner. "Glad I am to see you! Even though...well, you see what they've done to your home again. The bastards! Helped themselves. Made a dog's breakfast of it...our neighbors, that's who it was! Can you believe it? Nice folk we live amongst, eh?" The old man spat on the ground. "I fixed your gate, best I could."

"Many thanks, Andrus. Listen, I need your help again."

"Of course, of course, come in and sit down."

"I need you to take a message this time."

The old man sat wheezing on the steps of the Guardian's Palace that lead down to the kitchens and servant's entrance. He watched as boys in green livery ran in and out with packages and folios, careening up and down the stairs and cutting in front of each other. Carts with produce and merchants with goods went about their business stopping near the doors to un-load. No one paid him any attention.

"Ah shoulda' sent me nephew." Andrus grumbled.

After several attempts to grab at the flapping tabards of the boys he finally stopped a page before he shot past him and gave him the note pushing it into his hand with a coin.

"Lord Faolan, mind!" he shouted after the lad. "I'll know if yah don't!"

"Jenna!" the page smirked as he came up to her on the stairs. "A note fer yer precious Lord Faolan. Whadilya do fer me?" the boy said pinching the note between two fingers and swinging it in front of her eyes.

"Give it! You little puke!" She swiped it from his hand.

"Give us a kiss!"

"Ger off!"

The page pinched her ass before he ran off.

Faolan sat at his desk, poring over a scroll in front of him. The orange cat lay across one end flicking its tail lazily. Amused, Faolan held the animal still with one hand while pulling the scroll along beneath him as he read. The cat did not move. "You make a fine paperweight...lazy bastard..." he smirked.

Suddenly Faolan felt a pair of eyes watching him and he looked up.

Jenna stood in his doorway leaning against the wall.

"What do you want now, girl?"

"Ahm that glad ta' see you too!" She huffed sauntering into the room, rolling her hips and making her skirt swirl out as she did so. The cat sat up and watched her.

"You must have better things to do...but I seem to find you every step I take! And now you seek me out in my one refuge? Have I no place to hide from you or this damned cat?" he smiled. She immediately grinned and came closer holding the note behind her back.

She slid around the desk and whispered into his ear, "I've a message from Tanner." She turned and flicked it behind her like a tail.

"Give it here." Faolan stood up quickly and grabbed it. "Now get out of here, both of you!" Startled, Chores jumped from the desk and ran out. Instead of leaving, Jenna only went a few steps and leaned against the carved panels of the chamber, smiling at him.

He read the note. "How do you know Tanner?" he asked as she minced about the room touching his things.

"Oh, everybody knows Tanner. But...I thought he was a traitor now?"

"Shut your mouth, girl. And why did you read my note and where did you get it from, speak up! Did anyone else read it?"

Jenna reassured him that the page she got it from was too stupid to bother and it came from an old man.

"So...why did you read a note addressed to me?"

"Ah'm yer little spy, aren't I?"

Faolan grabbed her wrist and held on tight. "Jenna, you mustn't breath a word of this to any one, promise?"

"What? About yer meetin' with a traitor? Or about him bein' a hunted man? Or about him bein' in the city, walkin' about free like? Or all three?" Her childish teasing infuriated him. He squeezed her wrist. Jenna only grinned and following the force of his grasp turned her body around till she pressed up against him, pushing her back into his belly. "Hold me." she sighed, pulling his arm around her.

"Jenna! I swear..." he growled, smiling in spite of himself. He took her hand and spun her away as if in a dance then returned to his desk. "I'm serious. Swear to me you'll tell no one about this!"

"Oh, alright, I'll swear." she sighed aloud with happiness, her head spinning from his touch.

"I'm taking you into my confidence, Kitten." he said, staring down at the note.

She glowed at his words and leaned over with her elbows on the desk, gazing into his eyes.

"Affairs of state...you must trust me. Do you understand?" he said lowering his tone and saying the words slowly.

"An' I'd do anything fer you...do you understand that?" she said, boldly raising his chin with her finger and making him look at her. Standing up, she cupped her breasts and admired their contours, smoothing her blouse almost as if he weren't there. She turned, swaying her hips saucily and walked out of the room fully aware that his eyes followed her.

That night two men sat plotting beneath a plane tree in Andrus' garden.

The old man sat on an over-turned bucket near his front gate drinking tea, looking at the clouds as they passed over the moon and listening for footsteps or any other sign that Faolan had been followed.

"It was dangerous, your sending a note like that to the palace. Thank the gods my little spy intercepted it."

"Ah, Ruby's playmate you mean...Jenna. How is the little minx?"

"A nuisance, she dogs my every step. I've made too much of her. Dangerous."

"In more ways than one, I expect. But as to danger, how else was I to get hold of you? Throwing a torch won't work from my end. This was the only way. We're getting anxious. When do we strike?"

"A situation has fallen into my lap that we may be able to take advantage of but it means you must keep close watch and be ready to act when the time comes. Has Kora arrived yet?"

"No. But Arius, his men and the wagons to carry away the sick and feeble are already north of the city."

"His men?"

"Aye. He has his own troop of falconers, his father's men."

"Falconers, eh? I'd like to see that."

"Bloody circus but they're meant to disguise the purpose of the wagons. As if they're heading to Midwinter Market."

"Clever. And at least we can be sure which route the army will take, for you will force my father's hand to head north when they pursue the prisoners and they will pursue, we can count on that."

"You mean Rute."

"Yes, you see that too. Rute will be consumed with rage. Nothing will stop him. It is nearly spring and all is ready. They will follow you and their swords will be out. Pity the children and women if he catches up with them."

"Ah pity them already. But we mean to keep ahead of them. Pray to the gods Boru is riding already toward Guardia."

Faolan scraped his fingers through his hair. "To stop father before he even leaves home...this may work, but the other. This is a fool's scheme. So much can go wrong. Did you have a hand in it?"

"Aye, it sounds like me, don't it?...But no, it were Kora's idea."

"Hmmm. Well, we must follow where it leads...you must be ready to strike when you see my signal."

"What is it then?"

"I mean to bleed off soldiers from the army on a fraudulent mission, especially those troops camped nearest the hostages. Heading east for a few days, we'll be away long enough to give you a rat's chance of escape. When you see a great host move off toward the city lead by my standard, wait until nightfall and then make your rescue."

"A great host?"

"As many as I can pull away, but I must first convince my father of the necessity."

"Tha' would be brilliant." Tanner's smile faded and he kicked the dust with the toe of his boot. "Have you seen my wife?"

"I have kept a watch over them, as often as I am able without seeming overly concerned. Rute dogs my movements, he senses something. He knows I was against this war and against his being made general. He only needs proof and you will lose your inside man."

"Aye, an' you may lose yer head off yer shoulders...but tell me, how are they, the hostages?"

"They are tolerable, fed and clothed. Better off than they were at the jail."

"Alright, my friend. Be careful. You're father would be proud of you, you know, fighting from both ends of your shaft like this. You'll make a politician yet."

"If I'm not hung for a traitor."

"You'd be in good company." Tanner said rising and waving goodbye to Andrus.

The two conspirators shook hands and left one at a time through the garden gate, back through Tanner's empty house and out through the pantry window.

Andrus sat on his seat until he was sure they were well away, poured his cold tea onto the ground and hobbled back into his house.

Faolan lay sleeping, one arm hanging over the side of his bed. A single candle flickered against the walls of his room illuminating the tapestries of mythical creatures that hung there. An empty wine jug and a goblet lay on the floor. A stain of wine where the jug had fallen traced a circle there.

He snored lightly. Ever since finding out about Rue's death, drinking was the only way he could get to sleep and chase the memories of her from his mind.

A puff of air blew into the room as his chamber door opened and shut without sound. Jenna tip-toed along a wall holding her breath and stilling the gently moving tapestries with her hands. As

134

she came close to the bed she unbuckled her belt and laid it on a chair. The light of the candle sparkled in her eyes as she focussed on his sleeping form. She lifted her blouse over her head and let her skirts fall to the floor. The cold air quickened her skin and she slipped beneath the covers on the far side of his big bed. She marveled at the softness of the sheets and the silken coverlet lined with down. 'Must be nice...' she thought. Inching over to him she slipped her fingers lightly across his ribs, curling her arm around his belly. Pushing her body up against his back she laid one leg over his. Every inch of her flesh drank in his warmth. She sighed again, giddy with sensation and her own boldness. Becoming a little braver still, Jenna leaned over and touched her lips to his shoulder, then pulled back his hair to kiss his throat. Faolan's head moved back in sleep and his neck arched sensing her lips.

Suddenly he rolled over, waking with a start, grasped her under the arms and pulled her across his chest. "What? Who is this?" he mumbled, his voice raspy with drink.

"Doon't talk...just kiss me now." she said.

"Jenna! Good the gods! Get out! What are you doing here?"

She held his hands and tried to push them back onto the pillows, playfully straddling his belly as she did so.

"Get out of here before you are seen!" He said pulling the coverlet up over her naked shoulders like a tent.

"Who cares?" she said shaking it off again.

"I care!"

"I'm glad of that." she said softly leaning in toward him.

"No, I mean I care that you should not be hurt."

"You won't hurt me. I know you won't. Besides, I'm in your confidence, you said so."

"That is not what it means! Get out. Please. Kitten."

"Love me, I know you want to, I can feel you want to..." Jenna wriggled herself down on his groin as he grew hard beneath her. "love me or I will tell your father."

Faolan sat up and pushed Jenna off. "What do you mean by that you little cat?"

Jenna raised her eyebrows, pursed her lips and sat back, looking about the room. Rolling off him, she reclined at the end of the bed seductively, her head resting in her hand. She crossed her legs and admired her golden figure in the flickering of the candlelight. "Oh,

I was out in the stable yard last night when you were talking to those soldiers afore you sent them off. You know, I get around...I keep my eyes open. You're orders, remember?" she smiled at him. "I heard you talkin', you said 'disguise yourselves' and 'Leave no one alive' and 'do not be seen.' What might that be all about? You're up to something big, something dangerous, my Lord. You sent those men of yours out to do some terrible mischief." She whispered these last words flirtatiously, in spite of their seriousness, making her eyes wide, a smile just playing on her lips.

"What manner of wicked child is this?"

Jenna crept up the bed towards him and stuck her thumb in her mouth.

Faolan was speechless yet she was so comical that he could not help laughing at her.

"I'm no child an' you know it, take me, or I will tell on you..." she whispered, stroking his thigh as she came to him. She licked his skin and counted his ribs with her fingers while admiring the serrated muscles of his side. He grabbed her hand.

"Fool. Following me about will only make things worse for you. I should not have encouraged you. Knowing more than I wish you to know...is very dangerous." he said angrily. Putting his hands about her waist he pushed her away again. "Think what you're doing."

Jenna only laughed and fell back upon the pillows stretching her arms out and arching her back in delight as she looked around. "It's nice here...Ah like this bed, I've never been in a bed this big before." Her eyes sparkled with desire. "See thee, 'Your honor'...Faolan..." she dared again to whisper his given name. "Ahm' a woman, not a child no more," Jenna looked down at her own breasts and smiled up at him "an' I know what I want...ah wan't you, tonight, you've known mah feelin's long enoof. Come in to me, take me, Sweetheart, Ah' can be dangerous too if I'm not satisfied."

Faolan looked at the beautiful young creature lying next to him with her arms outstretched. He felt his blood pound and passion for her sweeping over him that he could not, no, did not want to control any longer. Aroused, he watched her pupils grow wide and dark. She drew back the sheet he held with one hand, slowly, letting the fabric caress his flesh. Giving it a last tug, she

136

triumphantly exposed his erect penis. His heart fluttered and he stared into her eyes. Everything around him faded away and he could only see her glowing body in front of him. The light from the candle seemed to dim and diffuse, obscuring everything. She did not seem to be the same girl. There was a sudden rushing noise in his ears and he grew dizzy as a face swam in front of hers.

Rue's face replaced Jenna's sweet features, her voice grew low and melodious, murmuring of her love, welcoming, enticing, not the teasing voice anymore of the serving girl but the woman he had loved beyond all telling and lost forever. Faolan, overwhelmed by grief and despair became enthralled with desire and fell on the girl like an animal.

Jenna gasped and cried out as he arched his back and took her forcefully to the full extent of his shaft. Her eyes filled with tears and she wrapped her arms about his neck, pushing her forehead against his.

"You damned little fool..." he cursed, sliding his lips across her face and down to her breast. "No man has known you...What have you done? What have I done to you?"

In the morning, cradled in his arms, Jenna lay with a peevish face looking toward the windows. Pale winter light stretched across the floor and smoke from the embers dying in the fireplace drifted up to the ceiling. She blinked at the stars painted above her in gold and cursed them. Her head pounded and her throat was sore as if she'd been breathing fumes all night. Her lower lip trembled with anger and confusion. Her flesh was sore and still throbbed with hunger for him but her eyes glistened with tears. While they'd made love that night he had touched her as no man had done before, tenderly, fiercely, as if he could never have enough of her and yet he seemed so far away...and he had desperately, constantly, whispered another woman's name.

***

The Matron swabbed a wet cloth over Brillie's forehead. The child had tossed and turned on her little cot in the elder Brilla's office throughout the night, calling out words Brilla could barely make out and gesturing wildly with her hands above the coverlet.

Something had driven her deep into a nightmare and Brilla could not shake her out of it no matter how hard she tried. To begin with the girl smiled and whispered tenderly reaching out and touching some un-known cheek as if caressing it. She lifted up her face to receive a kiss, not like a child in its bed saying good night, but as an adoring woman receiving her lover.

Brilla shuddered with repulsion watching her and could not understand what was happening. This was no sickness. The girl squirmed on her cot, spreading her little legs and holding up her arms as if to embrace someone. Brilla watched in shock as the little body contorted and mimicked positions a grown woman knew all too well. Finally she grasped the girl's knees, forcing them together and rolled her over onto her side. Covering Brillie with her blanket, the Matron held her down until she finally fell asleep.

Only three words could she glean from this obscene event, the girls flailing legs and ravings; "Wait for me." Over and over again these three simple words were said, sometimes as a desperate plea, sometimes a command. Later into the shank of the night the girl awoke and began to angrily cry out, cursing someone at the top of her lungs. She used phrases and spells Brilla remembered reading once, many years ago amongst the scrolls of Lauro's private library. Love spells. Binding love spells.

***

Faolan and his father rode in the cold wind of early winter through the army encampment. Everything was covered in snow. Activity had stopped. Soldiers huddled by the fires or in their tents.

"Have you heard from the men you sent to Bow Mountain? Was the apology accepted?"

Borchard grunted at Faolan's jibe. "Nothing yet, always a good sign."

"I don't think so."

"What do you mean, my son?"

"I must show you something." Faolan turned his horse off the main aisle toward the healing tent. Borchard followed him. Two muddy tracks led them to a standing cart. Orderlies with stretchers waited near by. Borchard rode up to the side and peered over the rails.

Several dead men lay stacked side by side. Their throats had been slit and gaped wide open like surrogate mouths. Their garments were black with dried blood. The year's last generation of flies crawled sickeningly about the bodies, humming, in spite of the cold.

"Your men at Bow Mountain, I think."

"How did this happen!" Borchard shouted, choking with anger. Clearly shaken by the sight, he pulled his horse away.

"Ambush? Surprised in their sleep? Who knows. We must do something." Faolan said. "We must find out who did this. Let me march to Bow Mountain before the campaign. I still have time to parlay with them and come back."

"You, my monk?"

Faolan tried to look hurt. "Father, perhaps a host of soldiers on their doorstep would cause them to regret their actions, perhaps there has been some mistake, brigands are always ready in the forests thereabouts as well as giants...before we accuse the whole of the Bowmountain clan of disloyalty, we need to get to the bottom of it. You were counting on them as allies."

"Let me think this out...What does Rute have to say?"

"The cart only arrived this morning."

"Find him and bring him to me in my tent."

"What are you playing at?" Rute paced the ground while Borchard stood in front of a brazier warming his hands. "Ah wouldn't waste a single man to know what happened there or what they were thinkin'. What do we care? A family of bull-headed, thieving...why they're only allies because we let them deal as they wish, talk about Saels breaking off from us? Has Bow Mountain ever been truly part of Earden?"

"Rute...they've murdered my father's men." Faolan cursed dramatically under his breath for the benefit of Borchard.

"Spies. Call them what they are...were. Sent to watch. They knew the danger."

"They were my men! Sent by me to assess the situation and they did it! Alive or with the gods. The Bowmountains are planning something or my men would have been spared as they have been in the past. This is not the first time I have had cause to distrust those cave dwellers." Borchard said truculently without turning from the fire.

"What if they plan to march on the city while we are gone?" Faolan said softly.

"Hmmm." Borchard strode to the tent flap and looked out at the snow. It was falling again and covering the many hoof prints and wagon tracks. "The city can hold them off. What can one family of rock weasels do to us? Let them crawl out of their holes, it's nothing to us."

"It's not their family I fear, but their friends." Faolan said.

"Ha! The Giant Men have never left their own country." Rute scoffed.

"Except to take back the farmland we stole from them." Faolan added. "Let me take a host, a show of strength. It is only a matter of a few days march, and we will see what we will see. Let me extend my hand, make excuses, take that cursed boy, Dane, back with me to train here, you insulted them, remember, for my sake, wasn't it?" Faolan stood by his father. "Let us be diplomatic, for once."

"Well, there's my monk back again." Borchard sighed. "Rute, what do you think? What harm can it do? We barely cast an eye to the east...Perhaps it's time we did. Eh?"

"Get an assurance of their loyalty. Fer all the good that will do..." Rute said grudgingly. "by all means bring us back a hostage, if you like. That would be some protection against rebellion. But I still don't see the need."

"Hmm. Dane, a hostage. That joke would make a cat smile." Borchard mused.

"Ever looking for a way to insult them...Father, really? In the last campaign they brought us five thousand men, surely, that's worth something." Faolan reminded him.

***

A very different host was gathering in the recesses of the pine forest above the Guardian's sleeping army. Stealthy Wild Men took up their positions on a ridge overlooking the compound of the hostages. Crouching down amongst the rocks, secure and secret, they hugged their furs about them and watched the sentries' movements about the enclosure like hungry predators stalking a meal.

Behind them, Tanner crouched down on the ground and drew a map in the dirt. Kora leaned over and studied it greedily, pointing and asking questions. Jak stood just behind her.

"I see you've got yersef a nursemaid." Tanner whispered.

"Yes. I use him to shoo people off when they're not needed."

"Like me, I suppose."

Kora smiled. "Yes, like you."

"An' who's gonna shoo him off?" Tanner said grumpily.

Jak leaned over Kora's shoulder with a grin. "No one, old man."

Kora batted him playfully with her fist, pushing him back, like a she-bear swinging at a cub.

Arius and his wagons drew close at the other side of the forest and camped, waiting for word. He knew, just beyond those dark trees was the ridge and Kora's men, and beyond that, the whole army of Earden. His falconers spent their nerves arguing amongst themselves, wondering what part they had to play in all this besides 'decoys'.

Tanner leaned up against a tree and jerked his head toward Jak. The young soldier glowered at him but finally approached, keeping one eye on Kora.

"When did all this happen?" Tanner asked.

"Wha'?"

"You 'n her?"

"It's not like tha', at least, not for her. Why? Are you jealous, old man?" Jak grinned at him.

"Doon't make me laugh, son."

"Ah thought..."

"There's yer trouble, then."

Jak stared him down. "What do you want?"

"Ah need you ta take a message."

"Ahm not yer bloody errand boy. Ahm' her body guard."

"Yes. You'll do this then, for her..." Tanner looked over at Kora who was poking a stick into the fire. Jak's eyes followed her every move.

"Ow do yah mean?"

"This raid...it's wicked tricky. She's got courage enoof, fer three men...but a lot can go wrong, an' even if we get them away, the whole army will chase after us by morning. Rute'll see ta tha'."

"Oo's Rute?"

"A bastard, an' the general in charge."

"What if ah' think you just want me away from her?"

"Yer that attached to 'er tit, then? Don't be daft, boy. Trust me, I want 'er safe as well. An' we need our army, here...we needed 'em yesterday...Now listen...You've got ta' slip away tonight, don't let 'er know, she don't think we need the help...but you know we do...an' ride like hell. Find the army! Bring 'em here!"

***

In the strong morning sun that reflected off the snow, Faolan and his host of five hundred men left camp. Shielding their eyes, and complaining about leaving their campfires, they rode back through the city and out the other side to the farmlands beyond. Crowds gathered to watch the parade and voices called out Faolan's name. They knew nothing of his mission, but a parade was a parade. Rute rode with them to the Eastern Gate then he turned toward the palace.

"I needs must speak with you, my Lord." he said, sending out the servants and shutting the door to Borchard's study.

"What do you need?"

"Your son. 'E's taken five hundred men...more than I thought..."

"Well, he's got to rattle their nerves, doesn't he? How can he gently persuade them otherwise?" Borchard half-smiled, growing weary of Rute's paranoia.

"So you're alreet with that many gone? I fear this is more than a mere flaw in his gentle character, this parlay."

"My son is compassionate, you know this..."

"I think there is more to it than that..."

"Do not come between me and my sons."

"Your sons?"

"You bother me like an old woman...get out and take your suspicions with you!"

Rute made for the door but stopping, said "How old are you now, my Lord?"

142

"What are you getting at?"

"Faolan desires the Guardianship."

Borchard looked sharp at Rute, then the wan smile returned. He moved the scrolls and papers about on his desk. "And he shall have it, soon enough."

Rute took a breath. "What if he plans to take it from you? What if he plots to stay behind when we march on Saels? What if he makes a pact with Bowmountain? Had you thought of all that?"

"Stay behind? My son will not betray me, he is loyal to the point of foolishness. He's a good boy..." Borchard's voice trailed off as if some memory took him to happier times. "Take your worries out of here. I will have no more talk of treachery unless you bring me proof."

Rute stormed out slamming the door behind him.

Borchard creased his brow and stared at the closed door. "And what would you not take if it was offered to you, my general? How high do you think you can climb on the shoulders of myself and my sons? What do you want, I wonder? And what of you, Faolan, my son...how you've grown. Are you plotting against me? An egg is one shade on the outside...but within...two colors." Borchard poured a cup of wine and stared out the window.

Rute stalked down the hallways looking for a way out, casting his evil eye on everyone he passed. His mind was troubled and it matched the convolution of his passage with every turn and hidden stairway. He never felt comfortable inside the palace walls. 'Too much like a prison...or a rabbit hole.' he thought. Loosing his way, he came upon Faolan's chambers and hesitated only for a moment. Looking about quickly to check if he had been seen, he slipped inside.

Snorting at the luxury he found amongst the furnishings he went immediately to the big desk, scanned the papers lying there and rifled through the drawers without finding anything of interest. He grunted his approval. Why would Faolan leave anything dangerous lying around? Still, Rute was convinced there was more to this sympathetic son than he let on.

A loud yawn came from the direction of the bed causing Rute to swing about and draw his dagger. He padded softly toward the sound. A broom lay propped against the foot board. Chores the cat lay curled in a ball on a pillow. Clogs lay where they were dropped and a pair of stockinged feet stuck out from beneath the heavy coverlet. Someone was sleeping beneath it. Rute crept up to the bed, threw back the coverings and grabbed a foot.

Jenna screamed. She lay fully clothed, hugging Faolan's pillow.

Chores jumped to the floor with a hiss.

Rute grabbed the girl by the arm and pulled her out. "What are you doin' in here?" he shouted at Jenna.

"Ahm...Ahm cleanin'!" she said, sticking out her chin and yanking her arm away.

Rute's eyes narrowed as he began to calculate. "Then what are you cleanin' in his bed?"

"Noothin'." she said backing away, her cheeks burning red.

Rute came forward before she could run and grabbed her wrist. He smiled as he tugged at the sleeve of her blouse exposing her shoulder. "Oh come now, mistress, a gorgeous thing like you and you have no reason to be here? I'll warrant you're keepin' his bed warm for him until his return." Jenna smiled shyly and then beamed a little, being called 'mistress' and treated like one. "So, you're his little sweetheart, are you?" Her eyes shifted to the side and her smile faded. "Oh? Missin' him? Gone off an' left ya pantin' ta fight more battles, eh?" Rute laughed a dirty little laugh. "Doon't worry, he'll be back, there's a girl." he touched her cheek. Her eyes were glistening. "Oh, there now, what's this, tears? We are soldiers after all an' never no good fer girls, you know tha'."

Jenna sighed.

Rute switched courses quickly and became the sympathetic uncle watching her every expression with interest. When she did not relax or acknowledge his guesses, he pushed her chin up with his fingers. Her eyes shifted again, this time her gaze came to rest on an open scroll that lay on a table beside Faolan's bed.

Rute walked over and sat on the bed reaching down and picking it up. He recognized the image of Rue on her golden throne. Rute patted the bed beside him and Jenna sat down next to him. "Love is not the smooth garden path for you, eh? Ah met 'er y'know...the woman in tha' picture. So he's still pinin' for that witch? How long has she been dead now? Still got her hooks in him? That's not healthy, nor natural. An' you so lovely an' willin'?"

Jenna grabbed the scroll out of his hand and threw it across the floor.

"'As 'E had 'is way with you, an' you so good-hearted?'" Rute fired her anger, blustering away like an enraged uncle. "They're all alike them nobles, you know tha' don't you, not like us common folk. No sense of honor, no loyalty...when it comes right down to it. Oh, aye, I may be a general, but I'm just like you. Born an' bred right 'ere in the province, poor but honest. We folk must stick together. They takes what they wants. I'll warrant 'E's used you in other ways as well, eh? Little favors, information...they can be bastards, them."

His voice was like the voices of home, Jenna thought, low born, suspicious, but loyal to each other. She nodded at everything he said.

Rute knew Faolan had a web of informants and now he knew the girl was one of them. "You know, a smart girl like yoursel' could do very well if she keeps her eyes open and tells the right people what they needs ta know...money fer yer family, nice things..."

"You?"

"Why not? Am I not a general and do the people not need to win this war?"

Jenna looked at him considering this, her gaze shifted to the desk.

"We're bound for battle this spring and many may die. Do you have family in the army? Young lads at home? What if we could stop it? Or win it quick-like, saving lives?" Rute followed her gaze, standing up and walking into the middle of the room. "A portion of the realm has already fallen away from us through their foolishness, father against son...what a tragedy." He sat down on the desk top and lowered his eyes, shaking his head as if in sadness.

Jenna nodded carefully as she slipped into her clogs.

"There are enemies within you know...they play a dangerous game, innocently perhaps...like our friend here." Rute watched her face. "Always trying to patch things up. It's not for nothing the Guardian calls him his 'Monk'. Tho' no monk would treat you as he 'as, eh?"

"Dangerous game." Jenna murmured in agreement.

"Aye, maybe even treachery."

Jenna picked up her broom and made swiftly for the door. Rute grabbed her arm. "What do you know?" His teeth flashed an evil grimace. "Tell me!"

Jenna squirmed in his grip. Her gaze dashed between the door and the desk.

"There's soomthin' in there, inn't? Soomthin' 'E wouldn't want 'is father ta see. An' you know what it is! Show me! Do your duty to Earden or I'll see you spend the rest of yer life in the dungeon beneath these floors listening to that dragon snorin'! An' maybe yer folks'd like ta stay there too!" Rute pushed her down in Faolan's chair. She sat shivering with guilt and fear. "You know how to open it up, don't you, little spy? Do it!"

Jenna gulped and slowly removed a drawer, placing it beside her. Then her hand searched for the latch beneath the desk top. A soft click announced the release and the top opened on a spring, sending the piles of papers flying and settling about the floor.

Rute dove in with both hands, rifling through the compartment. Amid documents unrelated to his interest Rute found the note from Tanner. When he came to the signature his eyes grew wide and he smiled. He put a hand on her shoulder and squeezed. "Fool ta keep it." he said. "When did they meet?" Jenna mumbled her reply. "You listen to me Jenna, my sweet, Jenna my willing, anything else you find out you bring to me. Do you hear? You'll be rewarded. But if you don't, I'll see you punished, an' yer family, too. An' don't let on to yer sweetheart when 'E cooms back. There's m'girl." With that he smiled, slipped the piece of paper into his jacket pocket and left. Chores slipped out behind him.

The sound of running feet in the halls of the private apartments made Borchard step out of his bedchamber door. Young Jemson stopped short. His new green tabard was disheveled and he held his sword and sheath in front of him like a prize fish.

"Jemson! Where are you off to?"

"Oh! Good moro, my Lord! Ahm' late ta' practice! Did I disturb you? I'm sorry." he said in a rush.

Borchard smiled and knelt down on one knee. Straightening the boy's uniform and looking into his eyes, Borchard placed his hands on the boy's shoulders."Taking a short cut? You've learned your way about, eh? But this is no way to begin your training. Now, tell me, how are you getting on?"

146

Jemson's eyes lit from within with a fire Borchard had seen before in his own children.

"Ah can't describe it! It's lak I was meant fer it. Ah love it! Feel mah sword arm!"

The boy showed the old man his muscle, then pulled back suddenly feeling foolish.

Borchard only nodded and felt the small bulge on his upper arm. "Impressive. Tell me something, young warrior...suppose I were surrounded on the battlefield, what would you do?"

"I would come to your aid, my Lord! I would stand back to back with you until the foe were defeated!" The boy almost shouted. Borchard looked very serious and Jemson eyed him curiously. "Is anything wrong, Sire?"

"No, young man. And 'Lord' is good enough for me, I am no king."

"Near enough." the boy said under his breath.

Borchard snorted with laughter. "Here, help me up."

Jemson stood still while the old man used his shoulder, struggling to heave his body upright. "Old bones and a young heart...we make a fine pair. Go on now." he said waving the boy away.

Jenna sat gulping and sniveling on the stairs leading down to the kitchens. Every footstep she heard made her jump.

"What on earth's the matter with the girl?" Devers said coming down the steps and leaning over her.

"Noothin'. Noothin's the matter." she stammered.

"Come on...come with me." he said picking her up by the arm and dragging her into his chambers at the bottom of the stairs.

"Sit down now...you're as white as a lily." Devers poured two brandies and watched while she drank hers down. "Now tell me what's happened."

"Noothin'. Ah don't know...But Lord Faolan...Tanner...General Rute...traitors..." Jenna blubbered and sniffled so badly he held her chin to stop her mouth.

"Start over and stop crying." Devers listened carefully sipping his brandy while Jenna confessed to crawling in with Faolan and sleeping in his bed after he had gone. Then she told him about the note and Rute's threats. "Calm yourself, Rute won't hurt you, I'll see to that. But don't you go telling him anything without you're first telling me. There's a dangerous game being played and your only one small piece on a board of Kings Men."

"But Ah'm Lord Faolan's little spy, 'E told me so."

"Not any more, you're not. And you're not Rute's either. Though you must pretend to be for both of them. Keep your eyes open and your mouth shut. Can you do that? Good. Now you work for me. Feeling better? Then get back to your duties and don't let me catch you tempting Lord Faolan with your charms any more or I'll have you flogged. I mean it. He's strong drink, he is. You stick to barley water if you know what's good for you. One bastard running about the place is enough."

***

Faolan rode hunched over against the cold at the front of his troops. He wiped the wet flakes from his horse's mane. He thought glumly of how long it would take him in his cot that night to get warm, of how he would pull his knees up to his chest and how they would protrude off the narrow camp bed. He thought of how he would glare at the brazier of dying coals and calculate whether it was worth the trouble to replace them.

The clop of his horse's hooves punctuated the air and echoed off a series of outcrops and ridges as they passed from the rich farmlands of Guardia and climbed slowly into wilder territory. As they did so the snow became lighter but more stinging. Deep scrub-covered ravines carved from soft stone lead in one direction like the burrows of wolf spiders toward the mountains of the north east. Bow Mountain stood in the distance above its fellows in a blue haze of storm clouds. All paths in this remote corner of Earden seemed inevitably to lead toward it. Beyond its frozen boundaries lay a land of conflicting territories, ignored by the guardians and only fought over by frontier folk and giants.

Faolan dreaded these long rides alone with his thoughts. Rue's face and form was ever beside him now; a specter either riding or standing on a hill watching him as he passed. She had begun to haunt his every waking hour, not just her memory but her form and her voice followed him. Her power was growing. He tried to think of it as an illness, the dizziness, the nausea, something that would

148

fade away. But when he thought of his brother and of his all consuming love for one woman, he cursed their shared disability. Not only that, but worse still, he loved a dead woman. 'What a fool, I cannot even enjoy the company of that serving wench...so willing…' he swore under his breath, remembering Jenna and the tears drying on her cheeks. Even she had been affected. How to put an end to it? He did not know. He tried to put his private life out of his mind. 'Soon Tanner and the Wild Men will make their raid,' he thought, looking behind him at the mass of troops he had stolen away. 'at least I have given those families a chance at freedom but what am I to say when I get to Bow Mountain?'

12

Bowmountain King

Tanner leaned over and touched Kora's shoulder as the sun rose. She stood up and wrapped her furs about her. He resumed his seat by the fire trying not to watch her stretch her lithe body as she shivered and yawned. It had taken all Tanner's strength not to crawl beneath the furs with her the night before.

The morning mist rose around the bases of the fir trees at the edge of the forest. A dark grey shape like a bear swirled the foggy air as it came out and approached the camp.

"My men have sent someone." she said with a cough.

The wild man came into the clearing and taking up a place by the fire, settled down on his haunches and warmed his hands.

Arius jumped from his wagon and joined them by the fire.

The wild man spoke first in a low tone to Kora. When she nodded he took some meat and roasted it without saying another word.

"What did he say?" Tanner finally asked.

"Faolan is at the head of a mighty host of soldiers moving off to the east, back along the road and into the city gates."

"Good the gods, I had hoped for a few more days..." Tanner said. "but that's our signal. He's taking them on a little outing, long enough away from the main force to aid our rescue."

"Then it's tonight?"

"Yes."

The wild man finished eating his meat, wiped his hands on his leggings and trotted back to the woods.

"I wish Jak were here..." Kora said.

"'E's a babby..." Tanner spat on the ground.

Kora knit her brows together. "He's no child even if I did want him, which I don't. What do you care, old man?" She smiled slightly, her eyes sparkling. "Are you jealous?"

"Nay, Ah take when it's offered, tha's mah motto. You said yersel' it were over." he shrugged his shoulders, then peered up at her. "Are you offerin'?"

Kora grumbled something under her breath. "No. I'm not."

"Miss me? Ah kin fix tha'."

She only glared at him.

"You do like him, then? Well, what's happened? Has 'E run off? Wouldn't a' thought it of 'im. Such a good-lookin' sprout too." Tanner cocked his head, watching her carefully as he poked at the fire.

Kora's eyes narrowed and her dark brows arched like a crow's wings. "I don't know where he's gone...I don't suppose you had anything to do with that? What did you say to him? You haven't hurt him have you?"

Tanner feigned innocence, pointed to his chest and made his eyes wide.

***

On the third day's march Faolan stopped his troops at nightfall near a river. Though they had climbed above the foothills they were still several miles from Bow Mountain. In the morning, he decided, they would turn around and march back, having had what he would describe to the green recruits as a 'training mission'. No need to go any further. In the mean time, Tanner and Kora would have rescued the prisoners or, they would be at the palace gate to greet him, hanging in chains.

152

It was impossible not to think about the raid even as he knelt that night in his tent, his hands clasped to his heart. A smoldering brand of cedar lay on the ground in front of him, the fumes trailing upward. He prayed to the Twin Gods of War and also to the Great Mother, entreating Rue, if she were there, to intercede for everyone's safety.

In the morning he made his speech to a surprised but relieved audience. As it ended and the troops were getting ready to walk off they heard clapping coming from the rocks above the riverbank. A strange voice called out demanding all of Faolan's men to sit on the ground or their leader would be killed. The troops panicked and made to draw their swords but Faolan gestured them to do as they were told and looking straight ahead, he pointed. A hundred archers dressed in yellow and black stepped out from behind their cover, into the sunlight. Their bows were drawn and all were aimed at the men. Faolan raised his hands and an officer came forward on horseback.

"You are Lord Faolan, are you not?"

Faolan nodded.

"I have been ordered to accompany you to Bowmountain, my Lord, our king wishes to speak with you. Your troops will stay here under our protection and your officers will come with you. Tell your men to keep camp here, no harm will come to you if they stay where they are. If they attempt to fight, retreat or send a message you're head will be delivered back to Guardia with the bodies of your officers to escort it. Your troops will never leave this spot alive."

With that Faolan and his four officers reassured their company and rode off flanked by Bowmountain troops. Faolan gave nothing away but questions and excuses boiled in his mind beneath his stoic face.

Bow Mountain stood alone, tallest of the peaks guarding the furthest reaches of Earden; a little kingdom of its own. For generations the warriors of Bowmountain had fought beside the soldiers of Earden, but their people and their king were jealous of their freedom and they kept their lives and their customs separate. It was a 'rocky' alliance as Borchard was fond of joking.

Faolan shivered as the cold crept between the layers of his clothing and his fingers grew numb in his gloves. It was a stark land, higher in elevation than the plains of Guardia and their path wound through it ever higher and higher. Finally, through blinding gusts, they approached a long causeway of stone carved from the very bones of the rocks. The wind sang as it dived beneath the slender stone bridge. Its arching expanse made Faolan hold his breath as he crossed. To make this wonder, he realized, the masons of Bow Mountain must have used tremendous effort. They had hewn away an entire mountain to create it! It lead up to a mighty structure of palaces and homes also cut into the cliffs. It reminded him somewhat of the School of Healing with its honeycombed balconies. His stomach turned at the memory for that is where he had first met Rue. Citizens gathered at the main gate in the wall that surrounded the city and stared openly at the strangers.

Faolan was astonished by their opulent dress and handsome faces. His father's flippant remarks over the years had colored his opinion of them and not for the better. He had always thought them little better than the boorish boys they sent yearly to be trained in martial arts and 'house-broken at our expense', yet another quip of his father's. He noticed as he rode through the main market street the many shops that sold bows and other weapons but also he saw fine musical instruments and time pieces. Shops displayed intricately woven woolen goods in bright colors with exquisite patterns, some with gold threads or jewels. Elegant ladies with servants carrying parcels stopped and stared at him as he passed. They had no coats as they walked in the wind but their winter dresses, lined at the neck and cuffs with fur, were made of this heavy, felted wool and the skirts stood out, away from their figures like bells. He was enthralled and just glimpsed, as they walked, neat, red leather boots with pointed toes. 'How Jenna would like a pair of those...' he briefly thought, smiling to himself like a newly-wed. Then his brows knit together and he shook the notion out of his head. He continued on, marveling at all he saw. This was a wealthy nation, small though it was. He had often wondered what the population did for trade. This land he had been told, was only fit to raise mountain sheep.

Turning from the market, his captors lead him up a steep ceremonial boulevard of blue stone, open to the sky. Beyond that, the steps and facade of a mighty palace beckoned.

Bowmountain King was standing beneath the arched and

elaborately carved entrance. His dark beard and piercing black eyes were complimented by a robe of grayish blue embroidered with silver. He looked to be all one with the mountain apart from his golden crown. Beside him stood Dane, the boy Borchard had rejected. He jeered openly at Faolan. Faolan gulped.

Bowmountain King waited for the men to get down from their horses, then he turned on his heel without a word and they were made to follow him into the palace. The great doors slammed shut behind them. Faolan breathed easier as the warmth surrounded him but he did not feel welcome. Noblemen bowed to the strangers as a matter of courtesy but did not smile, as they passed down the dark hallways. Faolan was very much on edge, not knowing whether they were guests or prisoners. Suddenly, they walked into a brilliant dining hall filled with courtiers. Unfriendly eyes studied him.

The king took his place at the head of a long table piled high with food and Faloan and his officers were offered seats below the dais. "Come, refresh yourselves, you must be hungry, then..." he said sitting down "after you have eaten, you can tell me why you turn up on my doorstep with a great legion of troops. What can we possibly have done to deserve such an unfriendly visit?" A councillor leaned in and whispered into the king's ear. "Someone has murdered a few of your father's men?" Bowmountain King stared at Faolan with a knowing grin. "What was that all about? But first, be my guest, eat."

Faolan rose and bowed, feeling ill at ease. He placed his hand over his heart. "My liege. You are truly king here, I did not know."

"I have that honor. The Guardians of Earden have never been very interested in kings of any sort, not our culture, or our titles. I am not surprised you did not know. Unless it suits his purpose, your father keeps things very much to himself. In fact, he still spreads the rumor that we live in caves!" At this the courtiers and noblemen laughed sourly.

"I would change this if I could."

"Yes, I have heard you are a peace-maker and a scholar. All the more strange then, this visit, or is it a threat?"

"Is there not somewhere more private where we may speak at length. I have much to explain."

"Indeed you have, but nothing more important than what you

must say in front of my family." Bowmountain King gestured toward Dane and his father.

Faolan took a deep breath. "Then let me first apologize for the actions of my father during Mid Winter Festival. He meant no great disrespect to your nephew, Dane." Faolan bowed to the lad's father who stood behind his son and glowered at him. Dane showed surprise but remained unbent. "My father has a fondness for my natural son and in deference to me, raised him up, perhaps importunely. Dane was, as a senior page, in charge of the lad but...how shall I put this, was less than welcoming to my boy." Faolan smiled at Dane who's face showed clearly this was a revelation to him.

The boy turned to his father with upward palms as if he would explain himself. "Had I known, father..." was all Dane had time to say before his father clapped him across side of the head with his hand, then the man bowed to Faolan.

"Forgive him, my Lord." Dane's father mumbled.

"Perhaps a trip back to the city is in order to resume his training?" Faolan said in an aside to the king.

The king nodded slightly. "We will consider it. But surely you did not come all this way just to apologize to one boy?"

"No. We need your help. Allies once more. We go to war in the spring, soon in fact."

"We have heard this. Against your own brother, and the new nation of Saels. But we have little interest in this tiny country on the edge of the sea so far from our own home. And if you will pardon our frankness, we value our independence as much as any nation, large or small...why not let them be? If it is all in the family anyway?"

"A good question, my liege. Though I fear there is no family left. I must tell you my brother is wrongly branded a traitor and there is no forgiveness left in my father. Indeed it is of this I would speak more with you in private."

The king nodded. "But first, let us dine together. I will send your officers back to their men in the morning with supplies as an assurance of our hospitality and your safety while you are here. They doubtless will feel more comfortable overseeing their troops."

The king gestured to two guards standing by. The great doors of the hall were opened and the noble women of his court were allowed to enter now that "...it was safe". the king joked. The women took their seats beside their husbands. Faolan was relieved to see the ladies clad in more comfortable fabrics that sung with color and embroidery but were soft and clinging. Jewelry sparkled on their necks and in their hair. Faolan and his officers rose and bowed in tribute to beauty.

The feasting lasted late into the evening with music and laughter resounding throughout the palace.

Bowmountan King motioned to Faolan and taking his arm led him outside to an enclosed staircase. They climbed many steps winding around the exposed side of the mountain till they came to a set of chambers perched like an eyrie at the very top.

"These are my private chambers, no one is allowed to enter, indeed you are the first person who is not a king of our realm who has ever set foot inside. Look, from here you have a clear view of the stairs and the causeway. No one can approach me or my kingdom that I will not see first. The king of this land must be ever watchful. That is my duty. We are said to have sprung from a family of eagles..." Bowmountain smiled and taking Faolan by the shoulder, walked him about the large room. In the gloom, many desks, tables, thrones and couches were scattered about, all heaped with scrolls and maps, helmets and shields and all thickly covered in dust except for one area. Only one spot was bright. A polished desk and chair stood in this cleanly swept section of the floor. Two free-standing iron candle holders blazed on either side. Bowmountain King sat down upon his unpretentious throne and grasped the handle of a broom which rested against the arm. He looked at it and smiled at Faolan. "My scepter, as you see. Please sit down. This is my place amongst my ancestors, here I sit and ask their advice. Believe me, they readily give it! I have only to ask and my mind is filled with their exploits, their successes and failures. Speak now, what you will."

Faolan took a deep breath. "Thank you for your surprising hospitality...and this great honor." he gestured about him.

"Come now to the point, as my fathers would say...."

"To the point then. My father has cast aside my brother, I think you know this."

The king nodded and poured himself a goblet of wine, pushing the tray toward his guest.

"He has been mislead by events into believing that Boru wants this war. Indeed I have found out that my brother's attempts to communicate through messengers have been twisted or turned away. Whether this is my father's doing or not I must ascertain, but it makes no difference now."

"I have known your father a long time. He was not always so easily led astray...nor so cruel, but I know he would not willingly suffer a jewel like Saels to be wrested away from him. Not one so hard-fought and won. Your own mother's city. He will have it back."

"I would stop this war if I could but I fear it has gone too far for that. In fact I know it has."

"What can we do for you?"

"Fight with us."

"You are not being honest with me..." the king said softly.

Faolan stood up and turned away from him looking out the window. "You see many things from your mountaintop..." Faolan turned back and took a deep breath. "Alright..." he said finally "I am a traitor to my father and my country, I am trying to tip the scales in favor of my brother."

"Ah yes, the murdered men. Explain to me why you had your father's men ambushed not ten miles from my doorstep and why I have been accused of this crime?"

Faolan gulped but hesitated no longer as he told of the raid and rescue attempt of his father's hostages which had already taken place for good or for ill.

"Thank you for that explanation," the king said. "but we are through helping your father hold together his guardianship. We have worries of our own. Time and again we have asked for his help to push back the giants from our lands and received no answer, yet we are blamed for their acts of violence. They have forced the folk of the Eastern Provinces from their homes...our settlers and yours. I have even sent emissaries to your High Council and they have agreed, but has he sent troops to our aid? No. Has he carried out their decisions? No." Bowmountain King looked at Faolan considering him from beneath his bushy eyebrows. "It is time for a new leader to sit upon the throne of Earden."

"We have no throne."

"Time you had one made..." the king smiled "or take one of mine." he gestured about him with a laugh.

Faolan looked at him dubiously.

"What if...as you say, I could find a way to help you end this war quickly...would you listen?"

"Of course."

"Good. Let us talk no more of this tonight, you have journeyed long, come, let us rejoin my guests and family."

When they re-entered the hall the torches had burned low in their sconces upon the walls and people had pulled chairs and benches up to the fireplace. They were passing cups of wine amongst themselves, sharing intimately, as was their custom and listening to the sweetest music Faolan had ever heard. A woman's voice drifted out over the heads of the players of stringed instruments who sat on the floor facing the singer. She was in a recess next to the fire and her face was in shadow. Her figure was full and an elegant gold necklace rose and fell on her bosom as she sang.

Faolan squinted into the darkened room and as his eyes adjusted he could just make out a younger woman standing behind the singer, her long blond hair flowed freely and her arms draped affectionately about the back of the chair as if in an embrace.

"My wife and child." The king said taking his seat amongst the guests and telling Faolan to do the same.

The song the queen sang was a long romance of many verses. Eagles, mountains and wandering lovers were prominent in its story. When it was finished the princess leaned down to kiss her mother's cheek. Her hair hung in front of her like a silver curtain. She looked up and smiled shyly at Faolan. He felt his heart constrict for a moment and he held his breath.

Then, as one, the guests rose and pulled their seats to the sides of the hall. The musicians began to strum a tune quick as a heartbeat. Faolan watched as the maiden strode to the center of the open space. He admired her willowy figure in its pale blue gown and the yellow hair, bouncing and swinging on her back as she moved. She began to spin slowly in the center of the room, looking about her, her arms outstretched and her fingers curling inward with the rhythm of the music as if calling for a partner. The pace of the tune quickened as she twirled and young men came out of the crowd surrounding her in a wide circle.

Faolan's fingers twitched nervously and someone gave him a gentle push from the back. He hesitated, then found without realizing, he had joined the circle of men. Each one in turn danced with the maiden and hoisted her into the air. The crowd cheered every time she was lifted. Her face shone with a fierce delight as each man took his turn. Some merely spun her around while others lifted her high above their heads showing their strength and kissed her brazenly about the neck and shoulders before putting her down.

Faolan stood open-mouthed. More men joined the circle and the music grew louder until the hall rocked with ecstatic sound. Faolan, stunned, stepped back to watch as her last partner, the man next to him, spun her wildly and threw her up into the air. She lifted her arms and her face toward the ceiling. To Faolan she appeared to be flying. The man caught her, cradled her in his arms and carried her quickly from the room. The guests exploded with laughter and cheered.

It was over. He watched as the courtiers dragged their chairs back to the fireplace moving around him. Faolan stood for a moment speechless as the crowd went back to small talk and a musician quietly strummed a lute. Faolan bowed to the king and left the hall.

Where had the couple gone he wondered? Was she at this moment being ravished in a corner by her chosen partner for the night? Or did the men simply take turns? This was the princess of Bowmountain? In a mixture of shock and desire just for a moment Faolan realized he might have been the one to dance last with her. Seeking a breath of cool air he walked to an open window and spied the couple sitting in an alcove. The courtier grinned, whispered in the princess' ear, rose and walked away with a bow.

The young woman looked up at him with a haughty smile. "I am Jermaine, and you are... Prince Faolan?"

"Lord Faolan, your highness."

"Oh." she said dismissively. "Why did you not join the Eagle Dance?"

Faolan's mouth went dry. "I am not familiar...I did not know..."

The princess laughed. "Perhaps your people do not dance?" she

160

said plucking a piece of lint from her gown.

"Yes, we dance." Faolan bristled and could not hide his look of disdain. "But I see you have partners enough..."

"Perhaps you did not like what you saw?" Jermaine rose and smoothed the contours of her gown with her hands, passing over her bosom and waist to her hips. She seemed to be admiring her own figure but cast a sly glance into his eyes. She adjusted her bodice, jerking the fabric to better display the two pink mounds of her breasts more attractively.

He could not hide his look of surprise, nor look away from her.

"You remind me of one of my father's librarians..." she said sitting back down with a peevish sigh. "So modest...Guardia must be a boring place. I will call you 'Scholar'. Come Scholar, take me to bed, as you have scared away my prey for tonight. Let me see what knowledge you have of that art ...if any."

Faolan stared at her and did not know what to say. "If you will forgive me, Princess." He bowed and left her sitting alone. As he retreated down the corridor he heard laughter from a pair of voices.

***

Brillie stood waving her cane at her brother as Jors ran up the beach toward her. She clambered awkwardly onto a rock as the wind off the sea ruffled her apron. Throwing down her cane she opened her arms wide and he grinned as he picked her up off the rock.
"Spin me around! Faster! Faster!" She cried as he hoisted her into the air.

***

In the morning Faolan met again with the king on a sunny balcony overlooking the city and the westward slopes. "Sire...a quick end to this war?"

"Ah...quick yes, but not easy, my son. We have decided to join you, but only you...your forces, not your father's."

"I do not understand, I have no forces, apart from these borrowed men."

"Come, come. You have spent your life amongst the intrigues of the palace, surely you can guess what I am talking about."

Faolan turned away, looked over the balcony and up as the mountain wind pushed feathery clouds swiftly across the sky. "You are asking me to betray my father...is that it, and what else?"

"You have already gone that far yourself...syphoning off this great host from your father's army...I am only following your lead...Have you never thought of Earden for yourself?"

"I suppose it will come to me in time...and it has crossed my mind that in some things my decisions would have been very different."

"Crossed your mind? No, my son, you've made up your mind, that much is clear. Reach out...you are ready, the time is right. I'll wager on that...and what of your life? Your own life I mean. What do you know you have? What if your brother wins this war? What becomes of you? The next Supreme Guardian...are you sure? And a bastard son? This is your line? Come here..." The king took him by the arm and lead him along the balcony. "Look down there."

Jermaine was walking along a gravel path in a small private garden. The ground was laid out in an intricate pattern which must have been pretty in warm weather but was now clear of plants. She walked about it like a single piece on an empty game board. Her fur cloak brushed the frost in little flakes from the low hedges of box and sage that surrounded the empty beds. She moved listlessly, examining what was left of the hardy herbs and stopping in front of the rose bushes which were her favorites. They were trimmed back and tipped forward. Earth and mulch covered their knees protectively until spring, like a warm carriage rug.

Bowmountain squeezed Faolan's forearm, bringing him back to the conversation. "What if I could give you a queen? Think on it...our two houses bonded in blood. We will help you to stop this foolish war, face your father and his council of old men or sweep them away, I care not which...and in return you will help me to force back the giants from our lands...just think, a new age...allies on both sides of Earden (would not your brother be pleased?)!"

Faolan stared into the king's eyes. "A knot looks simple enough when it is tied." he said sarcastically repeating one of his father's peasant sayings. "But I cannot abandon my father, I am his general...and you forget one thing. I am a Guardian as is my father, we do not reign."

162

"Well, my daughter must be a queen and I would give her to someone she cannot ride, do you understand?"

"Then you will have to look else where for a husband."

"Unless..."

"Unless?"

"Unless you make yourself a king."

"And how might I do that?" Faolan asked facetiously and with a look of shock on his face.

"For now, simply declare before my guests and my people that you will be one and that you plan to take what is yours."

Faolan looked at the king, cocked his head in astonishment and laughed. "And how might I do that?"

"Leave that to me. Good. It is settled."

Jermaine looked up at the sound of laughter coming from the balcony. Her father had been in deep conversation with the stranger for some time. She knew it was important because he hated the cold, yet this was his most private spot to do business. She shivered as she heard the old man's hearty chuckle. This was unusual and his laughter never boded well. He had gotten what ever it was he wanted.

She shielded her eyes from the sun and tried to make out the stranger's features. 'I know father worries about me. Could I really be looking at the face of my future husband?' she mused. 'No, it cannot be...father has promised me a king...no less...not this scholar, this 'Monk' as even his own father calls him. Far from a king…' His every move seemed solicitous, hesitant, more like a cautious emissary than a soldier. He was everything she disliked. She tried to make out his form in the daylight. Were his legs strong, was he well-muscled? She could not tell. She had felt nothing when he spoke to her in the dark of the corridor. Then she remembered her partner of that night and smiled. Her body still pulsed from the pleasures of love-making. This man Faolan, reminded her of her father's astronomer, 'cold and living only in his head…' she smirked.

Jermaine decided she did not relish the thought of his bloodless hands on her skin, yet he had had a bastard. 'He must know something…' she said to herself with a smile, kicking the snow on the ground with the toe of her gray suede boot. 'but then again, it doesn't take much to make a child...' Looking up at Faolan, she caught his eye. Strangely, gold stars seemed to be swimming behind his head. She rubbed her eyes. "The sun is strong today...and I'm getting a headache." she mumbled leaving the garden.

Night fell as Faolan reviewed the reports from his officers. The men were getting restless and he sent his messenger back without the answer they most wanted to hear, when it was that he would join them and they could leave for Guardia.

A loud, officious knock on his door brought two noblemen into the room dressed in clothe of gold. They looked about them with distain and finding no clothing of his suitable, picked up his heavy fur cape with the silver buckles. With a sniff they placed it on his shoulders and lead him from his room. He peppered them with questions as they hurried him along but they said nothing. At the grand entrance to the palace he was given a cup of mulled wine, and told to drink it down quickly as the doors were swung open. A blast of cold wind and snow hit him in the face.

The facade was ablaze with torches, their flames whipping in all the archways. Dark clouds covered the night sky and he could see no stars. All the citizens of the realm of Bowmountain seemed to be crowded onto the wide boulevard below. They held hundreds of lanterns and torches aloft. A great cheer went up. Faolan was stunned and looked about him for some answer. As his eyes adjusted he found he was not alone but surrounded by all the members of the court in their finest raiment. The women's jewels and necklaces sparkled on top of their heavy, bell-like costumes, which he had learned were traditional and in some cases passed down from generation to generation.

The king and queen came forward to meet him. Their crowns flashed brightly in the flickering light of the torches. On a stand to his left, a brazier burned with incense which wafted in a blue plume over the heads of the nobles and up into the sky. To his right a great book lay open on an iron stand and next to it a priest stood, also in clothe of gold, hooded and waiting.

Faolan did not know what to think, but neither was he afraid and he walked down a step to meet them. The king came forward with the priest and Faolan saw that in his hand he held a circlet of gold. Without pause he placed it on Faolan's head and turned him round by the shoulders to face the citizens. After a moment of surprise the crowd realized what was taking place and cheered again. Faolan looked at the king in some confusion.

"You are my heir." Bowmountain king said simply.

"You do me...too great an honor..." Faloan stuttered, looking about him in consternation.

"Wait..." the king said turning from him and looking down the steps.

The queen moved aside to reveal the princess standing behind her. Jermaine's face was down and as she raised it to look at him he saw that her eyes were dark as pitch and her lips were set in a blue line. She shivered with the cold, or was it anger? Her gown was of costly red silk, but very thin and shined almost on its own. A diaphanous over-dress of subtle colors blew about her in the wind and reflections of the torch lights shimmered upon it. It seemed to pulse with light and glow from within. Her long hair was dressed and on her head she wore not the circlet of a princess but a small gold crown of great age shaped like a cap. From its brim little gems were suspended. In the light of the torches they danced and sparkled.

Faolan's throat went dry. He could not take his eyes from her face and yet, the old feelings that haunted him began to return. He watched as her features swam, mixing and transforming into the face of his beloved. He swayed and grasped the arm of the king.

"Yes, beautiful isn't she, my son? Your queen. And why not?"

Faolan tried to speak, to tell the king that he was unwell but his throat would not let him. He stared into the face of Rue, all his dreams of her were coming true, their marriage, a life together. She had not died after all, so far away from him, where he could not save her, she was here, she was his, standing in front of him.

"Give me your hand, my son." the king commanded softly.

Without breath or thought, Faolan held it out.

Bowmountain King took a small dagger from the priest and quickly made a cut in the palm of Faolan's hand, then raising it, showed the crowd. A trickle of blood snaked down and felt, for a moment, hot on his arm.

Jermaine stiffened as she watched. Her mother reached out and grasped her wrist tightly. A noble woman came out of the crowd behind her and held her by the shoulders, pushing her toward the king. Near fainting, Jermaine looked up into the face of her husband to be. His smile surprised and alarmed her. It did not seem possible that this man who had clearly disliked her the night before was now glad to take her in marriage. She flinched as her palm was cut. The blood seeped across her hand as it was held up to the crowd. Together the couple were led to the book and their hands were pressed side by side upon a single page. The priest wrote something down and then held the book aloft for all to see, two bloody imprints and their names affixed as oath to the act. The priest walked solemnly back into the palace. It was done.

The king and queen and all their court parted around the couple and followed the priest inside. Faolan and Jermaine stood together on the steps as two nobles bound their hands, palm to palm with a red silk bandage. The courtiers instructed them to raise the symbol of their marriage to the crowd and as they did so the streets thundered, horns blew and torches waved in dizzy celebration.

Faolan stared around him, his mind coming back out of the fog. It was all over in a moment and he had hardly realized what was happening. He looked at the woman standing next to him, his wife, his queen. She was shaking with the cold but her face was difficult to read. She looked in pain, confused, and her knees were giving way beneath her. With his free arm he wrapped her in his cloak and helped her as she stumbled up the steps toward the palace. She jumped as the great doors were slammed shut behind them. She was even more shocked than he was.

The two were seated at the very middle of the high table in the great hall and it was the intent of old custom, Faolan was told, that they feed each other throughout the evening's festivities and that the bonds remain in place until morning. They sat side by side as if in a dream while all about them was laughter and music.

He offered her a morsel from his plate but she declined. She did however accept his goblet and drank it to its bottom, staring at him with fury. Picking up her own, she demanded it be filled to the brim. Instead of offering it to him she drank it all. Wine seemed her quickest avenue out of this misfortune. She stared down the hall at her lover of the night before and to her bitter disappointment saw him already embracing another woman. The feasting and celebration continued while her mood darkened.

Faolan watched her out of the corner of his eye as he tried to regain his composure and take in what was being said around him. Snippets of conversation and laughter at his expense floated about.

"Ride her or she'll ride you."

"Bowmountain is thanking the gods for this favor."

"He'd better!"

He knew clearly enough what was meant by all this, but his mind was not steady enough to scheme a way out of the marriage and perhaps he thought, he did not want to. Could she help him get rid of the ghost? He thought. Picking up his own goblet he raised it to the king and drank it down. When his gaze fell again full on Jermaine's face his foggy smile returned and he was under Rue's spell once more.

As the wine began to erase her shock, her breathing slowed and Jermaine took a moment to inspected her new husband. In spite of her predicament, she found his features handsome and regular. She liked a strong jaw, straight brows and blue eyes and he had an intelligent forehead. But her foul temper soon re-emerged with the loosening of the wine as anger at her father resurfaced. A handsome husband did not compensate her for being forced into a precipitous marriage ceremony with a total stranger. What did he mean to make of her? A fool? She glared at the king. She liked her life and her men. She thought with a smirk 'It's taken me years to train them...' She would not give them up. Then she thought with a drunken hiccough, How soon would she be made to leave her home as well? Her hand throbbed and she peevishly pulled at the bandage, trying to loosen it, spilling wine from her husband's cup as he held it to his lips.

After an hour on display, drunk and petulant she pushed herself up suddenly from the table dragging Faolan's hand with her. "Are you coming?" she slurred, thinking unclearly that she would cut herself free of him as soon as they were out of sight. Traditions be damned.

Faolan looked at her as he was dragged to his feet and saw this demanding young woman clearly for the first time all evening. There was something in her rebellious actions that fired him and he grinned at her as she swayed there, drunk and foolish. She reached out for her goblet but he blocked her hand instead. She lost her balance and fell forward. As if in an embrace and for the benefit of

167

their guests, he slipped in front of her and caught her, saving her from embarrassment. He lifted her up and throwing her nonchalantly over his shoulder he carried her from the hall.

"Don't let her untie that bond! Our custom demands it stay on all night!" the king shouted at him over the celebratory pounding on the tables and encouraging hoots of the courtiers.

13

A Staircase of Rose Petals

"Put me down you schtupid...guardian, lord, whatever you are!"
Jermaine shouted, wriggling on his shoulder and pounding against
his back with her one free hand.

"Where are we going?" he asked with amusement as he set her
down.

She teetered unsteadily holding onto the lapel of his coat for
support as if it were a handle or some other inanimate thing.
Looking dizzily about the empty corridor she threw her hand out
briefly and pointed at a staircase strewn with dried rose petals.
"Obviously." she scoffed and rolled her eyes, then grabbed his coat
again and tugged on it for emphasis. "The lasht of my roses...what
a waste." she looked at him, "But WE are not going anywhere! I'm
going to my room, ash shoon ash I get free of this stupid thing..."
she said yanking at the bindings on their wrists "and you can go to
Hell for all I care!" She stepped willfully away from him. "Give
me your blade...quick now!"

"I cannot...your father...it is your custom, not mine...and you are
my wife." The words stunned him as they came out of his mouth
and he stared at this struggling, peevish, drunken top as she spun
about on the stone floor slippery with flower petals.

169

"Your wife! I will not be bound to you, Scholar, what ever the priest may say! I'll cut this bond and run! I'll lay with as many men as I can get my arms around! I'll drink until I'm dead!"

"So intent on destruction..." Faolan mused.

"Jermaine! Hush now. What a fool you are!" The queen and two noble women came running down the long hallway. Their gowns were newly covered by red aprons, the sleeves of which were decorated with entwined scarlet ribbons.

"This way my son." The queen said giving her daughter a stern look. She gestured toward the staircase. As Faolan walked with Jermaine tagging along behind him, reluctantly as if on a leash; the queen drew close and began whispering hurriedly into his ear. "You have accepted my daughter graciously, I thank the Great Mother for this...for who else could have made it happen? But I warn you, my son...make her work for her pleasure tonight...break her heart open...no one has ever demanded a thing of her, in bed or out of it. These men of our court are all afraid of her...and my husband, he spoiled her from birth. She has had everything she desires these past years without ever giving anything of herself! Ride her spirit! And make her ride you tonight, my son, no, do not look away...you know what I mean, make her work for her own pleasure and labor to please you till she can do no more, reward her only when she gives of herself or you will have nothing but pain from her. Promise me..." the queen looked into his eyes at the entrance to the bridal chamber as Jermaine dragged him across the threshhold.

The couple entered a lofty room ablaze with red candles and bedecked with flowers. White banners hung in a row upon one wall. A fire was lit and a table set with honeyed fruit, almond cakes and wine. Two maid servants entered as Jermaine surveyed the bridal bed. It was also covered in petals. "Wayshted!" she said, swiping at them with her hand. "Well?" she shouted at the maid servants. "Get it over with!"

One came forward with a goblet on a tray and raising it to Faolan, bade him drink. It tasted sweet and earthy, made of the juice of beets and watermelon.

"A present from the king." the maid said winking at him. "Not that you'll need it, my prince." she whispered.

Jermaine dragged her husband clumsily by the arm till they

stood beneath the hangings. "Do you shee theesh sorry things?" she asked.

Faolan looked at her for explanation.

"Look!"

He gazed upon them. "There is nothing there, no embroidery, no crest of noble house, nothing, merely empty linen. Why do they hang here?"

"Look closer." she said. "Do you shee? Yes, they were cut from linen, fine sheets of linen." she said with a sigh. In the center of each was a much-faded blood stain, saved and displayed. "Relics from ancient bridal beds. Can you believe it? Generations of my women folk, married and bedded. There you see my mother's. They're pride and maidenhead for all to see. Given for their people. And what do I have to give them...my people...your people. Nothing." she scoffed turning back to the women. "Well? What are you waiting for?" she cursed at them.

The women drew out little silver blades from their pockets and began cutting away the sleeves above the couple's bound hands. Then un-buttoning and unbuckling, swift little fingers removed the rest of their clothing or cut it away until they stood naked before each other save for Faolan's boots and Jermaine's slippers.

Bowing and giggling, her ladies took away the spoiled garments and left the room.

"Well? Step out of those! You're not going to fuck me with your boots on!" Jermaine dragged him to the table unabashed. "I need a drink." she grumbled. Her body glowed in the light of the fireplace. She stood brazenly, paying no attention to him, shifting through the bottles till she found what she wanted. "Cherry liqueur." she said, pouring two drinks and handing him one. "Or perhaps you prefer my father's recipe...his insurance to help an old man's performance?" she laughed. "He's taking no chances...well husband? Is it working? Are you ready to perform?" She tossed the strong liqueur down her throat angrily and stood in front of him twirling the stem of the empty glass.

He was pricked by her insults but found his desire rising in spite of her surliness. His eyes traveled from her arched brows and haughty expression down her shoulders and up-turned breasts to her lithe body and he smiled in spite of himself at her little feet sticky with flower petals.

171

"I hardly know what to think, I find this all so strange."

"Yes, I don't suppose you thought of this as you were riding toward my father's house."

"If I had I would have turned back." he blurted out.

Jermaine looked surprised and for a moment he saw just the glimmer of hurt in her eyes. She slammed the cup on the table and turning her back to him, poured another drink. "I know you've had a woman before...I just hope you're not clumsy."

"Jermaine..." Faolan said coming close.

"Here, make yourself useful. Take down my hair, theses jewels are beginning to bite." He removed the crown and the star-shaped clasps and sent her hair cascading down her back and over his arm. He buried his face in it. It smelled of almonds. He pushed it aside and kissing her neck he pressed his body up against hers sliding his free hand along the soft curve of her hip and onto her belly. The touch of his warm fingers forced her to smile and she felt him rise against her thigh. "So, you did not need my father's beets and melon after all, Scholar."

"I think I can please you." Faolan drew her toward the bed.

"I am hard to please, and I am still angry."

"But not with me."

"Yes with you and my father. You are not a king." she said looking over at the two crowns lying side-by side on the table.

"A wife's duty is to encourage her husband." Faolan murmured. "If you want a king, start by treating me like one."

"And?"

"Perhaps if I love you I will do this thing?"

"You do not love me?" she said like a school girl while arching her neck and pushing his hand between her thighs.

"I do not know you!" he scoffed, removing his hand. Wrapping both arms about her waist he threw her on the bed tumbling on top of her in the process. "These bonds will surely kill us!" he laughed.

Jermaine giggled and her reluctant smile woke in him the will to change her, mold her, break open her selfish little heart. He leaned into her with his whole body, crushing her under his weight and kissed her mouth until she gasped for breath.

Jermaine's eyes grew wide and she wriggled out from under him, rolling away as far as she could, tucking her legs up like a child. "I'm...I'm tired. Let me sleep, Scholar."

172

"Ah, no. I have been instructed to make you work tonight. Ride me."

"You over step yourself..." she murmured pretending to yawn sleepily. It was a phrase that had worked before on men who demanded too much of her, or anything of her. A phrase meant to dismiss.

"Time to work off some of that wine...my little drunkard. Ride me." Faolan dragged her back like a sack of grain and pulled her on top of his hips kissing her face and neck, holding her in place until desire and sensation rose and her pulse began to throb. Finally her body sought connection with his and she mounted him with a gasp. His strong hands about her waist helped quicken her movements, making her cry out with pleasure as waves of sensation tantalized her. Her flesh turned pink with exertion. Their bodies warmed to the task as she lay down on top of him pressing and swiveling her hips. Shifting her position she arched her body backward placing his hands on her hips and holding them there with her own as she moved up and down.

Jermaine's face glowed with desire and something else, a softening of the look in her eyes as she stared deeply into his. It was as if a door had opened in the wicked labyrinth she called her life. A way out. She focussed on the blue depths of his eyes and ignored the burning of her calves and thigh muscles. Time slowed and the hours of the night melted into one as they melted into each other.

Faolan's mind began to wander, he fought against this, staring back at Jermaine and smiling, urging her on. Release for him did not come however. She labored on, moaning and crying out in ecstasy, beyond exhaustion, her skin glowing with perspiration. Willing him to finish so that she could stop but somehow determined to please him beyond all else; her fervor and his desire burned hard and hot as the night passed. Time and again something kept sweeping him to the very precipice of that 'sweet death' but then subsided. His ecstasy and sensation transformed into something else, the sound of waves crashing against a rocky shore far away, filled his ears. Delirium, coming ever closer and finally overwhelming him, as if he were drowning, he closed his eyes.

He was suddenly lying on a couch surrounded by the faces of Boru, his brother, Aolwynd and the girl who had nursed him so long ago, what was her name, his foggy mind asked? Their expressions were full of grief and they seemed to be listening closely to what he was saying. Then the strong smoke of burning herbs took him to another scene and he knew he was standing in front of Rue's throne in the prophesy room at the School of Healing. He clasped his arms about Jermaine in despair and stopped her movements, rolled her off and took her in his arms like a man dying. There were tears in his eyes. "Rue, my love." he cried out in pain.

Covered in sweat, gasping for air, Jermaine struggled to get out of his embrace. Frightened, she pushed at him. "What is this? Who is this Rue? What...what does this mean?" She tried to discern some explanation on his face in the light of early dawn.

"Don't leave me, Rue...my love..." he breathed.

"Leave you? Scholar...husband, you are my husband! Explain yourself!" She sat up and slapped his face. "Another woman. By all the gods! I should have known."

Faolan came back to the present and saw the shock in Jermaine's eyes as she gulped for air, drawing the sheets about her. The cold morning wafted in through a window prickling the drying sweat on her skin. "Did she whelp your bastard for you or did she drop you for a saner man? Of course, she left you. And that is just what I'm going to do." Jermaine reached beneath her pillow for the little dagger placed there for brides in case of emergencies. She deftly cut the bond between them and with a look of disgust, hopped off the bed, her legs wobbling from the night's exertions. She grabbed the coverlet and sweeping it about her shoulder like a queen, she grabbed her crown and a full bottle then shuffled out of the room.

Faolan lay back on the pillows exhausted, as an angry woman's voice from nowhere whispered into his ear "You have betrayed her. We will have our revenge on you, Warrior."

***

Cere and Lyla had great difficulty getting Brillie ready for bed. A breeze from the east chilled the air and the girl demanded her window be closed. She had been restless and petulant all day, ordering every one about from nurse to cook. She dodged her hair brush and refused to stand still during rounds in the wards, dropping Brilla's instruments on the floor and refusing to pick them up. With the last rays of the sun she began to mutter to herself and by bed time she was screaming "Bastard! He's betrayed her! He'll pay for it!"

Cere ran down the hall and called the Matron in. It took Brilla an hour to sooth her namesake. The girl tossed and squirmed, throwing off the covers. Brilla could make no sense of the insults and abuses Brillie spouted to persons unknown. Finally after a torrent of crying the girl curled up in a ball next to her and moaned "...he married her...what shall I do..." her little hands clutched at Brilla's apron as she fell asleep. Brilla felt a blast of cold air behind her and the girl whispered in a voice not her own "We will see him punished." Brilla knew that voice, it was Lauro's.

Aolwynd met the matron near the steps of the Temple of the Great Mother. Holding hands between them, Brillie swung playfully, hopping up step after step, her nightmares all forgotten. She seldom used her cane and her leg grew stronger every day with only a slight limp. Yet Aolwynd's face was worried for her daughter. Passersby whispered to each other as they crossed the plaza and pointed at the little girl. News of her strange behavior had spread quickly. The citizens of Saels were bothered by yet another rumor of the freakish people their new ruler had gathered about him. First his small troop of bed-mates, then the councilman's wife and now a girl possessed of voices and visions. Bad omens. Aolwynd also feared her daughter was possessed and that this was indeed a punishment cast upon her for loving Boru and leaving her husband. These ugly rumors had been whispered amongst the city folk before, but recently, as anxiety about the war increased, the girl's behavior and news of her prophesies had even been brought before a council meeting.

Brillie's demeanor became quiet and apprehensive as they passed beneath the portal of the temple. She pulled against her mother's grasp and twisted behind her, hiding her face in her skirts.

The Matron placed incense at the altar and lit it, kneeling down to pray.

Brillie began to snicker wickedly. Mumbling, she peered around her mother's skirts. "He's mine, you know, well...ours. You won't keep him...I'll see to that, you do know that, my queen, don't you?

A king for a queen!" Brillie giggled and hiccoughed.

Aolwynd bent down and held the girl. "What do you mean, my sweeting?" Her daughter's eyes seemed to be searching as if she were not in the temple at all but upon some precipice looking far off into the distance.

"What do I mean? Warriors and traitors and betrayers! That's what I mean! Didn't I warn you daughter? Yet you cleaved to him...fool!!" An old man's voice came out of the girl and then the melodious tone Brilla and Aolwynd recognized immediately as Rue's. "Forgive me, father! My love in bondage? How will he lead them? Listen my friends..." the little girl turned to Aolwynd and seemed to see her, "brothers and yet not brothers...do you remember what I told you? Oh, it seems so long ago...I see two fighting side by side and two bound in darkness. My love! I'm coming! He has her amulet? Is that all he has left of her?"

"What are you saying child? Who are you? Leave my child!" Aolwynd screamed in fright and shook her daughter causing her little head to bobble back and forth.

Brillie rolled her eyes to the ceiling and fell to the floor. Her mother scooped her up in her arms. "I'm taking her back...you cannot keep her anymore. She cannot stay in this place...Poison! It's all your fault!"

Brilla called out as her friend ran with the child through the garden to the council palace. Someone stirred behind a pillar as she passed.

The voices of servants assaulted Aolwynd as she hurried through the corridors toward Boru's chambers, entered and locked the doors behind her.

"What did the prophetess tell you?" they called after her.

"What of the war!"

"What did she say?"

"Tell us!"

When her daughter was safely put to bed and a guard posted outside her door, Aolwynd went back down the hall and crawled into bed beside Boru.

"Tell me what she said, my love." Boru asked, blowing out the candle and taking her in his arms.

"You too? It is all I have heard all day, even whispered in these

176

halls." she sighed. "Two brothers in the dark...A king for a queen...two fighting side by side...what does it all mean? I don't know. And the insults the people throw at me, a married woman who has cast aside her husband, their councilman and savior of the city...living openly with their new leader. What will become of me? Can not you delay your army for a few more days? I cannot bear this without you!"

"My love, we are ready to march." Boru pulled her across his chest and rolled her onto her back sinking his face into her neck. "I am always with you and now that you are with child...I must know that you are safe."

"How much safer with you than here amongst all this hatred? My love, take me with you!" Aolwynd dissolved into tears as Boru lifted her night dress and kissed the thighs already opening to receive him.

***

Bowmountain King sat alone in the darkness of the great hall. Footsteps roused him from his meditations. "Well my priest, what have you found?"

"I have read the blood signs for your daughter and her husband." The priest held the book and waited while the king adjusted his robe.

"Shall I call the court?"

"My liege..."

"I would have them hear your predictions."

"My liege..are we alone?" The priest coughed and looked about the empty space nervously.

"You know we are...Is anything wrong?"

"The signs do not bode well...Even in these few hours her print is fading, strangely. I do not understand it...and his, it is as if there were another hand obscuring it. I have consulted with my brothers, this over-shadowing...this fading...be wary my King! Keep her safe. I dreamt last night of a hawk hunting a dove and this morning..."

"Now you talk of dreams? Spare me! They are one! It cannot be undone. And this ritual of yours...is merely a nod to the old ways..."

The priest looked at him with horror. "They have only spent one night together...and she cut the bond before dawn...cast him out! There is still time!"

"This is a lie! Do you spy on my family? Be careful priest! My temper grows short! Why should I believe you? Remember your own dire predictions for my marriage and yet here I am, king, and my queen beside me still. I have my own reasons to believe he loves his lady and all will be well! Go back to your tower, wipe your own asses and read the stains!"

Bowmountain King stood on the steps of his palace three days later, surrounded by his court as he had on Faolan's arrival. "We will make ready to join you when the time comes if it must be that you return to Guardia. Hunting giants must wait, I see. Even now the air is ripening. Spring is upon us any day and soon the hills will be greening."

"I cannot abandon my father, I must stop this war in my own way."

"Will you ride alongside your father hunting a band of women and children until they are pushed into the sea? Take Guardia while your father chases shadows! The gates will open for you and we will ride in behind you! Take the palace while your father is far from it!"

"It seems simple when you say it."

"All the simple plans are best. Think on it as you ride. Send me word if you change your mind. But remember, I ride for you, my son and for my daughter's future. I will not march for your father."

Faolan mounted his horse. "I pledge you my allegiance, Bowmountain, as a prince of your realm and as your son-in-law...." Faolan looked about for Jermaine but she was not there.

He rode across the causeway deep in thought. As he reached the other side a rider came up next to him from beneath the shadows of the bridge.

Jermaine cleared her throat. "So Scholar...you are leaving me already?" She looked bitterly at him but the haughty demeanor was missing. "Should I call you 'Sweeting' and cry at your departure, begging you to write to me?" She stared ahead at the road. "After three nights..." she said to herself, then turning "Tell me...my husband, will we always share our bed with this Rue woman?" She stumbled over the name. "Do I look like a love-sick girl to you who will do anything to please her man or a queen?"

"Both." he said staring into her eyes and leaning in for a kiss.

Jermaine jerked her head away. "Well..." she stammered "answer me this...who tore the bridal hangings down from their wall and burnt them in the fire?" Shifting her eyes away from him she leaned in, taking hold of his collar and whispered "Did you do this for me...husband? Why?" The last words came out haltingly, as if they gave her pain. Without waiting for his answer she let go, yanked the reins of her horse and galloped off to where a hunting party was waiting.

14

The Vanguard

"General!"

Rute woke groggily, his hands gripping the edge of his desk. A red mark showed where he had laid his forehead against the wood. Pulling his body up with difficulty he craned his neck and shoulders to loosen the bones that had stiffened in the cold night air. "Ahm too old fer this." he grumbled knocking his empty dinner plate to the ground. "What time is it? What's the matter?"

Running feet and shouting could be heard outside his tent coming and going in all directions. The rattle of armor and weapons being hastily gathered alarmed him. Rute ran outside, his heart already pounding. Torches flew about all over the encampment like fireflies. Men shouting and cursing, rushed toward the north end carrying spears. "The hostages..." he said to himself. The blood pulsed in his neck and his face flushed as he barked at his squire. The man fumbled as he laced up Rute's sleeves of maille and fastened them to his leather armor in a panic. Rute shouted for his horse, jumped onto it and pulling out his long sword nearly took off the squire's ear as the man held the sheath up for him. He did not wait to buckle it about his waist but galloped away without it. Holding his weapon aloft he rode through the crowded aisles between the tents and scrambling troops. He reached the enclosure just in time to see the enemy forming a defensive line. A long muddy trail through the snow beyond them lead away from camp. A small vanguard of warriors were already fighting, holding back the tide of Borchard's troops. The bodies of two guards lay at each end of the enclosure where they had been killed earlier at their posts by Kora and Tanner.

Rute rode into the center of the action and immediately recognized The Viper and her company of Wild Men. He smiled and drove his horse like a spear through the combatants toward her.

She was standing back to back with another warrior on a small knoll fighting all comers. As he drew close, Rute could not believe his good fortune. "Tanner!" he cried and jumped down from his horse almost as if he were greeting an old friend. Running up to them he pushed Tanner's opponent out of the way. "Traitor!" he yelled looking around at his men for approval. Engaging swords and grinning mercilessly at each other their blades crashed and rung in the night air.

Kora finished her enemy with a slash of her single-edged sword and turning around paused in her action, hearing Rute's cry. For a brief moment she looked to Tanner's safety exposing herself to attack. A guardian ran up behind her and took full advantage, driving his sword into her right side below the ribs. A cry of dismay and anger went out of her. As she fell to the ground she made eye contact with Bela on the hillside behind her and sharing her thoughts he tried to run to her. The other Wild Men with renewed fury came plowing through the soldiers till they surrounded their fallen leader. Kora called out to her brother to go back, save himself and lead her people.

Bela hesitated, torn with guilt and grief but finally, ran back to join Arius and his men. The vanguard was broken.

Wave after wave of the Guardian's army advanced out of the camp like wasps out of a broken hive. Kora's Wild Men were forced into an ever tightening circle around Tanner and Rute who fought on regardless, ignoring everyone.

Arius's soldiers looked on from the hill in horror, then Arius called on them to split their ranks. Half went back through the woods to guarantee the hostages' escape, the rest battled down the slope trying to reach their brothers in time.

Yet one by one the rescuers were vanquished as Borchard's troops overwhelmed and surrounded them, a desperate circle of falling warriors within an immense circle of conquerors. Only Tanner was left alive swinging his sword over the dead body of Kora as if he were protecting her from wolves.

Rute held up his hand suddenly and backed away, leaving Tanner standing alone within a wall of enemies holding torches. "Put up your weapon, my friend. You're worth more to me alive." he said and motioned for his troops to close in around his prisoner.

Tanner dropped his sword hand to his side and crouched over the body at his feet. He took the bone amulet from off his neck and placed it in Kora's hand, closing it with his own.

"Lost two wives in one night, eh? There's a feat worthy of a song..." Rute was in rare good humor as he ordered Tanner to be dragged away.

"Your honor...the hostages...shall we pursue them?" a soldier asked.

"Sun's up soon. No rush. We'll find 'em dead, litterin' the ground like a trail o' horse drops. How far can they get in this state, they're half gone already." he said with a laugh and a yawn.

Rute pounded impatiently at the door to Borchard's private chambers as the sun rose. "My Lord...forgive me, It could not wait! I have someone who'd like to bid 'good moro' to you." He rushed into the anteroom and in his zeal continued right through to Borchard's bed chamber. Behind him two guards dragged Tanner. His defiant face was swollen from beatings and his clothes were bloody and torn.

Borchard rose from his bed in haste, disturbed and annoyed. Servants ran in and quickly lit candles and covered him with a robe; shooing a young woman from his bed. She hopped down and stood hiding her nakedness behind a bed post peering out at the commotion and yawning sleepily. Borchard waved his arm at this discourtesy by Rute and the guards. His attendants forced Rute and his soldiers to retreat. It was hard to tell who was more upset by this lack of decorum, the Supreme Guardian or his servants.

Borchard kissed the girl's hand and squeezed her rump as she left with the servants, a sheet wrapped about her like a cloak. "Later..." he whispered into her ear with a smile "I've something for you're efforts..."

Borchard marched into his anteroom, the skin turning red at the base of his neck and rising into his face. "What is the meaning of this?" he barked. Rute grinned at the niceties of his leader's private life. Then he covered his mouth and coughed as the old man glared at him, waiting.

"Tanner...my Lord, paid a visit to our camp tonight, paid a visit and made off with our hostages."

"What?"

"They're all gone..."

Tanner smiled in spite of his pain and watched Borchard's face.

"But I'll get 'em back." Rute said hurriedly.

The Guardian sucked his teeth. "Did you pursue?"

"Mah men'll be leavin' soon.. We'll scrape them off the frozen ground where they lay."

"By my troth! You are too full of yourself my General! You take your chances and my patience too much for granted."

Rute flinched and Tanner laughed. The guards yanked Tanner about and one of them hit him in the back of the neck with an elbow to silence him.

"How did all this happen?" Borchard asked as Tanner raised his bloody head and stared sullenly into the Guardian's eyes.

Rute jerked his head toward the prisoner. "'E 'ad help."

"Ah yes, the Wild Folk, you told me."

"Them, yes..." Rute gestured to the guards to take Tanner away. "And another."

"Have you any prisoners?"

"Asides 'im? Nay, an' that wild bitch is dead, thank the Twins, but tha's not what I mean." Rute watched as the door swung shut and they were alone. "Yer son, my Lord. Without 'is help it never coulda' happened."

"Boru of course."

"Nay. Yer own General, yer sweet monk, Faolan! Aye! Killed yer spies an' used it as an excuse ta leave us weaker, sap our forces fer tha' rescue! It were all a ruse." Rute pulled Tanner's note from his pocket where it had been his lucky talisman and handed it to the Guardian.

Borchard's visage turned to stone as he read it. When he'd finished, he struck Rute full in the face. Rute grimaced with

184

surprise at the shock of it and felt for his dagger but instead simply bowed, his whole body trembling with anger as he left the room.

"Get them back do you hear me?" Borchard screamed through the door as he threw the note into the fire.

15

What the Eagles Told

Boru leaned his elbows against the parapet and watched as a lone rider moved slowly down the plain toward his army's encampment and the city of Saels. The man was hunched over his saddle, an arrow sticking out of his back. His horse wandered, grazing on bits of tender grass that had escaped the bitter touch of winter. Boru called down from the wall and waved to his soldiers.

Jak fell into the arms of the men sent to retrieve him.

Boru was waiting outside his tent as they laid the soldier down upon the ground.

"My Lord..." Jak croaked.

"Easy..." Boru murmured and gave him water.

"My Lord...Tanner sent me, two days ago...the raid...he begs you to hurry...even now they may be pursued...he worried..."

"You rode all this way in two days? The gods! Calm. Calm yourself. We are ready to march. We had word. We know of the raid."

Jak grabbed at Boru's lapel. "Then I am too late..."

"We have even swifter messengers than you, my friend." Boru cast his eye at the eagle resting on its post near his tent.

"The hostages?"

"They are away. That is all we know."

"And Kora?"

"A great heart, a great attempt. They fought bravely. The hostages escaped but there was a deadly battle and we have had no word since then."

Jak grasped Boru by his lapel and moaned. "Kora..."

"He saw no prisoners. The eagle master witnessed a funeral pyre before he sent his bird on its way, but he saw no prisoners."

Jak lost consciousness.

"Take him away, see to him." Boru said to a soldier.

"Where am ah?" Jak asked as he was carried up the steps of the House of Good Women that night.

"Close your eyes and rest, you will soon be in a comfortable bed, soldier, you have done your duty."

Jak swiped at the woman's sleeve and grasped it tightly, pulling himself up and nearly tipping over the stretcher and the men who held it. "No I've not! I've let 'er die! I know it! I left 'er! Why'd I listen to that ol' man? Ah should 'ave been there ta fight fer her, ta fight with her! Ah let 'er down an' now she's dead! You...'Good Woman', can you bring 'er back? No!" He shouted angrily.

Brilla peeled his hand away and stood back as the men carried him inside. Cere and Lyla were waiting by the entrance. "Take him in. Give him a strong sleeping draught. Get him settled on his stomach, I'll get my instruments and be right there. I'm good with arrowheads." Brilla reminded them.

***

Shaking with fear, stumbling and running, half-starved women carried their children up the snowy hillside away from Borchard's encampment. Arius' men herded them as quickly as they could picking up the ones that fell and urging on the elderly and the sick. Hissing encouragement, the men looked back over their shoulders for any sign of movement in the Guardian's camp.

It was not long from the time Tanner and Kora had crept over the fences, murdered the guards and slit the side of the hostage's tents to the first sounds of alarmed troops. Gesturing silence they got them moving and out to the strong arms of the rescuers ready and waiting to drag them over or under the fence posts. The black silhouettes of their pursuers soon enough were dashing across the flames of the many campfires lighting torches and gathering weapons.

Tanner, Kora and her Wild Men took up their positions, spreading out in a V-line across the hillside pointed at where they thought the heaviest onslaught might come. Their vanguard was all that stood between the fleeing victims and Borchard's waking army.

Stealth and The Night were ever gods and allies of the Wild Folk but both were fading fast in this endeavor and Dawn was approaching. The Wild Men sent their prayers that she would sleep on.

Tanner could hear the screams of the horses and knew that soon hundreds of soldiers would be coming at them. "Ah couldn't see Cherry...she moost be there...she moost be..." he said coming up the hill toward the vanguard.

"Do not worry, my brother...she is safe. We will see her safely away." Kora drew her sword. Watching her, the Wild Men cast their bear skin capes back from their shoulders and drew their weapons. Borchard's soldiers came around both sides of the hostage enclosure in waves as the last of the women and children disappeared into the pine forest. Tanner drew his weapon and coming close to Kora took her arm and swung her around, pressing his broad back up against hers. "Stand w' me." he said quietly.

Ruby was waiting, wagons hitched and ready for the first of the hostages to emerge from the forest. The early mists were rising in the open field before her. Voices coughing from exertion and children's cries suddenly broke the air. The oxen shifted nervously, snorting great clouds of steam.

The old and the sick were loaded quickly into the wagons along with the small children. Ruby noticed there were no babies amongst them and their numbers were fewer than they had hoped. Many had died. Winter and ill use had taken its toll.

Ruby stood up in the driver's seat and scanned the scene in desperate hope. She dropped the reins.

"Move off! Your cart is full!" Arius called to her, running up from the cover of the trees.

189

"Ahm not leavin' without my Moother!" Ruby shouted. "Ah haven't seen her!" Her voice echoed loudly in the still air.

"I will wait for her! Move off!" Arius yelled, anger and fear rising in his voice.

Suddenly Ruby jumped down from the wagon and ran back toward the woods.

There were only a few stragglers left to be seen. A Wild Man stopped her. "There's no one behind me." he said gruffly holding her arm.

"No!" Ruby tugged to free herself and ran on. "She must be there!" Darting through the pines she followed the muddy path of foot prints through the freezing slush of early spring. She passed another soldier. "There's nowt but dead behind me..." he said.

Ruby ran on, her arms and cheeks scratched by low branches, her clothes soaking and cold, wiping the tears from her eyes so that she could find her way. The trees confused her and in the mist that was rising they looked like tall figures until she drew close to them. She began to see the already cooling bodies of the dead, beside the trail, those for whom rescue had come too late.

Suddenly in the distance she heard the urgent voice of a child. She followed the noise.

Sitting with her back against a tree, a woman held two children, one in each arm. Beside her stood a ragged boy. It was Ruby's brother. Ruby ran up to them. Cherry was alive but so weak she could go no further. Her head was tilted back against the tree trunk, her face gaunt and her chin was sharp as an arrow point. Her eyes were closed. She was barely breathing.

Ruby picked up a child and cried out to her mother to stand up.

Cherry opened her eyes and smiled. "Go on, Sweeting, go on...I won't last. Ruby my heart! Tell your father..."

"No! I won't leave you here! Get up!" Ruby yanked at Cherry's arm.

"Let me go, love..." her mother sighed.

At that moment Arius came rushing through the trees toward them. Picking Cherry up in his arms without a word he carried her while Ruby dragged the two children and forced her stunned brother to move ahead of her.

"Hurry! There isn't any time! Dawn is here, they'll be on us!"

190

"Moother! There's some women in Brillie's room!" Jors cried as he ran into Boru's chambers. His mother was still sleeping. He grabbed the covers and threw them back pulling her by the arm.

Aolwynd rushed to her daughter's room. Two women had Brillie between them and were dressing her in a grey shift. They were smiling and whispering encouragements into her ear. Brillie's eyes were very wide, confusion and fear raced across her face one after the other. She cried out when she saw Aolwynd and tried to wriggle out of their grasp but their arms were strong. Aolwynd recognized the temple's deep blue tattoos adorning the women from wrist to shoulder. They served the goddess.

An older woman clothed in silver-grey stood looking out into the garden with her hands clasped behind her back.

"What are you doing?" Aolwynd cried.

"She is safe, do not worry, she is ours." the old woman said turning and smiling.

"Take your hands off my daughter! I demand you leave here at once!"

"Demand?" The priestess showed no anger, no fear, only a mild surprise as if she had never expected such a reaction.

Aolwynd stared at her. Jors hid behind his mother's skirts but pushed her forward, urging her on. "Who are you?" she asked.

"Alaine, I am Alaine. I serve the Mother...and we are taking your daughter so that she may do the same."

"Give her back! You have no right! It is the law...no one can be forced to serve!"

Alaine moved into the light and warmed her back in the heat of the sun. She was very pale, her skin was nearly translucent and her eyes were like two black beads. Her tattoos were faint with age and looked like mere tracings beneath her skin. "Do not be afraid...you may see her at any time, but she belongs to the temple."

"No!" Jors cried coming around his mother and drawing his dagger. "Get out of here, you old bitch!"

Alaine's women stood up and backed away still holding Brillie but the old woman only held up her hand. "You love your sister and are proud of her, aren't you? So are we. You're sister is special, you have no idea...such a gift...We have not seen such a one in many generations. Even she surpasses the Queen of Rue Mountain, our gift from the Great Mother, untimely taken from us. May she serve in Cloud Heaven. But here, in the same age is another even greater queen, a seer for our people. It is our right, nay, our duty...we may take your girl and teach her to serve, so says our custom, so says the council and the old law."

"You went before the council about my daughter? Why was I not told? We have the right to be there! No! I don't care! Give her back...I'm warning you!"

"Demands...warnings...threats? If you were a queen, perhaps you might persuade them that she has a future in marriage to some prince...but even then, I think not with that damaged limb. And then of course, you are little more than an adulteress, a concubine, at most his mistress, one of several playmates...no more."

Aolwynd blushed and tears welled in her eyes. Jors stood, shamed and angry, not knowing what to do.

"Come, come...be comforted." Alaine crooned as the women walked Brillie from the room. "Brilliana will wield great power, one so rare, one so precious as she. She will help her people. I will teach her to harness this gift before it destroys her...ah yes, she is dangerous. Even you have seen this surely? And mother, what hopes did you have for this crippled little bird? In the temple a limp means nothing, strange voices that tell of the future do not frighten us...who would you find to marry such a one?"

"Where are you taking her?" Aolwynd asked as if the breath had left her body.

"She will be back amongst the Good Women soon enough. Calm yourself. She will not be moved to the temple until the full of the next moon. We must prepare, ceremonies of this weight take time, you know. I have much reading to do, she is a vessel, she is a Goddess Queen, there are rituals to be performed...visit her tomorrow. You are free to do so, but I warn you, it is done. The people wish it."

Servants rushed in after the old woman left and lifted Aolwynd from the floor to her bed. Jors sank down, his back against the wall and cried.

Brilla checked item after item from her list as she loaded the wagon. The netted shelves within had been fitted with all manner of medicines and supplies, tinctures, bandages, crutches, aprons, a small tent and camp bed for herself. The horses stamped their hooves and sniffed the cool night air.

"This is foolishness! What are you thinking of?" Cere blurted out as she ran down the steps of the hospice.

"You would not understand, Cere, please, I must go."

"What would I not understand? Who do you think you're talking to?" Cere shouted.

Lyla came down the steps slowly with the Matron's surgical bag.

Brilla took Cere by the arms. "I'm going with the army, it is my duty. You and Lyla will take over for me. I trust you completely."

"Leaving us to deal with what? Coward! That's not the way it's done! You cannot simply walk away, the Goddess...your vows...you are bound here, as are we all...and the girl..." Cere huffed and blustered but Brilla only jutted out her chin, turned away and placed the bag in the cart.

"The army is leaving at dawn and I must go with them. I am compelled...I feel...do you not see Her hand in this? I can."

"And what is that?" Cere asked, pointing to the arrowhead hanging about Brilla's neck by a strap of leather.

"A good luck token."

Cere and Lyla clung to each other as Brilla climbed onto the driver's seat, snapped the reins and headed down the road toward the city and the Eastern Gate.

Grasping her shoulder and kissing her neck, Boru threw his leg over her hip and tried to turn Aolwynd over in their bed. Her knees were tucked tight in protest and she tried to hold back a sob. "Get away from me..." she moaned.

"Don't do this. I have so little time left with you...how can I leave with you like this?"

"Then don't. I don't care about the war...Earden, your father...only my daughter...my children...promise me you'll find our son and Jors...he is not a soldier, you can see that, look after him will you?"

Boru smiled, rocking her backward inch by inch, playfully. "Come now...my warrior, my shadow..." he pinched her shoulder till she flinched. "of course I will."

"And Brillie...what becomes of her?...I am afraid..." Aolwynd rolled into his arms and pushed her forehead into his neck. "I love you. Don't go."

"I must. If only to bring back your husband so that you can divorce him..."

"Don't. It's too sad to be funny. I have hurt him and if our son comes back alive it will only be because of Jem. I owe him so much, and I am so afraid."

What is it you fear?"

"It is as if I have lost everyone, everything...If I lose you...I will be alone."

"And I fear nothing...anymore...those years of loneliness are over because I have you. Now open to me, give me something to dream on while I journey...it will be too long before I hold you again in my arms..."

Torus knocked gingerly at the door while it was still dark. "It's time your honor...your squires are here waiting to dress you."

Aolwynd blinked back her tears and wiped her eyes. "Alright." she called, sitting up. "Alright. He's coming."

Aolwynd watched the soldiers dismantling their tents with the dawn, putting out their fires and embracing their families. The Army of Saels was ready to march. She stood on the battlement hugging Boru's fur cloak about her. She buried her face in it and tried not to cry. He had forbidden her to come down amongst the chaos and had given her his cloak as a token of his love. "...like my own arms around you..." he had told her.

By full light the troops were marching. Boru rode in front followed by his retinue and generals. He rode so far into the distance that Aolwynd could barely make out his face. Somewhere amongst this mass of soldiers, Jors was riding with him.

The Lord Protector of Saels, her beloved, stood up in his saddle for a long moment and scanned the walls of the palace. Aolwynd held up both her arms high into the air and hoped he could see her. Her first gesture to him when they had found each other again, and now she prayed, not her last. Her body ached for him already. Would she never reach for him again, would this child she carried ever have a father? She wondered these things as she scanned the distance. Apple trees were just putting out their blossoms like a pink mist over the hillsides.

A surround of refugees and families cheered as the last of the army began to move. The long lines of soldiers converged slowly into one and as they marched more troops came out of the great mass of humanity below the walls of the city. The thunder of their footsteps resounded and their pace quickened implying urgency.

Aolwynd stood blinking away tears in the morning light until even Boru's cloak could not keep her warm. She went back to his rooms and looked about the empty chambers, crawling back into bed. Jors was gone, squire to Boru. She had railed against it but Jors had insisted and Boru agreed. Brillie was taken from her, and her first born...somewhere in danger with her betrayed husband. She closed her eyes and moaned, ignoring the soft words of the servants. They plied her with breakfast and dainties but she rolled over and buried her head in the pillows. Searching for Boru's scent, some warmth remaining from their last night together, she gave herself over to grief. The sheets were cold and so was she.

Finally in late afternoon, she dressed and called for her horse. The whispers of the citizens meant nothing to her now. 'Let them snicker, I love him.' she thought. 'How dare they judge me? Haven't I given everything for this city...this country...now even my children...a queen could do no more.'

Cere and Lyla met her with open arms in the only place where she still felt welcome.

"I have come to see my daughter." Aolwynd said rather coldly.

"Yes! Isn't it exciting? And don't worry, the rash will go away."

Aolwynd looked at them in confusion and hurried up the steps into the building.

"She's around here somewhere..." Cere said as they flew down the hall after Aolwynd. When they entered the girl's room it was empty. Brillie was no where to be found. Women were sent scurrying, searching cupboards, storerooms, kitchens, the gardens, even the wards of the men. No one had seen her since bedtime the night before. She was gone.

"She's always hiding, don't worry." Cere said in passing.

Only hours before, Jors had tiptoed along the dark hallways of the hospice ducking into doorways and making his way to his sister's room. He could hear her sniffling as he waited for Cere and

Lyla to finish putting her to bed that night. Their lantern bobbed away down the hall leaving only one candle burning in the child's room.

Brillie lay with her swollen arms above the coverlet like an old cloth doll. Her forearms had been dipped in the blue dye of the dogwinkle shell, an initiation rite preparing her for life as a votive of the Great Mother. All the Good Women had gone through this before they entered service at the hospice but she would go further still, swallowed up by the temple. With her final vows sacred tattoos would begin to creep up her arms one after the other as she completed her lessons.

Brillie stopped hiccoughing and crying when she saw her brother. "They killed a dove in front of me an' wiped it on mah face! Oh Jors! It was horrible! Ah doon't wanna be a priestess! Help me, Jors! I promise I'll never say anythin' scary again!" Brillie threw her arms about his neck. There were pinkish welts where she had dug at them. "It itches terrible! The old woman said it will go away...but I'm scared of her! She smells funny an' she was mean to me!"

"Shhh! Ah've no great love fer tha' ol' witch meself." Jors rocked her back and forth as he'd seen his father do countless times. He held her arms up, examining them. "Good the gods! What 'ave they done to you?" He stood up and found her old clothes, pulling off her night dress and kicking it and the new grey shift under the bed. "Get dressed...yer comin' with me."

Brilla steered her wagon into the tail of the column with the others and followed the long line of soldiers and equipment marching away from Saels. The drivers stared with mouths agape at this woman driving beside them who wore the blue and white uniform of the Good Women. Saels had never needed an army surgeon, in fact, Saels had never needed an army. She nodded at them but did not worry about their reply. They would be glad to see her when they lay bleeding on the ground, she thought. She also wondered if her passenger was awake yet.

Brilla had known last night without turning around that she was not alone in the wagon. She had seen Jors creep up to it and help someone over the tailgate. She guessed who it was. It gave her a strange kind of comfort and she knew her sudden need to go with the army had the approval of the Goddess. As if she and Brillie had some role to play in all this, apart from tending to the sick and wounded. She did not know yet what it might be but the compulsion was strong and she knew better than to fight the Great Mother, who knew all and moved all things.

Jors rode back through the troops and bade her 'Good Moro' coming along side the wagon.

"Lookin' for your package?" she asked. Jors looked up with a start. "Don't worry, it arrived unscathed, and the hives are going down."

"What package?"

"Your sister..." Brilla stopped the cart and looked in the back but the girl was gone.

"Where is she?"

"Who?"

"Brillie! Where is she?"

"Ah doon't know what yer talkin' about..." Jors answered her, swinging his horse around and galloping off.

Thin blue arms had flung themselves about Jor's neck as he pulled her out of the cart only hours before. "Jors!" Brillie whispered. "I love you! Don't leave me!"

The boy waved his hand at her as if batting away flies. "Shh!" he warned. They silently crept between the tents. Jors brain worked feverishly, trying to think what to do with his little sister, where she might hide. She tugged at his sleeve. "Ger off! Stay here till I kin coom back fer yah." Jors left the little girl as dawn came up in a group of camp children gathered around a fire. "Fit in, will yah? An' doon't start no fights. Ah'll be right back."

"He serves the gods." Brillie whispered to the children, who looked at her with curiosity.

"We all do." came Rue's voice from the back of her mind.

197

16

"...Safely Away..."

"Where is she?" The priestess said striding angrily into Boru's chambers.

Aolwynd sat in her robe in the courtyard, kicking idly at a dead frond from one of the palms. She looked up vacantly.

"Do you know the punishment for obstructing temple votives in their duties?"

Aolwynd just smiled at her. "She's somewhere in the hospice...your women said..."

Alaine paced back and forth. "She's not there! You've hidden her! We will find her! In the meantime the city will have to offer sacrifices...great sacrifices! You cannot play this shell game with us! Give her back!" The priestess spoke rapidly to herself. "I promised the Mother. Now I must appease her, the one your daughter has insulted...and Brilliana cannot turn away from such a gift, it is unheard of. I need her. And you will be punished!" The old woman wrung her nobbled blue hands and stared at Aolwynd, waiting for some manner of reply. When none came she whispered to herself "Mother must be appeased." and left.

Bela rode up beside Arius and reaching across the horse, grabbed his arm, pulling him to one side out of the way of the wagons. Bela looked long and hard into Arius' eyes, took a deep breath and said "We are leaving."

"What do you mean?"

"I am taking my men...what's left of my men and we're going."

Arius stared at him, holding his horse Traveller back as the wagons passed them by. "You can't! I need you!"

"It's enough. Haven't you had enough? What part do we play in this foolish war between Borchard and his own son? What part do you play? Why are you doing this? You are no longer a puppy, following along behind that man. You've given him enough. Come away with us now, bring your Ruby, your wife! You could be one of us. We have a good life in the forest, free...forget all this...what do you owe them?" Bela gestured at the bent and shuffling figures as they passed.

Arius watched the families of Boru's men as they struggled along, cold, exhausted, clinging to each other. He could not believe what he was hearing. "I cannot believe you do not see what is in front of your own eyes. Don't. Don't go, Bela we need you...we need to make a stand...I must see them safe."

"I'm saving what's left of my men, they have wives and children too...They've been left alone too long." Bela took another deep breath. "I gave my sister...that is enough." He reached over with an apologetic smile as if to make peace between them and grasped Arius' shoulder. "We will guide Ruby across the mountains. But then we go." Bela turned his horse and fell into the column.

As the parade of wagons and hostages drew into Nortown, the first town out of Guardia on the Northern Road; the people came out of their houses to gawk, but only for a moment. Quickly they ran inside and returned with food and blankets. Their empathy immediately bubbled over into anger at the stories of hardship, abuse and suffering they heard. All knew of Borchard's unjust war and harsh revenge upon his first born son whom they knew and loved. Resentment soon grew into whispers of rebellion.

Arius and Ruby urged the townsfolk to make haste in their acts of mercy for they were every moment expecting Rute and his troops to come after them. Relatives searched the wagons for their own as the vehicles moved slowly toward the end of town. When none could be found among the survivors a great wailing went up and the men folk ran for their weapons to join the company.

Arius set his men to watch at the gates and took Ruby aside. "Keep them moving. Take them by the mountain road and don't stop till you get to the pass and the road to Saels."

"Don't you order me about! What are you saying?" Ruby blubbered as realization crept in.

"Bela will guide you. I'm staying here. Someone's got to hold them off...we will make a stand for Boru. You go on."

"Don't be a fool! Your falconers and a handful of townies? What good would that do?"

"Ruby...I have to do this...I am his man and you will have a chance to save your mother if you do what I ask, if you stand with me...the hostages will never get away." He lowered his forehead onto hers. He did not say '...and we will all die.' though it was in his mind. "The town will stand with us."

Ruby pounded her fist against his chest and moaned. Arius wrapped his arms about her. Monk jumped from one wagon to another calling nervously.

"You love him...it's true...more than me...this damned war...but I can't...I can't go on without you..." she said softly. Arius pushed up her chin with his finger and looked deeply into her blue eyes now rimmed with red. He smiled and kissed her. "Yes, I love him. If a child could have picked his own father...I would have chosen no other but as I would die for him, I would live for you. And as to you're not being 'able to make it without me'...that's a lie. You've more courage, and you're more pig-headed than me for sure. If anyone can get them home you can. And we must get them home."

"Home?"

"Yes. Our home. Saels."

As the sun rose higher, Ruby and the hostages headed west out of town. Bela rode before them in a sombre mood. All she could see was the rounded, furry back of his cloak. His men rode in the rear, guarding the last of the wagons. After an hour the caravan

201

came to a logging road that lead south and climbed the cliffs into the mountains. Bela pointed toward it. The road was rough and narrow for wagons, meant more for teams of horses pulling timber and used only by mountain folk and Wild Men. There was some hope however that Borchard's troops would pass it by and continue on the broader and speedier path heading toward the sea.

Arius ran back to his men. A crowd of townsfolk stood with them holding pitchforks, spears and hatchets. "We've 'ad enoof of this bloody war mongering! Lord Boru's been all the Guardian we've ever seen! The rest 'av been butchers 'an' thieves. Aye! Close the gates! We'll stand w' Boru's men!" they cried.

Arius held up his hand. "Nay. I'll not have you turn to open rebellion, not yet. Let us be smart...Lord Boru's army is even now marching upon Guardia. Pray he comes soon. But he may still be days away from here...those of you Nortown folk who wish to fight, there will be time to join us. For now let us prepare."

***

That morning the trail of the hostages was easy enough to follow. Thawing patches of snow held the slushy imprints of many feet. Rute's soldiers rode along leisurely expecting at any time to come upon a clot of exhausted prisoners too worn out to carry on. Passing the already stiff and frozen dead covered in a thin layer of frost, the forest looked like some neglected garden filled with statues that had been toppled over. There was some nervous, sympathetic laughter and grumbling complaint from the men which was quickly reprimanded. The rest of the way the guardians rode in dogged silence. Coming at last into the sunshine they were shocked to find the deep ruts of several oxen wagons and signs of encampment so near their own army. Surprised and dismayed they dug their heels into the flanks of their horses and rode on at a gallop. On the Great Northern Road the signs were lost but it was obvious which direction to take. The company of guardians reached Nortown by mid morning and were yet again amazed to find the town was barred against them. The captain rode forward and pounded his fist against the heavy wooden doors.

An old man's voice called from within. "Oo goes thar'?"

"Open up in the name of the Guardians!"

"Hold on! Hold on!"

They heard huffing and wheezing, then groans and curses as a shock of white hair and a boney hand appeared just above the stockade wall, then a wizened face showed beneath it and finally a thin white beard. "Oo goes thar?" he repeated, looking over the heads of the soldiers into the distance as if he did not see them.

"Open up Daddy or we'll break it down...or go 'round you!"

"Ye' can try ta go round but them cliffs might get in yer way...Alright! Alright! I'm coomin'! Just doin' mah duty by me town. It's fell times around here, ye' ken! Thar's a war on!"

"Open up!"

"'Ere! Ow' do I know you ain't Lord Boru in disguise...'im that was our own dear Borchard's son an' now we're goin' to war against?" The old man pointed at the captain with a toothless smile.

"I'll have your head for a traitor in a minute! You're obstructing my duties! We're after the hostages!"

"Sausages? Ain't no sausages here yet...that there stall won't be set up fer hours...this here's a market town, ye know, we've got to get up an' ready! Missed yer breakfast did yah?" The old scarecrow laughed and looked down at imaginary townsfolk with a nod, pretending to have an audience. "Can't eat raw sausage!" He said to no one. "You'll git sick if yah do, why I remember one time...."

"Twins! Give me strength! Hostages! Hostages! You doddering old nobhead! Who died and left you gatekeeper? We're after the Guardian's hostages, escaped last night... they must have come this way! You! Soldier! Climb that gate and knock that old idiot off the wall!" the captain shouted.

"Alright! Alright! Hold your water!" Taking his time, the old fox disappeared and made a great complaint of aching bones all the way down loud enough for all to hear. Then he leaned against the inside of the gate and waited as long as he dared. Shouting for imaginary help, he slowly opened the gate.

The captain and his men galloped into the main street and were immediately slowed by sellers stalls, wagons filled with produce, cages of chickens and tethered pigs clogging their path. It looked to be an ordinary market day but there were no customers and those behind their goods stared with sullen faces. The soldiers urged their mounts through, kicking and lashing out at whatever obstructed them. Shadowed figures stood in doorways and behind curtains, watching.

Arius stood on the outskirts of town waiting behind an outcropping of rock for the guardians to come. He pulled at his collar and debated whether to remove his heavy leather jacket. He felt for the hilt of his sword, then felt for it again. Beads of sweat rose on his upper lip. Would he stand or run, he wondered. Then he thought of the man he had killed over a year ago, of Rute's partner in love and war and of Rute himself. If he was there he would have to fight him...the general of Borchard's army, to the death. Funny images passed through his mind as he watched the road. Ruby's red lips appeared before him, their first kiss, the night they had met, the chandelier swinging in her mother's kitchen and the jokes they had made as Tanner made love to his wife on the floor upstairs. Then he thought of his return to Saels with a thousand men behind him, of Monk flying above his head like a banner and finally his mother's face, Dor, now dead in her grave. Tears rose in his throat.

"They're coming!" one of the men whispered.

As the soldiers left the town Arius counted them.

"Ten...twenty..." and a captain leading them that he did not know. Arius breathed a sigh of relief. "Good. It's little enough..." he said out loud to his men. Coming out from behind the rock he drew his sword.

***

The east gates of Guardia opened and the setting sun reached out beneath the archway and blinded Faolan for a moment as he rode in followed by his troops. When he took his hand away from his eyes, Rute was there in the middle of the street waiting to meet him. Rute had been there all day grinning and talking to himself in a low voice, watching the guards and making them nervous. He fell in next to Foalan and the two generals rode side by side at the head of the company.

Those citizens who paused in their business to watch them could not have had more different reactions to the two leaders. Faolan drew welcomes and warm smiles while Rute saw only their turned backs.

At the West Gate Rute drew Faolan aside and let the soldiers pass by, continuing on to rejoin the army. "We are ready to march...your father too." he said. "Did you clear up that mystery of murdered men? Smoothed some feathers at Bow Mountain? Ah see you've brought that boy back with you. Ever the diplomat, patching things up..." Rute spat on the ground. "You've heard of course, that the hostages escaped..." Rute watched Faolan's face but he only registered surprise. "Ah...you didn't know then? Huh. Any road, yer father wants to see you."

"Now?"

"Aye. At the palace."

Faolan and Dane followed Rute through the streets of the city. Rute jumped from his horse as they approached the guard's entrance. "'Ere! You two wait here, I won't be a moment." Rute disappeared through the archway but immediately returned with ten men. They rushed upon Faolan and dragged him from his saddle. With fear in his eyes, Dane backed his mount away from the tussle. Before Faolan could draw a weapon he was being carried away. Dane quickly turned his horse and galloped out of the courtyard as the guards pulled Faolan into the shadows.

Rute stood with his hands on his hips. "Git that boy!" he yelled as a soldier mounted Faolan's horse and sped away after Dane.

"What is this!" Faolan yelled trying to get free of the guards.

"Yer under arrest by order of Lord Borchard..." Rute grinned in his face as he strode into the guard room. "Traitor." he whispered in his ear. "Ah know what you've been doin' an' you won't muck up my plans anymore...Take 'im away."

Faolan was dragged through the back corridors of the palace in haste. They had been emptied of servants and the torches had been put out. No prying eyes saw them taking the prisoner away and no voice cried 'Foul!'. Rute could not help grinning as he sauntered along behind them.

Down a cold, spiral staircase they went to the palace prison. After descending several levels, the walls opened up into a large circular room. The ceiling rose and curved toward the center like a beehive at the very top of which was the small carved likeness of a dragon. Near the top three small barred windows let in a pale equivalent of light and fresh air. A conduit snaked down from a fourth window and attached itself to an enormous bellows being worked by a prisoner. Fresh air and bad puffed in and out. Between the cell doors hung iron rings and chains.

Guards snapped to attention. Rute entered and signed the book handing the prisoner over to the jailor. Faolan was quickly thrown into a cell and he slid across the dirty straw and slammed into a corner. The heavy door clanked shut and then came the finality of a key setting the lock.

Faolan rose to his knees and shook his head. Stars swam before his eyes.

A soft laugh and a voice came out of the shadows. "Well met, my friend."

Faolan jumped as a hand grasped his shoulder. "Never fear...settle in...make yersel' ta home. Tell me your tale and I'll tell you mine..."

Faolan squinted as his eyes adjusted to the gloom. "Tanner! By the Twin Gods! Tell me we have not failed!"

***

The captain of the guardians split his forces when he saw the ambush waiting for him outside the Nortown gate. He sent six men on in pursuit of the hostages.

Arius cried out as the riders galloped past him but he was soon too busy defending himself to stop them.

Ruby's caravan climbed the mountain road. The oxen complained as they pulled the heavy wagons upwards over ruts and rocks, jostling those inside. Finally the terrain leveled off and they traveled some miles until sundown. With Bela's knowledge they came to a plateau hidden by trees where they could rest the night.

Bela motioned Ruby away from the others and whispered in her ear. Her eyes grew wide with fear and disappointment. He was leaving them. Going back to find what was left of his people. They had been away so long, he said, he and his sister, he knew not what had happened to them or where they were but he would search until he found them. His people had paid too great a price, he said. To her great dismay Bela mounted his horse, joined his men and rode off without saying anything more, disappearing into the night.

Feeling overwhelmed, Ruby gathered the hostages into little

groups, close together and told them to watch over each other. She forbade any talk at all nor fires lest they be discovered. Monk flew about nervously until he settled above a silent, exhausted group passing bread and cheese. When he was not offered any he let out a solitary, disappointed squawk, flapped his wings and went to sleep.

It was during that first night that Ruby began to hear the noises: a snuffling, curious grunting and broken branches all around the perimeter of the camp. At first she thought it was Bela coming back, perhaps with meat but when she ventured to call out to him there was no answer. She finished her watch late that night and crawled into a wagon with Cherry but found that she could not sleep. The wagon began to rock as it had when she and Arius made love. Then she realized some stinking animal was using it to scratch its back. The grunting and heavy breathing was very close now and continued until shuffling footsteps diminished into the woods and dawn came.

They were moving again in the morning without breakfast, eating their bread on the way. She questioned the others delicately so as not to scare them but they had all been too tired to notice anything, not even the pungent odor that still clung to the side of her wagon. By mid-morning Ruby began to hear the rustling again, twigs breaking and the sound of brush being parted. They were being followed closely by some thing that kept out of sight.

In early afternoon they heard hoofbeats.

Expecting Arius, Ruby halted the wagons and waited. Suddenly around a bend in the road came the guardians at a gallop. The women began to scream and then the children's high pitched cries joined them.

Out of the thickest part of the brush an enormous she-bear rose up on her hind legs and stepped forward into the road in front of the soldiers, displaying her claws and teeth. Two men turned their mounts immediately and fled back down the road. The oxen screamed as the bear let out a roar that sent chills down Ruby's spine. The rest of the guardian's horses shrilled, reared as one, threw their riders to the ground and galloped off. A small knot of shaken men were left standing together to battle the fearsome beast. Suddenly, the bear looked back at Ruby, caught her gaze and jerked its head as if to say, clearer than any words "Be off! Save yourselves!" Ruby sat stunned for an instant then cracked her whip over and over again on the backs of the frightened oxen until they dug their hooves deep into the earth and lurched forward. The terrible cries of the bear's victims electrified the hostages and they began to run. The foul roars of the beast and the desperate shrieks of dying men drove them on and echoed throughout the mountains.

Frightened and shaken, the hostages moved on in a daze, putting one foot in front of the other. Ruby moved her wagon to the side and took up the rear, constantly looking backward over her shoulder but there was only the sound of wind through the leaves.

Higher and higher they climbed. When they reached the summit that night they found it was held by the Eagle Masters. Cries of joy and relief came from the women and children. Dressed in the blue livery of Saels they welcomed them to their campfire. Immediately a message was tied it to the leg of an eagle. Walking to the edge of an outcropping, the man let the bird go. The children followed him. From where they stood they could see far off in the darkness, a dim orange flickering of torches on the horizon. The city of Saels beckoned to them.

Around the fire, Ruby had her first chance to inspect her charges. She saw the thin arms and sunken eyes of the women and the big bellies of their children meted out to them over months of captivity. Barely two hundred wretched souls had survived, half of Boru's families had died in camp. She heard stories of how the elders had given up their rations to save the young and how quickly the sick had died, removed from their midst and left untended by the soldiers.

Ruby lay near her mother that night with her siblings between them. She could not sleep for a long time, hatred consumed her. She was too exhausted to listen for noises.

Monk grew more and more restless as the wagons turned west and made the long descent onto the plain. Ruby had noticed the further away he got from Arius, the more unhappy he became. Finally he swooped forward and back again above the wagons, urging them toward the city. When they reached the flat lands, giddy with new green; Ruby paused and looked back toward the mountains. She followed Monk's dark wings as he left them. He was returning to Arius.

In the blue of the fir-covered cliffs, she saw a large black shape standing on a crest of the road they had traveled. It rose up onto its hind legs and stood still for many moments watching them, then it dropped down, dove into the brush out of sight and was gone.

The city of Saels and the refugee's camp lay within a day's journey, they would be there by nightfall. The sea was a grey smudge just beyond it.

17

Sacrifice

"Thank you for coming so quickly, Alaine."

"Kabul." the priestess haughtily acknowledged him as the councilors of Saels rose from their seats and bade her sit at their table.

"Tell me why the people are pounding at my door? This offense against our goddess...what do you know of this?"

"Rumors are spreading...there have been signs, Kabul, dead birds on the steps of the temple."

"Not put there by you, I hope..."

Alaine stared blankly at him. "The people are afraid, my dear Councilor General. As they should be! We have been dragged into war, we are overwhelmed by refugees...we need the Great Mother's protection, and now this girl, this precious gift to us has insulted her...has been hidden from us! She would have grown up under my protection and taken over for me when I died! She would have blossomed into the greatest Seer to ever serve the gods! The whore did this!"

"The Lady Aolwynd?"

"Of course! She is the axis around which everything has turned! And now, she is against even this great gift to her people!"

"How do you know she is behind this?"

"Who else, The Seer is her daughter! She is all she has left. Her sons are gone, her husband..." Alaine spat on the floor. "and her lover has abandoned her..."

"Please, Alaine, we are at war...he leads us, be respectful. What else do you know?"

The old woman smirked. "The Matron of our hospice has abandoned her duties...did I not tell you so many years ago, she was not worthy to fill Lauro's shoes?"

"Curb your venom, if you can...sometimes I think that stain has gone to your brain..." Kabul pointed to the old woman's arms.

Alaine stared at him as if she would kill him for his sacrilege.

Kabul sighed, unwilling to continue the fight. "Brilla had our permission to join the army."

"That was for me to decide, not you!" The priestess slammed her open palm against the table top sending their scrolls and papers flying. "She will also be punished."

"By you or the goddess?"

The priestess grimaced.

"Ah well, what do you suggest we do?"

"Send a party to find the girl."

"And what, in the meantime do we do to quell the people's anger, or if we cannot find her?"

"I will offer a great sacrifice."

Kabul looked at the priestess with disdain but said nothing.

Alaine stormed out of the city chamber. A collective sigh came from the council.

"A difficult woman."

"At the best of times..."

"And getting more dangerous with the years..."

"Many say she is close on the doors of madness…"

"Yet behind those doors lie prophesy." the old woman called back from the archway where she had been standing in the shadows.

***

Jenna walked along the upper corridor to Faolan's rooms, her heart pounding. She remembered his lips that night, tasting like strong wine, slippery and sweet. Then she thought of the woman's name he had whispered and the dizzy, ugly after effects of their love-making. 'I don't care...' she said to herself, hugging her shawl about her to keep out the draft. She would do anything to feel his body close to hers again, bite his neck and taunt him till he rose with desire for her. Anything. She put Rue's specter out of her mind. "I'll cure him of her..." she spoke aloud and with a coquettish smile she pushed open the heavy door. The anteroom and bed chamber were just as she had last seen them. No muddy boots, no cloak slung over a chair to announce his return and no Faolan. "The soldiers are back, something is wrong..." she whispered.

Jemson hung over the battlement counting the tents of the army as they deflated upon the ground. They reminded him of the jellyfish he and Jors used to poke with a stick on the beach near their home. This made him think of Jem and he scanned the tiny figures as the soldiers gathered their things together in preparation for the long march to Saels. Borchard's army was going to war. Dah was somewhere down there, he thought. Jemson gulped back a sob and kicked his practice shield and the sword in its scabbard lying next to him.

"That's no way to treat your best friend!" Borchard said coming up the stairs and out into the sunshine. He breathed in the brisk spring air.

Jemson hopped back from the wall and bowed. His expression was peevish.

"What ails you, son?" the old man asked, smiling and picking up the sword. "A good blade." he said taking it from its sheath and wielding it about.

"Only a practice sword."

"My son's sword!" Borchard said as if the boy should have known and been grateful.

"Which one?"

Borchard glowered at the boy whose innocent face betrayed no meanness in his question. The old man relaxed. "Here, let me see." He hefted the short sword in his hand and looked closely at the pommel and the blade. "My eldest...I had it made for him when he was your age. Yes, those were good times...but you need to practice if you would be as good as...Boru." he hesitated as he said the name. "Practice and rest, practice and rest. The muscles, you know. They burn and then they are stronger."

Jemson stared at the blade as it was given back to him. "I want to go with you...grand..." The boy stopped himself before he finished the word and pointed out over the field. "and Dah's out there soomwhere. I want to be with him."

"Ah yes, you're 'father', the cook." Borchard said slyly with a penetrating look. "I would be better served by that man in my kitchens...ah well."

"I want to serve."

Borchard rested his arms upon the wall and looked out over the fields. "You serve my son, remember? You're duty is to him."

"He's gone."

"He'll be back." Borchard said sternly.

"When?" Jemson cried. "I can serve! I can buckle armor and dress a warrior! I can fetch weapons from the smithy! I know things now!" the youth looked up at the Guardian, pleading.

"What do you want, son..." Borchard grinned at him, waiting.

Jemson knelt down on one knee. "Take me with you...My Lord Borchard. Let me serve you in his place till he comes."

"Well..."

"Please! Don't leave me behind!"

"So alike you are..." the old man mumbled, casting his thoughts back and remembering his sons. He basked for a moment in memories of their sword practices and of his tales of battles fought and how they hung on his words. His brow wrinkled and he grew sad. "Alright...until such time as your uncle joins me, what's one more squire under foot, more or less?"

"Thank you, Grandfather!" Jemson leapt into the air, whooping for joy, then suddenly he stopped and caught his breath, biting his lower lip.

Borchard could not help but chuckle before he turned deadly serious. "Do not speak of this to anyone, I will keep your secret, but do not...call me grandfather...you have no right."

Another boy came running up the staircase, sword and shield in hand.

"What's all this?"

"Practice, my Lord. I've come to find him." The boy jerked his head toward Jemson.

"Scoundrel! Off you go!" Borchard cuffed him then turned back to survey his army. The boys ran down the stairs. Left alone, the old man raised his eyes to the west, to the mountains.

Again he heard footsteps on the stone behind him. "Ah! Striker! How is that shoulder?" he said turning to meet the man as he slowly walked up and bowed, his arm in a sling. "Are you healed enough to take on your command?"

"My Lord..."

"General?"

"I fear riding is beyond me now..."

"It does not matter. You will be well enough for what I have in mind."

"My Lord..."

"Come and look. Is it not glorious?" Borchard spread his arm out with a sweeping gesture and looked down upon the swarm of troops. "Tonight I will celebrate with my men and tomorrow we sacrifice before the gods of war. This will be my last campaign, doubtless. So long ago, do you remember? I melded these provinces into one realm, by my own hand...I will not see it sundered...my sons...How different were my plans for them...but they chose their own way and I have mine."

Borchard turned back and touched Striker lightly on his good arm. "You will keep safe my city while I am gone and wait for Faolan's return. Send him on to me immediately he comes...I need to talk to him. I need to be sure of something and he has been too long away. If Bowmountain rides with him, close the city gates and let them go round. Hold the city safe until I return. But I cannot believe it."

"Believe...?"

"Oh, bits of paper, the mechanizations of a greedy mind...a man without subtlety. But I cannot wait any longer. These hostages have turned a town against me...have you heard? Before this sick spirit of rebellion goes any further we will stamp it out and have a clear path on the Northern Road to Saels." He looked back at the palace walls. "About the city. Hold it for me and squash any rumors, any hint of treason from the citizens. I have already hung men loyal to

215

Boru at the western gate as an example. Be merciless if you find any more vermin or hear any complaint. I would have peace."

"Peace, my Lord?"

"If not peace while I'm away...then quiet."

"Through fear?"

"How else?"

Striker bowed and backed away without showing the Guardian his concerned expression. "As you command."

Rute pushed past him on the stairs. His face was a jubilant mask. This disturbed Striker even more.

"Well, boy? What do you think?" Jemson stood in attendance beside the Guardian's chair looking out over a thousand campfires. Borchard's tent had been moved to a knoll to better command the festivities of the moro. The old man sat on a throne between two braziers for warmth as stewards brought trays of meat and served him wine. When he had filled his plate and handed Jemson a rabbit's leg he gestured them all away. Jemson gnawed at his meat as Borchard continued. "Tomorrow, the parade and then we march."

"Parade?"

"That's right. Best dress, best armor, best horse. Show the people what you're made of. Through the city and out the Northern gates. Reassure them you're in charge, eh? Or warn them. Remember that. And a sacrifice to the 'Twins'. Need their favor, eh? No more luck at my age. Need the gods." Borchard stared into the night, suddenly growing solemn. "All alone..."

"Lord Faolan..."

"Eh?"

"You're missing him."

Borchard bristled. "He'll be along...he'll be here. Leave me now. Go see to your duties." The Guardian called for more wine and more coals for his braziers.

"Alan..." Master Fructus Bell whispered as he tossed and turned in their big bed at the end of a busy night in the kitchens. Besides the banquet in the great hall before Borchard and his retinue left for the encampment, Master Bell had had to prepare a feast to take with them. He was keyed up and exhausted at the same time, and something was on his mind. "Alan!" he whispered more forcefully, shaking Devers awake.

"What is it, my love?" Devers answered peevishly.

"I need to think something out."

"Oh, the gods...what now?" Devers sat up, adjusted his nightcap, flipped his pillow to the cooler side and closed his eyes. Soft breathing immediately returned as Devers drifted away.

"It's something you told me the other day..."

"Ummm."

"Alan...wake up or I'll tickle you."

"Don't! Alright, I'm awake but it had better make sense, it's not another one of your dreams?"

"It's about the jailor..."

Devers sat straight up in bed, now fully awake, and jealous. "You told me that was all over! You bastard!" Devers said rolling out of bed and putting on his robe.

Fructus Bell jumped out on the other side. For a big man he could move very quickly when it was necessary. "Don't be a silly girl! We are one, I love you, nothing has changed that. No...sit here and listen to me...something's wrong down there..."

"Where?"

"In the prison...where did you think?"

Devers stared at Fructus' naked body and nodded toward his genitals.

"Gods, what a fool you are. No. I'm serious! Come back to bed, I have to talk, and it's cold."

The two lovers went back and huddled together, plumping pillows and making a nest.

"Now will you listen?"

Devers nodded.

"There's been special food requested."

"What?"

"Yes. You know him, he don't care what we send down to him (one of the reasons I left him!) and the prisoners get only bread and slops. But now he's asked for bread and meat and fruit."

"Fruit?"

"Aye. Like they're paying special care of someone. It's not for him, he hates fruit. Must be for one of his prisoners. Strange. He don't usually care if they live or die. In fact 'E prefers it. My feelers are out...I keep thinking of our little Lord Faolan an' how he loved fruit with 'is meal. An' then you said t'other day you'd had a letter from Dane's uncle, about the Bowmountain boy, how he hadn't heard from him, that the boy always wrote to tell them he'd arrived safely, yet this time...nothin'. Well, where is he then?"

"I don't know my love, but I think you're right, there's something very wrong and we're going to have to find out what it is. Perhaps that boy is down there as well...we could have a war on our hands both before and behind! Let me kiss that brilliant brain of yours! " Devers leaned over and kissed Fructus on his forehead.

Master Bell smiled. "As long as you're kissing, don't stop there." he whispered as he raised the bedcovers.

Clever as a spy, Jenna crept along the back passages of the palace carrying a tray that Master Bell had set up for her. Beneath a cloth were a roasted chicken, bread, oranges and a bottle of the jailor's favorite brandy. As she came closer to the prison corridor the guards stopped her but she smiled her prettiest smile and said "...for the jailor." They soon let her through. It was obvious they had let pass special platters from the kitchen before this.

Down the spiral staircase she went holding the rope bannister with one hand and balancing the tray with the other. She'd never been in this part of the palace before. The walls were damp and at any moment she expected to feel the breath of the fabled dragon on her neck or hear its snore.

Suddenly she came out into the flickering torch light of the jail. Not a snore but a wheezing sound came from the prison bellows where a half-naked prisoner was working, pumping his legs wearily up and down.

A muscular man in a leather vest studded with brass sat sweating within the confines of a circular desk at the very center of the room. His collar was open, exposing his thick neck. His face was somewhat flattened by a broken nose but his eyes were sharp. He was writing in a large log book and asking questions over his shoulder. Behind him, a smaller man with a face like a weasel was leaning against the wall. He was dressed in dirty livery with his arms crossed and his eyes closed, answering back sarcastically and yawning.

The jailor looked up as Jenna minced over to him setting the tray down. "Well?" he said.

Although Devers had told her to say "...with Master Bell's compliments." Jenna had a sudden inspiration. She curtsied and said "Meat and fruit for the prisoner...the brandy is for you, 'for services rendered'...with General Rute's compliments, your honor."

The little man opened his eyes and let out a laugh like a bark. "Fer services rendered! Ha! Tha's rich! You'll be lucky that's all you get, holdin' that one down here..."

"Shut up, you idiot!" the jailer shot back. "What's all this?" he asked, standing up and looming over the girl.

Jenna grinned sheepishly and stepped away from him quickly. He smelled. "Meal...from the kitchen."

The jailer took hold of the bottle and mumbled something. "'G'way wi' yah, back up out o' here...it ain't yer place ta coom trippin' down 'ere. What's 'E doin' blabbin' to the kitchen an' sendin' a girl...'E's a bigger fool than I thought. I'll see 'im soon enoof...settle 'oor business, an' mah account. Yew tell yer boss 'E can't pay me off w' a bottle o' brandy."

"Aye, think o' the chance we're takin'?" the little man said coming over and slamming a ring of keys on the table. He poured himself a drink.

"Oh…" Jenna purred."then you're in charge?"

"No! I'm Jailer here! 'E follows my orders." the big man snarled.

Jenna dimpled her cheeks. "I'll bet you have some real important villains down here."

"None more than that one..." the little man said coming over to her and looking her up and down.

"Idiot!" the jailer spat at him and coming out from behind the desk in a rush, took Jenna by the shoulder and shoved her toward the stairs. "Git! This ain't no place fer you. An' doon't come back. Tell yer General Rute I'll be expectin' somethin' more for me troubles than bread and cheese...this ain't no small thing I'm doin' fer him. Ah expect ta git paid!"

"Aye..." she overheard the little man saying as she shrunk against the walls of the staircase out of sight "treason goes both ways y'know...an' the price is high."

Once she had sauntered past the guards, Jenna ran all the way through the palace, back to the meat kitchen and stood in the doorway of Master Bell's little office panting from exertion.

219

"What is it Jenna? Take your time."

Jenna held her finger up in the air till she caught her breath.

"They've got him, it must be him, an' Rute's to blame." she said gulping, pushing Chores out of the way and collapsing onto a chair.

***

Ruby lead her caravan of wagons into the sea of people beneath the walls of Saels. Cries of relief and despair sounded in equal measure from all sides as arms were raised to help the hostages down. Before Ruby could give any orders, organize anything or decide who should be sent on to the hospice they were whisked away. It was as if the community of refugees were at last given some way to help, some purpose, some task that would help relieve their own suffering. They fell on the victims, carrying them all off to their tents.

Ruby looked about her suddenly not knowing what to do with herself. She made her way up the main aisle blinking in the sunshine at the remains of what had been a great migration and a waiting army. It was but a third of what it had been. Children ran amongst the empty squares of trampled grass and jumped over the cold, black scars of dead campfires.

Aolwynd stood in the place where Boru's tent had been, like a priestess at some sacred site, surrounded by the abandoned posts of the falconers. She watched as Ruby stumbled across to the spot where Arius and she had lived their first days as husband and wife. Her eyes filled with tears and spying Aolwynd she ran across to embrace her. She sank to the ground, her knees buckling under her.

When Ruby awoke, strong sunlight was on her face. She found she was resting in a comfortable bed with a view of an enclosed garden.

Aolwynd sat beside her in Boru's bed chamber.

"Where am I?" Ruby whispered.

"You are safe, they are all safe. The gods have blessed you. Rest."

"My moother...the children..."

"They're being looked after. Rest yourself."

Ruby sank back into a dream in which Arius rode through the forest, wounded, cut by a sword, and a great she bear walked beside his horse.

"It is time we came to some decision about these people..." Councilor General Kabul said.

"We must take them in. That is all." Aolwynd said softly.

The old men around the table grumbled and looked at each other. Taking orders from the Lord Protector's mistress was not to their liking even if she was long known to them, perhaps because of it. Many resented her treatment of her husband and held it against her from the very beginning, and now, gossip and rumors about her reached them daily, fueled by fear of the strangers that had flooded their streets.

"My Lord Boru and I are in agreement on this..." Aolwynd looked about her and smiled at the sullen faces.

Kabul coughed. "Yes, but where are they to go? Our streets are no fit place to house so many people."

"They sleep on the cobblestones, the poorer sections of town are over run with them like rats." one said.

"Yes! And some of them are thieves!" said another.

"Or lazy...they won't work but sit about and drink, talking in their funny accents."

"And their food smells funny."

Aowynd stared at them as if seeing their true natures for the first time. "Enough! We are at war, gentlemen! This is no time for fear or prejudice! Any day we will see Borchard and his army coming over the horizon! We can wait no longer, they must all come inside. I will see to it."

"My lady..." Kabul said "perhaps, as an innkeeper you are used to treating strangers as if they were family...we are not. In Lord Boru's absence WE decide what is best for our city...not you. We lock or unlock the gates according to what is best for our people."

Aolwynd glared at them as her cheeks bloomed with color.

"Have you heard from your husband?" One councilor dared to whisper loud enough for her to hear. "I hear he fights with Borchard's army..."

Aolwynd ignored him and slammed her fist upon the table. When she spoke her voice was cold as stone. "You talk of our

221

city? We are no longer a city, councilmen. We are a country and these are our people, all of them, strange dress and funny accents be damned...we will find room, we will give them sanctuary!" With that she left the chamber.

Within the next two days she was as good as her word. With the help of the Good Women, the remaining refugees by the wagon-load were being moved into the city and housed where ever there was an inch of space to be begged or bought. No one was to be left outside the walls. The families of the guardians especially, were invited to stay at the hospice, in the wards or in tents upon the grounds.

Ruby slept soundly that night in Boru's big bed with comfortable dreams of Arius' arms about her while Aolwynd sat outside dozing in a chair. The sound of the breeze rustling the palms in the garden lulled them both and covered the quiet footsteps of someone entering the room.

Arius was enfolding Ruby in his arms and she surrendered to his embrace. Ruby mumbled "My love..." in her sleep. He crushed her face to his chest. The pressure of his warmth surrounded her, overwhelmed her. She found it hard to breathe. Ruby began to struggle. Arius was holding her down trying to suffocate her. Ruby gasped for air and awoke to find a woman's hands holding a pillow over her face. She cried out, coughing and wrestled the thing away only to find the hands quickly grasping her neck. Boney fingers dug into the soft flesh of her throat.

Aolwynd rushed into the room through the garden doors. Moonlight spilled in and illuminated a grey figure crouched over Ruby like a nightmare, her knees on top of her chest.

Alaine looked up and let go of Ruby. "You!" she screamed.

Aolwynd leaped upon the priestess and dragged her off onto the floor by the hair. The two women wrestled, rolling about. They knocked a table over and wine spilled, staining their gowns. The priestess' eyes glinted, full of madness in the moonlight.

Aolwynd caught her by her garment and pulled her up.

"What are you doing here, demon!"

"You! You are my sacrifice!" the old woman said through her

clenched teeth.

Wrenching away from her, Aolwynd ran to the bed and reached beneath a pillow for her dagger.

Alaine ran at her screaming and before Aolwynd could reach it, Alaine had it in her hand and had pulled it from its sheath. They fought for it, crashing into furniture, slipping on rugs. Servants ran in the doors and stopped in their tracks

"Call the guard! A sacrifice! For the people! For the goddess!" Alaine shouted as she bent Aolwynd's arm. Tangled together they slipped on the spilt wine and tumbled to the floor.

Ruby screamed and jumped from the bed helping Aolwynd to her feet. Alaine pulled herself up by the bed post. "You must pay, you whore! Give back the child! And whelping another bastard? The goddess will take that too!"

Shrieks and footsteps resounded in the halls.

Alaine lunged at the women and wrapped her tattooed arms about Aolwynd's waist, smiling and squeezing hard. A look of surpris and shock passed over her face. Ruby had forced her hand quickly between them, wresting the blade, turning its point backward upon the priestess. In the act of crushing Aolwynd to her, Alaine had forced the blade into her own abdomen. Her hands loosened first, then her arms. She fell back onto the marble with the stunned look of the dead frozen upon her face.

"We 'av ta get away from here!" Ruby cried, tugging at Aolwynd's sleeve.

"She attacked you! We have nothing to hide."

"Doon't be daft! Their comin'! They hate you! You're blamed fer everythin'! Get out! Let's go! Now!"

News rushed from one servant to another throughout the palace and was carried out into the city. By daybreak the whole population knew their high priestess was dead, murdered by the Lord Protector's mistress.

This was catastrophe. Saels was at war, Lord Boru gone, the city overrun by refugees. Who had brought him back here in the first place? Who had brought this bad luck upon them? It took no time at all for the answer to spread from neighbor to neighbor. One person...Aolwynd. Her uncontrollable lust and her hand grasping for power...surely all these fell deeds were her fault. There was no appeasing the God Mother now except by more blood. Aolwynd's blood. The pounding on the doors of the council's chamber increased and more voices shouted for her arrest.

Two cloaked figures walked silently through an unusual morning fog, making their way between the last of the refugee's tents.

"Moother..." Ruby hissed.

"What is it? Ruby? Is that you?" came a voice. "Av you come to take us into the city?" Cherry rose from her cot and held open the flap. Ruby and Aolwynd quickly entered and let it fall behind them. Their cloaks were near drenched with mist. Cherry went to light a candle.

"Doon't." Ruby whispered. "Let the children sleep. Leave it dark."

"What is it? What's wrong?"

"We're leavin'. Aolwynd an' I. There's trouble an' it's best we're away."

"Ah doon't understand..."

"Sumthin's happened...we've killed the priestess...ah doon't 'av time ta' explain. I've brought you someone to look after fer me." Ruby handed her mother a bundle from beneath her cloak.

"It's Arius' nephew, His an' mine...well. All of ours, let's say, fer now."

Cherry stared at the baby and tears came to her eyes. "He looks so like...if it weren't fer the dark hair...You know, I lost the other one...in the jail, he started to fail...it was so cold...an' I lost mah milk, we were lucky not to lose any of the oother children."

"I know...Moother, I know. You did your best..."

"But why? Where are you headed?"

"East."

"No! The war? Don't be a fool! Stay out of it!"

"Ahm goin'. An' Aolwynd's goin' with me. Goodbye, Moother. We 'av ta get away from here afore they start searchin' the camp."

"Wait! Wait right here. Hold the babby." Cherry pushed the restless bundle at her daughter, threw on her shawl and disappeared from the tent. She came back within a few minutes, out of breath. "Alright." she said taking the baby back. "If you must go...he'll go with you."

Ruby and Aolwynd looked at each other as they stepped out side.

The early sun was coming out and made the mists pale. someone was driving a wagon up to the front of Cherry's tent. One of Boru's soldiers got down and leaned nonchalantly against its side, one foot crossed comfortably across the other. He yawned, smiled and touched his finger to his helmet.

"Good moro." he said softly. "At your service, if you'll 'av me. Ahm well enoof now ta travel an' ah need to get back to mah post. As it happens, mah post 'as moved on. Ah were a guard outside Boru's tent, or was until..." Jak looked vaguely sad, as if he'd missed something, or someone. "Ah don't suppose you ladies would care ta give me a lift?" he asked softly.

He climbed onto the wagon seat, not waiting for an answer and took over the reins.

"You're not drivin'." Ruby said hopping up and taking the straps out of his hands. Aolwynd climbed into the back.

They had only moved off a few yards when horsemen appeared, galloping up the aisle. Cherry cried out a warning and disappeared with the child.

In the swirling fog the horsemen slowed as they approached, calling out "Halt in the name of the Council!"

Aolwynd reached up and grabbed Jak's shoulder "Keep going no matter what you hear. Tell Boru what's happened to me. Go!" Jak looked at her in confusion but nodded. With that she climbed out of the tail gate and stood brazenly in the path of the riders. The horses sensed her presence and reared up, neighing and prancing to a stop. Jak and Ruby pulled away, their wagon lost to view in the fog that strangely blew away soon after they left the camp.

Aolwynd's heart was jumping in her chest as the sun revealed her presence.

"Get out of our way, woman!" one soldier shouted. She stood her ground as they skirted about her.

"Gentlemen...aren't you looking for me?" she said.

The men quickly reined in and one jumped down from his mount. "Are you Aolwynd Melior?"

"I am."

The man's leather armor creaked in the cold as he reached out to grab her arm. He hesitated as if he was afraid to touch her. "Coom with us now, my lady, the council would like a word."

"So polite." She said as he helped her onto his horse and climbed up behind her.

"Fer now." he said.

End of Volume Three
The Guardian and the King

Volume Four – The Seer

About the Author

J. Carter Merwin lives in Castleton, Vermont and runs a small gallery with her artist husband, Tom. They have three dogs and two cats, all rescues.

She is a member of the Romance Writers of America and the Womens Fiction Writers Association.

81587563R00136

Made in the USA
Columbia, SC
04 December 2017